EPIC

by

Robert J. Smith

To Gwen
Lit's Time to put on
the 'Sunday Clothes'
in memory of all
the good times
Best Wishes
from Robert J
Robert J Smith
December 2004

Robert J. Smith was born in 1927 in Cricklewood, Northwest London.

The outbreak of World War Two caused Robert to have a rather difficult time with regard to his education. Due to the war he was shunted around six different schools, one of which was burnt to the ground during an air raid in the London blitz.

He volunteered for the Royal Navy in August 1944 when he was seventeen and five months and served until December 1947.

Before his retirement in 1981 Robert worked in the External Telecommunications Executive finishing his career as a Leading Technical Officer at Bearley Radio Station in Warwickshire.

Epic is his first novel.

Epic

by

Robert J. Smith

Publisher
Mediaworld PR Ltd
Best Books Online

To my wife Eileen for her love,
patience and understanding.

Introduction

Today we take for granted the role of the computer in our lives. A useful tool, and every day important tasks are being controlled by computers. Various reasons for this control are given. To save time and money are the main reasons. Some altruists believe that the computer is an essential progression for the well-being of mankind. It must also be noted that there are many jobs at which the computer excels, and a lot of work is now being carried out by computers that could not be done by human beings.

A time may come when we hand over the reins completely to our computers and allow them to control our daily lives. Allow them to make important decisions with regard to our freedom. Allow them to dictate policy on human affairs. To give complete and utter control to computers, or a computer, is a very dangerous thing to do, as future generations may discover.

Ask yourself a question - Why are we on this planet?

Is it to work? Is it to play? Is it just to exist? Is it to become servile to our own technology? 'Servants' not 'Masters'.

Or is it to live peaceably together on what is really a very beautiful planet.

The human race is now beginning to worship 'All things bright and material'. Materialism is now the priority, and traditional human values are giving way to 'Pride of Ownership of Material Things'. Looking to the future, and of our own safety in that future, we must recognise the danger of not being in control of our own destiny.

Chapter 1

The Adelphi, a large vessel specially designed for exploration in coastal waters, lay quietly at anchor just off Lowestoft. In the main lounge Bob Hollis, a tough thirty-five-year-old oceanographer and captain of the Adelphi, is briefing his crew. Beside him stands marine biologist Janine Cooper a shapely brunette in her mid-twenties. Bob and Janine are members of the Centenary Oceanic Society, a 'Society' founded at the turn of the century in the year 2000 A.D. and currently celebrating its one hundred and fiftieth anniversary.

"This briefing is hardly necessary," said Bob half smiling as he cast a glance at the assembled crew. "We've waited a long time for this moment, and to win the Oceanic Society's competition to visit the Headquarters in Australia was more than we dared hope for. But win we did, and in three days time we will all start on what may prove to be the journey of a lifetime."

Bob was feeling particularly proud of himself at this moment. He felt it was in a way pay-back time for all the setbacks he had encountered during his twenty-three year career in the service of the Society.

As a child Bob had been placed in one of the Societies schools after the Epic Special Police had taken his parents into custody. He was never told why his parents were taken away, he was only ten years old and all he knew was that the police had arrived at his home late one night arrested his parents and took them away. Welfare officers invaded the house, took him screaming from his bed and into care at one of the Society's 'homes'. He never saw his parents again. Bob was enrolled as a cadet and put into a class with thirty other boys, he was the youngest, the ages ranged from ten to sixteen, all the youngsters had been taken into care just like Bob, and in most cases *their* parents had also mysteriously disappeared. There were only boys at the school, girls were sent to a different school. He had received a good education, not only an academic education either, for he had to hold his own at the school and stand up to the

2

older boys, or be their slave.

As a gritty youngster Bob held his own and was known throughout his school days for his courage. He was at first bullied by the older boys and courageously took many beatings but he soon made it known by his defiance that it was not worth the trouble of baiting Bob Hollis.

Bob eventually became the school's head boy and when he left, it was with honours and a promise of a good career within the Society, a career that had taken him all over the world and underneath the many seas and oceans. Yes, this was a proud moment, winning the competition meant that the Adelphi was now considered the best run ship in the Society and the quality of service delivered by the crew was of the highest standard.

His crew of ten, eleven if you included Janine, started chatting excitedly amongst themselves, Bob continued his speech. "Okay… okay… quieten down and listen. The Centre has arranged for us to join an expedition to investigate a new crevice that has just been discovered near the Challenger Deep. Today, we take the Adelphi to Felixstowe, and there we dock. Tomorrow, that's April the twenty-eighth, the whole ship's company will get a final briefing from the Centre's officials in the morning, and in the afternoon you will be free to collect whatever personal paraphernalia you think you may require on the trip. By the way, any equipment we require will be supplied, so don't go taking a mini-lab with you. Any questions so far?"

"How are we going to travel to Australia?" The question came from James Hadley, a muscular Apollo from Glasgow, James was Scottish but with only just a hint of a Scottish accent. National dialects worldwide had become diluted. With so much integration intermarrying and interleaving of all ethnic groups all races and all creeds, what else could have happened. Races now so closely embraced each other that things like national dialects and cultures suffered substantially in purity and had become one great pudding-mix in the process. Worldwide the English language had taken over almost entirely and foreign nationals had to create Societies within *their own* countries to prevent the demise of *their own* language.

"Good question Jamie," answered Bob who would have told them anyway. "On the thirtieth of April, we all gather, that means deck-hands as well, in the Maplin Terminus B departure lounge at 22.30hrs. Then at 00.00hrs we take the Colossus direct to Australia... Four hours later we will be sitting down with the Centre's representatives in Melbourne and our great adventure begins."

Chris Bonham, a handsome twenty-five-year-old diver, let out a loud 'Yar-hoo' and punched his fist in the air shouting. "Yes! Yes!"

Hans Valdeckan, a giant red-headed Dane with sky-blue eyes and an easy smile gave Jamie a hearty slap on the back which nearly knocked him over.

"Steady on Hans," said Jamie. "You don't know your own strength."

Bob Hollis opened a bottle of champagne and glasses clinked as Chris Bonham tapped a ruler upon the desktop calling for quiet.

"Listen folks, listen... I think we all know that without the efforts of Bob and Janine we would never have won the competition. I know we have not always seen eye to eye with them, but with their persistence and devotion to duty they pulled us through." Hans and Jamie readily agreed, Chris continued. "Therefore, I would like, on behalf of the crew, to raise our glasses in thanks to you both."

Chris, Jamie, Hans, and the rest of the crew all raised their glasses in a toast of thanks to Bob and Janine, who stood there, arms linked, smiling like Cheshire cats.

The anchor chains rattled as they were hauled up from the sea-bed by sturdy winches through hawseholes in the bows and fed neatly into the cable chambers. The deck-hands hosing down the muddied links as they came up with the smell of the sea-bed strong in the air. With the anchors safely and securely stowed the Adelphi got under way and journeyed towards Felixstowe, cruising forty kilometres off shore. It was a splendid day for a sea trip, slight swell, gentle breeze, and a few wispy clouds floating effortlessly across the sky. The Adelphi stole gracefully past Southwold and Orford Ness. Bob Hollis looked at his watch then called up to the bridge. "Hans, we're getting behind schedule. Full speed to Felixstowe."

"Okay skipper." Although Danish, Hans had not a trace of a Danish accent, which was not surprising considering he came to England when he was only three-years-old and had spent most of his life in Southeast London. The Adelphi leapt forward at a modest 20 knots, and was now making good progress towards Felixstowe.

Janine was in the laboratory checking her latest batches of sea-water under a microscope. Dozens of small carefully labelled plastic phials containing sea-water collected from around the shoreline off Lowestoft were ranged behind a safety rail along a shelf in front of her on the bulkhead. Chris and Jamie were taking things easy, lounging about in the leisure-quarters aft and telling tall stories to each other about the good times they had had last week ashore in Lowestoft.

Bob was in his cabin writing a report when he was literally thrown the full length of the cabin, some six metres. A gigantic jolt, horrendous grinding of metal to metal, and the Adelphi reared up at a terrifying angle, then crashed back into the sea with a bone-shaking judder and a thunderous roar like an explosion.

"What the hell's happened?" shouted Jamie, racing out of the rest room heading for the bridge, followed closely by Chris.

"We've hit something in the water," said Hans with a grimace as Jamie burst into the wheelhouse, Hans was nursing a bruised arm and there was a trickle of blood coming from a cut on his forehead near the temple and trickling down the side of his face. "It was floating just below the surface. It looked like a huge container."

Chris Bonham followed Jamie into the wheelhouse. "I think we're sinking," he said. "Have you sent out a May-day?" Hans still a bit dazed shook his head.

Jamie rushed to the radio. "Where's the mike…. Where's the bloody mike?" he yelled, and started looking all around the place where the radio and microphone were usually housed.

"There it is, on the deck, over there in the corner," shouted Hans. "It's been ripped off. I must have pulled it off when I was thrown across the wheelhouse.

Find the skipper, he'll know what to do." Chris dashed off to find Bob Hollis.

The ship, already listing badly, was well down in the bows. "At this rate I reckon we've got about fifteen minutes," said Bob. "Get to the sub. Chris, Jamie, check on the rest of the crew bring them to the sub, and hurry, see you there."

Bob quickly collected the ship's log then with Janine and Hans made for the sub and began operations for release. After five agonisingly long minutes Chris and Jamie turned up with the other crew members They hastily climbed aboard closing the hatch behind them. Bob pressed the release button and 'Minnow', the ten-metre long submarine used for under-sea exploration, was quickly lowered out of her berth through doors already opened in the bottom of the Adelphi's hull, then catapulted in a flurry of air bubbles into the North Sea, gliding clear of the stricken Adelphi.

Bob took Minnow to what he considered to be a safe distance away, remaining five metres below the surface from where they watched the death throes of the ship that minutes earlier had been their home. The Adelphi drifted sadly past. Bob followed the ship down thirty metres to the bottom. He was about to surface and report, when he noticed on his large navigation screen the cause of the accident, a steel barge. The impact had ruptured the side of the barge, and torn a great hole in the bows of the Adelphi.

Chris, Jamie, Hans, and Janine gathered at the forward observation window and switched on the powerful searchlights normally used in the exploration work. They all stood by the great convex window gazing out at the barge. "I've seen those barges before," said Hans. "They're loaded in London, loaded in covered wharfs that go right in under the Epic Building, they've got auto-navigation systems. I've seen them coming down the Thames and off out into the North Sea. No one seems to know what the barges carry or where they go. The police block every inquiry. Every thought on the subject is blocked."

"Why aren't we being blocked now then?" asked Jamie.

"I don't know do I?" blustered Hans. "Maybe it's because we are under too much water, or maybe it's because we're inside a metal skinned sub, - Maybe a bit of both. Maybe it's…" Hans floundered to a standstill.

"Maybe you're right," admitted Jamie. "But now's our chance to find out what's inside the barges, find out what they're carrying.

What about it skipper?" Jamie turned to Bob who was sitting at the control console studying the screen.

Jamie became quite excited at the prospect of discovering what the mysterious barges contained, this one in particular. Bob was also intrigued by the idea.

"Good idea, I've got to know anyway, for the official report. That barge must have run into trouble two weeks ago, remember, when all craft had to seek shelter from hurricane Echo 72? Look, the motor unit's been torn away, and the cargo section's been left damaged and drifting. Janine, I want you and Chris to get into wet suits and take a look inside the barge, it's too deep for Fletcher's Gill, you'll have to use cylinders. Try to find out if it's got a name or a number."

Chris and Janine struggled into their wet suits and donned the aqua equipment. "You'd think that after all the time mankind has been skin-diving, someone would have invented something less cumbersome," said Janine.

"We've got Fletcher's Gill which is okay for shallow waters," explained Chris. "But compressed air mixtures in cylinders are still best for the deeper dives, different mixtures for different depths." Janine and Chris, climbed into the air lock, secured the watertight door, and carried out the usual equipment checks. All was well. They signalled to Bob, flooded the compartment and slipped through the outer door into the cold greenish heavily silted coastal waters of the North Sea.

Visibility was less than ten metres even though the sun was shining brightly above. The barge loomed large and foreboding, and it wasn't just the coldness of the North Sea that made Janine shudder. The barge had a two-metre gash in its side, and a faint brown haze staining the water surrounding the hole. Chris spoke to Janine over their intercom and told her he was going to enter and that she was to follow.

Powerful torch beams pierced the dim interior of the barge, the dark stain was much more pronounced. Janine followed Chris in through the shattered plates and swung her torch beam around inside the barge. In the torch-light she saw a sight that momentarily froze her with horror. She felt a mixture of terror and nausea, eventually she screamed, lost her mouthpiece, lost hold of her torch which twisted crazily on the wrist-strap wildly throwing its beam in all directions, lost her direction, and threshed about in sheer panic. Although also sickened by what he saw Chris kept sufficient control to grab hold of Janine, replace her mouthpiece and guide her to the exit.

Two semi-hysterical aquatic explorers scrambled their way back to the submarine. It was quite some time before Bob could get a coherent report from them. Janine, still shaking, wrapped in a blanket, gave an account of the excursion into the barge. "I'm sure the stain was blood. The lower half of the barge was filled with mutilated human remains, torso's with bits of white flesh hanging from them in shreds, arms, legs, heads, hair, eyes, - all lying about as if they'd just been dumped there. Flesh, floating about like bits of rag."

As she recounted this horrific story, her voice pitched higher and higher until she broke down in a flurry of sobs and tears. She clung tightly to Bob and buried her face in his chest as if trying to blot out the memory of her ghastly experience in the barge. Bob gently held Janine in his arms and consoled her. Chris carried on with the story. "I was as horror-struck as Janine, she diverted my attention by losing her mouthpiece. I could see she was getting into difficulties so I grabbed hold of her and made for the exit. I never want to see the inside of that barge again."

"So that is what happens to them," exclaimed Hans. "Hundreds, thousands, probably millions of people have gone into the Epic Building and have never been seen again. Any enquiry is immediately blocked by Epic, and I suspect the only reason our thoughts are not being blocked now is because we are under twenty metres of sea-water and tucked away inside a metal can."

"I think you're right," said Bob. "Anyway, I want to see for myself and try to assess what happened to those people. Jamie, you come with me, the rest of you stay put until we get back."

"We won't have to be very long skipper," exclaimed Jamie.

"Why not?"

"When we were sinking, the mike had been torn away from the radio, so I used my cerebral implant and telepathed a May-day to

Epic."

"But we don't need any rescue boats, we've got the sub," said Bob as he went to the control panel to take 'Minnow' to the surface.

"How was I to know that? As far as I was concerned we were sinking, I didn't know whether you could even launch the mini-sub out into the water," answered Jamie defensively.

"Yes of course, sorry Jamie, there was no way you could have known, you did the right thing. Perhaps now we may get some answers," said Bob as he opened the hatch. He walked out into the sunshine and stood on the broad flat deck of the submarine followed closely by his crew. "What are we supposed to do now?" he said to his crew, not so much a question but more of a general statement of his bewilderment.

"We'll just have to wait and see what happens when the boats arrive," said Janine, painfully stating the obvious.

On the surface in the bright sunshine, with the sub gently rolling on the calm sea and the slight breeze carrying a saltiness in the crisp clean air it was difficult to imagine the horrors seen by Chris and Janine in the barge. They waited some minutes, grouped together on the deck of the sub as it slowly rose and fell with the swell of an unusually calm North Sea. Bob noticed a mobile surveillance satellite high in the sky, just a speck in the distance off the stern quarter. It was heading their way. Bob told the crew that boats would be arriving any minute.

Suddenly the great head of Epic appeared, hovering fifty metres away and forty metres above the water on the starboard side of the sub. The giant head, looking imperious like Julius Caesar the great Roman Emperor, and he was angry.

The giant head spoke, its voice booming like thunder across the waves: *"Stay where you are! Stay where you are!"*

Bob sensed danger and immediately ordered his crew below deck, as they turned to comply a powerful force emanating from the surveillance satellite struck them. The voice of Epic continued to boom out instructions and the satellite was forever coming nearer. They all rocked and reeled about holding their heads in pain, and then they heard the staccato rattle of guns being fired. Bolts of high energy struck the seven deck-hands who were standing aft of the hatch killing them instantly and knocking them off the deck into the sea. Bob and the rest of his crew were shielded from the blasts by the subs superstructure. Bob struggled against the pain and looked at the bodies floating away in the sea. There was nothing he could do but he struggled to the edge of the deck to try and reach them.

"Stay where you are," boomed the voice of Epic. *"Stay where you are."*

The men in the sea were all dead. Bob Hollis stood up, an overwhelming feeling of hatred for Epic temporarily overcoming the pain. "Get below," he ordered, forcing himself to act by sheer willpower, fighting against the searing pain that was pulsating violently through his brain. He shouted at what was left of his crew. "Get below! Get below!" The guns rattled out again, miraculously no one was hurt, and the bolts of energy ricocheted off the steel hull dissipating their charges harmlessly into the sea. Bob bullied his crew until they were all safely through the hatch and below decks.

With the metal hull shielding them from direct contact with Epic the pain lessened. "We must dive," gasped Bob still reeling from Epic's devastating attack. He forced himself to concentrate on a plan of action and struggled to the control panel and sent the craft in a steep dive to twenty metres below the surface. He again spoke to his crew, which had now been reduced to just four people Hans, Chris, Jamie and Janine. "The rescue boats will be here any minute, except that I don't think they will be intent on a rescue, we'll either be arrested or they'll just blow us out of the water. Let's get out of here."

Bob set a course to the Southeast, not knowing at that particular moment just where they were heading. He reasoned that if the rescue party made a search they would assume the submarine would head towards the nearest shoreline.

"That should keep them busy for a while," he said to the crew as he steered the sub Southeast skilfully skating over the sea-bed manoeuvring round outcrops of rock and forests of weed to avoid detection. Bob stayed on the Southeast course for an hour, putting ten kilometres between themselves and the barge.

The 'Minnow' did well, although not designed for really deep water, it was quite safe up to depths of two hundred metres. Janine, still a little pale, recovered her composure and thought the best way to get back to normal was to keep busy, and set up the area on the computer screen. "Here we are," she said as a survey map of the area appeared on the screen. They all crowded round, looking over her shoulder at the screen. "Look Bob, we're near a fairly deep ravine. There's a sizeable cave about fifty metres from the entrance, down the ravine on the left. As she said this, the screen displayed bright yellow lettering, flashing in the left hand corner which read, 'GRADE ONE BANNED AREA'.

Hans read from the screen. "Grade one banned area. Oh no! If we're caught here that means mandatory life sentence in Atlantis." Everyone had cause to fear the prospect of being sent to Atlantis; a penal colony built on the ocean floor mid-Atlantic. No one ever returned from Atlantis.

Bob switched on his monitor and saw the contoured map of the area.

"Yes I see it. Let's go and have a look," he said, ignoring the warning.

He was just about to set off when Hans shouted. "Just a minute skipper, I've got something coming up on my screen. Coming this way on the surface."

Bob, still seated at the control console, switched screens and saw a line of vessels heading straight towards them. "I don't think they're from the rescue party, they're coming from the wrong direction." He linked the computer to the screen then back-tracked to find their point of origin. "Looks like they came from the Thames estuary. Wait a minute. They don't look like rescue boats. Hans, can you get a clearer picture?"

Hans adjusted the controls on his console and fine-tuned the signal. "There you are skipper, that's the best I can do."

"That's good enough," said Bob. "I was right, they're not rescue boats, they're barges."

"Barges!" exclaimed Chris.

"Looks like it," answered Bob. "And now is the best chance to see where they go.

I think we ought to follow them."

The others agreed and busied themselves with their various duties.

Keeping close to the bottom, Bob followed the barges. The ravine deepened after ten kilometres, the 'Minnow' following its quarry at eight knots.

"Look at this skipper!" shouted Hans. Bob looked at his screen. He could see a cluster of buildings coming into view dead ahead, right in line with the direction of the barges.

"Jamie," said Bob. "Get to the observation window up for'd, see if you can get a better view? I'll keep easing forward."

"Aye aye skipper," said Jamie.

Jamie reached the observation window in the bows of the submarine, and immediately reached for the intercom. "Just look now skipper."

"Thanks Jamie, I've got it on the screen." Bob closed to within thirty metres of the buildings, and with the submarine poised five metres above the seabed an unbelievable sight met his gaze. He observed what could have easily passed for an airport had it not been sixty fathoms under water, but instead of planes there were large amphibian submersibles gliding about. The whole area was in the form of a brightly-lit square, and at each corner he saw the base of a gigantic circular tower.

The square was a hive of activity. Out of the gloom on the far side came a procession of amphibian submersibles, gliding along, returning from some mission further down the ravine. Androids, looking just like humans walking about and busying themselves in what appeared to be their natural habitat. Most of the returning submersibles went into large openings at the base of one of the towers. Another stream of submersibles appeared out of similar openings in the base of the tower on the opposite side of the brightly lit square, and went gliding off down the ravine, eventually disappearing into the blackness beyond.

Bob cautiously eased the sub nearer, trying to get a better view. Twenty metres up from the seabed and seated on top of the towers, he could see the underside of an enormous building. Bob gazed for some time at the incredible scene and then spoke half to himself and half to the crew. "I'd like to hijack one of those vehicles and see what they're carrying. It might give us a clue as to what goes on in that building." The others were silent, still mesmerised by the sight

12

of the under-water activity unfolding before their eyes. Bob ignored their silence and continued.

"It's too late to try now, we'll go back to the cave and wait until morning." Chris, Jamie, Hans and Janine nodded their assent, and absentmindedly murmured their agreement, unable to tear their eyes away from the incredible sights being enacted outside the observation window.

The cave mouth was just large enough to allow 'Minnow' to pass through, but once inside the entrance there was plenty of room to manoeuvre. All the crew had seen wondrous under-water sights in their travels, but in the glare of the sub's searchlights they were entranced by the sheer beauty of nature's architecture. Massive rock columns, supporting a corrugated roof that reflected a coloured kaleidoscope of light in a multitude of dazzling beams and cascades. Great sweeping curves of rainbow rock carved out perhaps by some long forgotten ice age. No one spoke as they slowly travelled round the cave. Deep inside the cave Bob stopped 'Minnow's' engines, and, with a 'darkened ship' the crew settled down for a well-earned rest.

Food and drink had never tasted so good and they sat round the table chatting, they all had tales to tell and nostalgic memories sprang to the surface, memories of the old days, even the occasional joke was cracked. Eventually conversation ran low, fatigue began to take its toll, and they turned in to sleep the rest of the night away. Next morning Bob steered the sub out of the cave and down the ravine to where they had previously located the buildings. He kept well away from the towers and directed the sub further on down the ravine; they travelled along what appeared to be an undersea 'road'. It was a road not meant for 'wheeled' vehicles, more a 'clearway' for the submersibles. It was also well lit by lights anchored at the 'roadside' at intervals along its edge. Bob picked a spot off the road by the ravine wall, hidden from view by a mass of seaweed.

They hadn't waited long before powerful lights approached from the direction of the building. A large submersible glided into view, steered by an android. "How the hell are we going to tackle that?" queried Jamie.

Bob answered slowly. "The android was in an open cockpit?"

"How does that help us?" questioned Chris.

Bob moved over to the chart table and outlined his plan for tackling the huge underwater transporter. "Three of us will swim out to the roadway." Bob pointed on a modified chart where he had pencilled in the buildings, the towers and the roadway. "Now," he said, acting out the action as he outlined his plan. "If we used a long line, say about ten, fifteen metres, twenty at the most. Anchored it to a rock at one end, and had a running noose at the other, sat quietly in wait for one of those vehicles to come along, then climb up to the cockpit and simply slip the noose over the android's head. When the line tightens, the android gets pulled out and we take over the vehicle." Bob looked round his crew to see what reaction they would have to his idea.

They all looked amazed. Jamie tittered a bit and pulled a face. Hans said it sounded so simple it might just work. "They aren't travelling very fast," added Chris. And finally they all agreed to try Bob's plan.

"How's your arm Hans?" asked Bob, remembering that Hans had been injured when the Adelphi struck the container.

"Fine, no problem," answered Hans, doing a few exercises to prove a point.

"Okay then," said Bob. "Hans, Chris, both of you will come with me. Janine and Jamie stand by here in the sub, and be ready to move off fast as soon as we get back."

Chapter 2

Bob, Hans and Chris struggled into the aqua gear then went to the stores and sorted out a twenty-metre length of line. "Depth over fifty metres," said Bob looking at the depth gauge. "We'll need the Helium/Oxygen mixture and re-breather packs, that'll give us thirty minutes to do the job, if we haven't done it by then we'll have to leave it until later or forget it."

They entered the air lock and waited for the pressures to adjust. Then they all swam the ten metres from the sub to the edge of the 'roadway'. Hans and Chris tied the line round a convenient spur of rock, Bob swam off dragging the line after him and found a useful clump of weeds by the roadside in which to hide. He sat there waiting for a submersible, absent-mindedly fingering the running noose at the rope's end, his mind turning over all the possibilities of Epic's role in all this horror. He waited in the cold greenish darkness on the seabed of the North Sea and was thankful the re-breather packs gave no telltale bubbles.

Ten minutes elapsed before the first vehicle came along and a greenish dawn appeared at the end of the road caused by the bright headlight of the approaching vehicle. Bob waited until the submersible drew level then swam quickly out and up to the open cockpit, quickly thrust the noose over the driver's head and pulled tight. The submersible travelled four or five metres before the line pulled tight and all the time the android struggled frantically to loose the noose from around its neck. As the line tightened it half pulled the android out of the cockpit where it then stuck, held firm by a safety harness, half in and half out of the cockpit. The line tightened further and suddenly tore off the driver's head; off it came spewing green fluid like clouds of smoke. The submersible slewed round out of control and charged across the ravine, finally crashing into the ravine wall. Chris and Hans followed Bob over to the crashed vehicle and opened the container section.

Inside were several large watertight crates. Bob spoke to Hans and Chris over the intercom. "We'll never manage to break these crates open without proper equipment," Bob looked at his watch. "And we haven't time to go back to the sub and get it."

Hans had wandered to the front end of the container. "Hey, skipper, come and look at this." Bob swam speedily over to where Hans was waiting, followed by Chris. The impact with the ravine wall had caused one of the crates to break open revealing smaller packages inside. Hans pulled out one of the packages. It was a plastic bag marked 'Fertilizer 25Kg'.

Bob looked at the other packages. "They all look the same," he said, pulling out more of the packages. "We'll take one back to the sub and get it analysed."

Back on board and safely decompressed, Bob took over control of the sub from Jamie, who as soon as Bob, Hans and Chris returned, had started the return journey to the cave, once again widely skirting the towers. The sub gained the safety of the cave without incident, they could all now relax and analyse the situation.

"Great stuff skipper," said Hans.

"Went like clockwork," said Chris.

"Did it?" answered Bob, strangely quiet.

"What's the matter Bob?" asked Janine. "What went wrong?"

"Nothing *went wrong*…. It's just…" He paused, buried his face in his hands and shuddered. "Oh God! What the hell's going on?"

The crew all gathered round. "What's the matter Bob," said Chris. "Something's wrong. You've hardly said a word since we left that submersible."

Bob straightened up; he looked at them all. "When I put the noose over the android's head the line tightened and pulled its head off."

"We know that skipper, nothing to worry about though, it's only a piece of machinery," said Hans.

Bob looked directly at Hans, then at Chris. "You weren't there… not as close as I was… it struggled… and screamed. I couldn't hear it but I knew it was screaming. You see it *wasn't* an android… It was a human being, modified to live under water. That *green fluid* was blood, which as you well know would look green at a depth of sixty metres." There was a gasp from Janine and a series of comments from the rest 'You are joking', 'You're kidding,' 'No, that cannot be,' then silence.

"Do you mean to say that all those creatures we saw back there by the towers were humans not androids?" asked Jamie.

"Looks like it," answered Bob.

They all sat there motionless and took stock of this new situation. Janine, looking puzzled said. "Going back to the barge, I cannot understand why there wasn't more blood. There was discoloration of the water, we all saw that, but that barge was half full of mutilated bodies, and the bits of flesh I saw were nearly white, that barge was intact until we 'holed' it, so where did the blood go? What does Epic want with so much blood?"

Bob made known another observation. "That package we took from the submersible, the computer analysis confirms that the contents were of human origin."

They all began to realise the awful reality of what they had accidentally discovered. "You realise this means that we cannot go back to the mainland without risk of arrest."

"It begins to make sense now," said Hans. "Epic doesn't need people anymore, now that he's got androids. During the last ten years there's been a massive increase in the number of jobs the androids have taken over."

"But we now know that they were not androids we saw back there, were they?" pointed out Chris.

"No they weren't were they?" answered Hans.

"Perhaps the androids don't work very well under water," offered Jamie

"I must admit," said Bob. "I never gave much thought, about population levels but I think you've got a point Hans. Has anyone studied them recently?"

No one had. No one had paid serious attention to *what* the authorities were doing, whether it was population levels, or androids, or what jobs they were doing or anything. Janine said she thought the human population levels had gone down a bit. Jamie jumped in with a suggestion.

"Let's put it on the computer," he said. "Set up population levels for the last thirty years and see what comes up." It was worse than they had thought. The computer confirmed at first a steady decline, and then a sudden fifty per cent drop in world population levels over the last fifteen years.

For a few minutes it was like Bedlam. Bob called for silence. "All talking at once is getting us nowhere… Janine, what have you to say?"

"Me! What can I say? I don't know any more than the rest of you. Why didn't someone raise the question of falling populations or androids doing the extra work long ago?"

"We don't have to think very hard to answer that question," answered Bob.

"Since compulsory cerebral implanting fifty years ago, no one has been free to follow any controversial line of thought."

Janine suddenly got very excited. "Hey guys, I've just realised something."

"What's that?" they chorused.

"We're free… free to think exactly as we please… don't you see. The very fact that we are holding this conversation and not being *buzzed* is proof that the police are not able to monitor us… Epic cannot find us… we are free."

"Yes, but for how long are we going to remain free?" muttered Hans. "As soon as we surface we'll be picked up by the Special Police and finish up in the barges like those other poor devils."

Janine stood up. "If it's any help," she said. They all turned to face her, willing to listen to anything that might help them out of their present situation.

"If it's any help. Professor Burgess once said to me, that if I was ever in trouble with Epic, I was to see him personally, face to face. 'Don't phone; don't write, don't use a computer', he said. I never gave much thought to it at the time." She looked at the rest of the crew, their faces all looked drawn, as did her own.

"Who's Professor Burgess, and where is he now?" asked Bob.

"I don't know where he is now, but he used to lecture at Oxford University, I met him there when I was studying Marine Biology. Just a minute… I remember now, he used to have a big house, at a place called Burcot."

"How the hell are we going to get to Burcot?" shouted Jamie. "As soon as we surface we'll be picked up, and we don't know if he'll even be there."

Janine replied quickly. "His house at Burcot is very close to the river, we could use the sub."

"Don't be daft, we'd never get the sub that far up the river, what about the locks?"

"Sounds like a fairly good idea to me," exclaimed Bob. "We will have to take a chance of him being there. Listen to this… If we use 'Minnow' as far as the London Basin, two of us could then take the micro-sub the rest of the way, keeping below surface all the time to avoid detection and follow the other craft through the locks." There was a hesitant murmur of approval. "Okay then, Chris and Janine, you two will go in the micro-sub. Chris because you have the most experience with the micro-sub, and Janine because you know the location of the professor's house, you also know the professor."

The crew warmed to the idea and the next few hours were taken up in a flurry of excited activity. Food supplies, maps collected, depths checked, possible river traffic checked, where to wait for boats to go through the locks, and so on.

Next morning Bob took 'Minnow' to the mainland as far as the mouth of the Thames, he then waited for the tide to turn and went in on the incoming tide. He stopped opposite Rainham Marshes at a place called Frog Island, and gave last minute instructions to Chris and Janine. "When the time comes to leave the micro-sub, cover your head with layers of metal foil, the thicker the better, it may help to nullify the implant's transmissions. I've included some in your supplies. I don't know whether it will work, but it's all I can think of… don't forget… I expect it will take about four days to reach Burcot and find the professor, then you have the return journey… so commencing on the eighth of May, and every evening for a further week, we'll surface at 22.00hrs one kilometre off Sheerness and look for your signal."

On the surface visibility was very poor, it had been raining heavily throughout the previous night. Heavy clouds were still masking the unblinking eyes of the surveillance satellites the glowing apricot-orange spies of the Special Police, that hung in the sky overlooking the countryside like holes in a giant colander, watching every movement.

Saying goodbye is always a sad business, and these goodbyes were made infinitely worse by the uncertainty of the mission. Was this to be the last goodbye? Would they ever see one another again? They had all become such close friends, now bonded together by circumstance.

With goodbyes said, handshakes and embraces completed, and last, long looks taken Bob brought the sub to the surface and opened the forward hold that housed the micro sub. Chris and Janine already aboard were then cast off into the muddy waters of the Thames, a Thames swollen by the recent heavy rains. Chris switched on the Computer Assisted Laser Observer Unit (CALO), which gave a de-fuzzed picture of the surrounding area and placed it on a visual display unit. It showed the micro-sub in mid-stream, close to the bottom, travelling toward London.

They were in high spirits as they travelled along, perhaps in a type of euphoria enhanced by a fear of the unknown. Through the Pool of London at Wapping, on past Tower Bridge, then London Bridge, and the bridges of Southwark, Blackfriars, Waterloo, Westminster, Vauxhall, and Chelsea, all passed without incident. It was at Chelsea they picked up a fairly large pleasure boat, and *shadowed* it all the way through Richmond Lock and on to Twickenham, where they spent their first night, resting on the bottom, all lights out except for the merest glow from the instrument panel.

They both sat quietly in the cockpit and ate a simple meal. "How did you become interested in diving?" asked Janine.

"That's easy to answer," said Chris.

"It was just after I had had my implant seed inserted, I was six years old. As a reward for being brave my father took me on holiday to Polperra in Cornwall. It was then a protected area, with a rugged coastline. My father took me down to the local beaches and we had tremendous fun exploring the mysterious pools and caves. I was completely fascinated by it all and it just went on from there. I studied my diving techniques at Dartmouth, and four years ago went on an expedition surveying the ocean floor beneath the ice cap at the North Pole... We lived under the ice for a whole year... That's where I met Hans and Jamie. After the expedition we all joined the Adelphi, that was over two years ago."

"What do you mean about Polperra? You said it was then a protected area, what happened to it?"

Chris was reluctant to reply at first, to what was a painful memory connected to his childhood. "We had such fine times at Polperra, my father and I, we went down there every year after I had my implant, for the next four years, that's when I got really hooked on underwater exploration. When we went down on the fifth year it had all changed. We, of course, knew nothing of the change and carried on as we had always done in the past, swimming diving, exploring. My father swam into a cave and accidentally stumbled across some secret activity being carried out by the authorities, the Epic Secret Police I believe. He was arrested, I was taken into care, and I never saw my father again."

Janine was shocked and embarrassed with Chris's answer to what she thought was a polite inquiry during conversation into a puzzling incident, and one she thought that could have had a simple explanation. "Oh my God! I'm sorry Chris. I didn't mean to pry into your private life, honestly, you must believe me, if I had known I…"

"Don't worry about it," answered Chris. "I've got over it now, and I am grateful for all the good times I had with my father, I have my memories of him. Anyway let's change the subject and put that part of my life aside. As I said I joined the Adelphi just over two years ago and since then had a simply wonderful time doing things I really enjoyed doing. And six months ago we were told to expect a top of the range oceanographer, then you turned up."

Janine was not going to let a remark like that go unchallenged.

"What do you mean by that?" she replied hotly, ready to do battle.

"Oh!.. Sorry ... I didn't mean, oh dear, look, oh, you see, we were expecting a man, and, and, and er of course you're not a man, are you?" Chris was verbally back-peddling for all he was worth trying to cover up his 'faux pas'. Janine almost burst out laughing at the sight of Chris threshing about trying to find the right words. She liked Chris and had strong feelings for him.

She reached across the cockpit and touched his hand. Chris quickly drew his hand away. "Why did you do that?" said Janine looking hard at Chris.

Chris answered, his voice showing embarrassment tinged with emotion.

"Janine, you are a very attractive woman, and believe me I've got more than just friendly feelings towards you, right back to when you first came aboard." He paused, looking directly at Janine, his eyes searching the contours of her face, as if hoping an answer to his feelings would be reflected there, he continued. "But you are Bob's girl and…"

Janine butted in quickly. "Whatever gave you that idea?"

"Well, right from the start you and Bob went out together, and you kiss him," blustered Chris.

"Kiss him!" exploded Janine. "They were only little pecks on the cheek. Bob and I go back a long way. I used to be his girl friend years ago, but now, as the saying goes, we're just good friends. Do the others all think the same?"

"Yes of course they do," said Chris, brightening a little.

"Thank God for that, I began to think I'd got bad breath or something."

Chris with renewed eagerness leaned towards Janine, he held and caressed her hand. She patted his hand gently, then moved his hand off hers. "Now is not the time Chris," she said.

"You're right, of course," admitted Chris with a wry smile, but a much lighter heart. They both decided that sleep was the next thing on the agenda, and settled down for the rest of the night.

A few hours sleep and they were ready for work, turning their attentions to planning the day's travel arrangements, Janine showed Chris the local area on the computer screen, "Teddington Lock is next, then we go through Molsey, then Sunbury. I'm worried about this Desborough Channel. I'm hoping it's deep enough, and if we stay near the bottom there shouldn't be any sign of movement on the surface."

"It won't matter anyway," answered Chris. "If we can follow that boat again the turbulence caused by the micro will go unnoticed."

"Yes of course, well, that takes us on to Shepperton, and bearing in mind that we have three locks to go through I think that's about as far as we'll get in one day."

Janine was right, and the second night was spent at Shepperton, with the micro-sub on the riverbed as on the previous night.

During the night they could see flashes of light through the transparent hatch illuminating the muddied water above them. "Must be quite a storm going on up top," said Chris after a particularly vivid display of lightning.

Had they known, the storm was widespread and severe, by the early hours of the morning the current had strengthened to such a degree that the micro-sub began to bump along the riverbed. Chris had to keep the drive-motor running at half speed just to keep stationary. It was nearly mid-day when the first boat came struggling up the raging river and manoeuvred its way into the lock.

"Come on," said Chris. "We can't waste any more time, we'll follow this one through the lock."

On through Chertsey to Penton Hook. They waited hours at Penton Hook, all the time being buffeted by the fast flowing river. The new 'host' showed no signs of moving on, and as they were unable to negotiate the locks without surfacing, had to wait for the next boat through before they could proceed any further.

It was at Runnymede that the mission nearly ended in failure. Swirling currents, where the Colne Brook joined the Thames, caught them unawares and swept the micro-sub off course and then under the keel of a large barge careering downstream out of control on the other side of the river. The cylindrical sub rolled helplessly along under the keel, rolling over and over like a log. Smashing off its stabilisers and rudder, the weight of the barge nearly crushing the micro-sub between its keel and the riverbed. Eventually the barge passed over, but the micro-sub was completely out of control and finished up tightly wedged under a jetty.

Chris struggled to free the sub, but no matter what he tried, the sub remained firmly trapped, water seeping in fast through damaged joints all over the hull.

"How long have we got?" asked Janine.

Chris answered as he checked some of the instruments. "A couple of hours at the most I would guess."

"I suppose we *can* get out?…Can we?" queried Janine nervously.

23

Chris looked at the CALO screen. "I think so, there doesn't seem to be anything directly above us by the hatch. The sub seems to be trapped fore and aft by those timbers." Chris pointed out to Janine the massive wooden piles and trestles that supported the jetty.

"Can't you increase the air pressure to keep the water out?" suggested Janine.

Chris balked at the idea of Janine telling him what to do and replied slowly.

"Yes I can do that," came the terse answer from Chris.

"Good, let's do it then," said Janine. "We'll stay here until it gets dark, then go the rest of the way on foot."

"Are you mad? It's a *hell* of a way to go, we'd be picked up by the police before we got two kilometres up the road," argued Chris.

"Not if we wear the foil hats," parried Janine. Chris continued to argue.

"We don't know if they even work, it was just an idea of Bob's."

Janine not giving way argued back. "Well I think we ought to try it, *if you don't mind*? Anyway we can't stay here forever, we've got to try something."

Janine was getting angry at Chris's reluctance to take the initiative. "You balance the pressure, and I will sort out some things for us to take with us when we leave."

"But Janine... Oh all right, if that's what you want," answered Chris, unhappily caving in under Janine's onslaught. Janine collected two waterproof backpacks and filled them with items she thought would be needed for their journey, clothing, maps, a couple of torches and a compass. She then turned her attention to making the two foil hats that Bob had suggested might help them escape detection by the Epic Special Police.

Meanwhile, Chris, after balancing the pressure, was surveying the damage when Janine wriggled her way back into the control section and climbed into her seat. "How's it going?" she asked.

"Fine," said Chris with a touch of sarcasm. "Except that we will have to leave by eight o'clock tonight."

"Why is that?" asked Janine.

"I suppose you do know how we get our air supplies?"

"Of course I do," replied Janine. "We extract oxygen directly from the water through a membrane why?"

"It's not working," answered Chris. "When we were rolled along the bottom, the water inlets were crushed and nothing's getting through to the unit."

"Can't you bypass it somehow, get water through from another source?"

"No, it's a sealed unit, no chance of getting to it without the proper tools. We're on emergency air supplies now, and providing these leaks don't get any worse we've got about eight hours left." Chris's voice was serious, and it conveyed to Janine the harsh reality of the situation.

The air supplies held out until ten o'clock, when they eventually had to vacate the sub. Janine showed Chris exactly where they were on the map and the location of the Professor's house should they get split up.

Leaving the sub would be hazardous, with no natural light and the river too muddied for the visibility to be more than zero. Also with the jetty around them consisting of timber piles driven into the riverbed it would not be practical to use a 'buddy' line, because of the danger of entanglement. Which meant that they would have to eject separately into the river. "After I clear the sub," said Janine. "I'll go down-stream until I get clear of the jetty... I'll wait by the bank." She leaned over in the cockpit and, as best she could, embraced Chris. They donned the foil hats, then the helmets complete with 'Fletcher's Gill', a unique chemical device worn in the mouth, enabling the wearer to 'breathe' under water for about twenty minutes without the encumbrance of air cylinders. They gave each other a final check over, and then Chris switched off the power. The water came in fast, and it was not long before the hatch could be opened.

Janine went first. Out into the inky black water, hands holding tightly to the slimy timbers of the jetty, carefully feeling her way, powerful currents tearing at her all the while. She decided it would be best to make for the 'river' side of the jetty rather than the 'land' side. Which proved fairly straightforward, and once clear, she made her way down-stream to the end of the jetty to wait for Chris.

Chris had not fared so well, He too thought of making the 'riverside' of the jetty, but as he climbed clear of the sub, lost his handhold on the slippery timbers and was swept helplessly along under the jetty, getting entangled with weed and wires. In total blackness it took him twenty exhausting minutes to blindly disengage himself. He knew that his 'Gill' could fail at any time.

Meanwhile Janine, already at the rendezvous, was getting desperately worried. Twenty-five minutes had elapsed since they had left the micro-sub. She waited nervously at the down-stream end of the jetty, holding on to a mooring ring set in the side of the jetty for all she was worth, struggling against the swirling floodwater that constantly threatened to sweep her away. She began to wonder if she should attempt to return to the micro-sub to see if Chris needed help. An involuntary cry of relief sprang from her lips when Chris, in the grip of the floodwater, was swept round the end of the jetty. She grabbed hold of his arm and pulled him to safety. They helped each other out of the water, and as they walked along the deserted jetty in the rain Chris explained what had happened to him.

Chapter 3

Through the rain at the far end of the jetty they could see a weak yellowy light shining above the doors of an old boathouse. "Just what we wanted," said Chris. They walked along huddled arm in arm against the rain and made their way to the front doors of a black and white building, a wooden building in much need of repair. The roof and top quarter of the building were black, the walls were white, or should have been, but mostly they were discoloured to a dirty looking grey. Right at the base, and for about a metre up, the walls took on a greenish appearance due to a build up of algae.

Above the doors also illuminated by the light hung a sign, again in black and white but a lot cleaner and newer looking than the rest of the building, stating that this was the headquarters of the Runnymede Rowing Club, and gave a telephone number to call for enquiries.

The large double-doors at the front and under the light were of course locked, and all the windows along either side of the building were much too high up to reach from the jetty's timber flooring which was made of blackened beech planks with small spaces between each plank. Behind the building and reaching the whole length of the jetty there was a high earth bank thickly covered with shrubs and brambles and topped with poplar trees. They discovered there were no windows at the back either.

"Pity we've got to break in," said Chris as he picked up a piece of rock from the bank. He then walked round to the large double doors at the front of the building, and smashed one of the small panes of glass in a window at the top of one of the doors. Chris then lifted Janine up so that she could reach down inside and open the door.

Janine found her torch and swung the beam around to get some idea of the inside geography of the place. Several rowing skiffs were ranged along either side, and above there were a dozen or so pairs of oars in racks lining the length of the roof.

"Let's get out of these wet suits and change into some dry clothes," suggested Janine.

"I've no dry clothes, I have absolutely nothing," said Chris. "I lost my backpack somewhere under the jetty, I've nothing to change into."

"Well we can't walk about like this," said Janine. "Not if we intend going cross-country. Look, I've got some spare clothing, I'll see if I can sort out something that will fit." Janine put her torch on a shelf and rummaged about in her backpack where she found some silky underwear and a wrap-around housecoat.

Chris disdainfully held up a pair of flimsy panties and said. "If you think I'm going to travel across England dressed in these, you're very much mistaken."

"Oh come on Chris, you'll look beautiful, with your long brown hair and lovely hazel eyes, you'll get away with it easy... if you don't talk."

"I don't seem to have much choice, do I?" said Chris sulkily, and donned the female apparel. "What am I going to do for shoes?"

Suddenly the door was wrenched open and the lights were switched on. A heavily built man stood solidly in the doorway, pointing an energy gun directly at them. Janine, holding a short boat hook stepped back a little, and Chris, just stood motionless with his back to the man. "What have we here," said the man, in mock comedy. "Two girls out for a bit of sport eh? I'll give you sport... just get yourselves over here." Chris turned round, and the man's jaw dropped at the sight of a tall woman with three days growth of beard. "What the..." he started but never finished his sentence. Janine taking advantage of the situation struck him hard on the head with the boat hook.

The man's gun clattered down as he fell unconscious to the floor.

"Thought we were done for then," said Chris with relief.

"And we would have been, had not your 'charm' been so distracting."

"It was a lucky break really wasn't it? Now I won't have to wear your clothes," laughed Chris.

"What are you going to wear then, sail-cloth?"

"No, of course not, I'll change clothes with him, solves the problem nicely." chuckled a much-relieved Chris.

Outside the boathouse the man's car had been left open and the engine running. "He must have been in a hurry to catch us," said Janine. "We must have tripped an alarm when we broke in."

Chris agreed. "It's lucky for us he came along, we'll travel in style now."

He then climbed into the driving seat, and studied the controls. Janine foraged about in her backpack for a map.

"Here we are," she said. "Up onto the road, turn right, that should take us towards Windsor."

"I have a better idea," said Chris. "When that chap comes round he'll report the assault and the car as being stolen, the police will be on the lookout for us and it... Now, *this* car is equipped with an auto-follow facility. If we wait until another car comes along, put this vehicle on auto-follow, it'll follow that car wherever it goes. We on the other hand, double back to the river, and pinch one of the motorboats. There's bound to be one moored along the bank, and with a bit of luck it won't be missed for a while, not until morning anyway."

Janine was quite pleased with Chris, he was at last showing a bit of initiative. "What a good idea," she said, making a deliberate effort to give Chris's ego a much needed boost.

The car was duly sent on its mystery tour, then they doubled back to the river, giving the boathouse a wide berth. A suitable motorboat was found moored to a jetty about one kilometre upstream and with a little 'doctoring' they got underway. They set off, and in spite of the swollen river made ten knots against the current.

"We picked a good one," said Chris.

"You picked a good one you mean," cut in Janine. "I had little to do with it."

She stood beside him in the wheelhouse and put her arm round his waist, he looked at her and smiled. "You do look cute in that woolly hat."

"So do you," giggled Janine. She had found two hand-knitted woolly hats in the boat's locker. They were the ideal headgear to cover the foil hats she had made from the metal foil Bob had put aboard the micro-sub. The lock gates proved no real problem for them in spite of the swollen river, and with no other traffic at that time of night had a clear run up-river until they came to Goring lock.

Goring lock was a 'manned lock', and the would be sailors had to go into the lock-keeper's office and report. The lone lock-keeper viewed them with suspicion. Perhaps he didn't like the look of Chris, dressed as he was in a pair of baggy trousers four sizes too large and hanging in great folds round his waist. Or the tatty roll-necked jumper, that fitted like a tent, or maybe it was the expensive looking orange, green and white ladies woolly hat with a large pom-pom that seemed strangely attracted to the front, and hung stupidly down between his eyes. And he was not entirely convinced as to where they were taking the boat. For when he asked for their destination, Chris said, "Oxford", and Janine said, "Shillingford". Then to compound the error they *both* reversed their answers.

"Now what is it to be?" said the man with pen poised. Chris was about to answer when he received a sharp kick on the shin from Janine.

"Ow!" he shouted.

"How's what?" asked the man.

"Er... how's the weather been around here lately?" blurbed Chris.

"The same as you've been getting, now come on and stop playing games."

It was obvious the man was getting riled.

"We're going to Oxford," said Janine, "but a friend is meeting us at Shillingford, that was why we confused you."

"Right then, ultimate destination... O.x.f.o.r.d... Now, can I see the documents for the boat?"

Janine hadn't thought of documents. "Documents! Oh! My friend has them, that's why we're picking him up at Shillingford," said Janine quickly, realising that her mental agility had got them out of an awkward situation. Meanwhile, Chris had moved aside, thus avoiding another well-aimed kick from Janine.

"I see," said the man. "And what might your friend's name be?"

"Clarke," said Chris.

"Smith," said Janine simultaneously. Another searing look from Janine and Chris retreated. "His first name is Clarke, and his surname is Smith," said Janine, still looking hard at Chris.

"Right," said the lock-keeper. "If you'll just sign here," he indicated the bottom line on the paper. Janine signed Gloria Bentley.

"Thank you Mrs Bentley… or is it Miss?" he said with a quizzing look.

"Miss," said Janine with a confident smile. The lock-keeper gave Chris a knowing look, which Chris could not decipher as being either one of admiration or derision. The lock-keeper allowed them to proceed through the lock with a proviso that they reported to the River Thames Authority when they arrived at Oxford, to which they readily agreed.

They travelled all day and cruised safely past Dorchester. Janine said, "Only two kilometres to go now."

They had made good time in spite of the river being in spate, arriving at Burcot late in the evening of the fourth day. Chris steered the boat over to the Burcot bank, crunching in under some over-hanging branches, which provided perfect cover, he secured the boat and leapt ashore.

The rain had stopped, and the sky was almost clear of cloud. It was an hour after sunset when they made their way up through the bushes and trees that lined the gently sloping bank, carefully picking their way by the orange glow that came from the giant surveillance satellites that hung in the sky eighty kilometres above the Earth's surface.

Chris stopped halfway up the bank. "Now, where are we exactly?" he said. "Do you recognise anything?"

"Hold on a minute Chris, we've only been on the bank two seconds," gasped Janine in surprise.

"Sorry Jan… must be getting edgy," said Chris apologetically. Janine was in a forgiving mood.

"Let's go through here and see more of the place." She led the way through the bushes, and eventually came to a narrow grass verge by the side of a white-curbed road. "I think this is the way," she said, pointing left. "You remember that Lido we passed about a kilometre back? As far as I remember there was a road that ran past the Lido, followed the river for a while then forked away to the right. The Professor's house was on the corner of that right hand fork."

"So we're almost there then?" shouted Chris enthusiastically.

"Shush! Keep your voice down, someone might hear and alert the police," cautioned Janine. They were about to step out onto the road when a car with powerful headlights came roaring towards them. They darted back into the bushes, the car, bearing the black and gold insignia of the Epic Special Police, roared noisily by. "Do you think they were looking for us?" asked Janine.

"No, I don't think so," said Chris hopefully. "They walked along the tree-lined road, hiding at intervals to avoid being seen by passing traffic. "There's the house, the big gates, I remember them," said Janine.

The gates were not locked and once through they walked up a long crunchy drive, edged with huge laurel bushes. Eventually they came to a large old-fashioned Manor house surrounded by a sizeable walkway paved with grey flagstones and broad stone steps leading down to the drive. Walking slowly up the broad stone steps and across the grey flagstones they came upon an imposing iron-studded oak-panelled door. Standing there in front of the door for a moment, their hearts pounding with mixed feelings of fear, relief, tension and excitement. They held hands tightly and Chris touched the bell push.

No sound came from inside the house and they wondered if the bell was working. Chris was about to try again when the huge door slowly opened and they heard a low whispered voice bidding them to enter. Into a dimly lit hall they stepped, the door closed silently behind them ending its travel with an ominous click. The voice, now a warm, vibrant, compelling voice continued. "Welcome, now will you please move to your left and proceed down the corridor. Enter the lift and press button number three."

Down the corridor they went, walking slowly and cautiously. Janine began to take notice of the trappings. They were walking upon a rich rust-red deep piled carpet bordered on either side by highly polished parquet flooring. They went past antique tables with little drawers and beautifully inlaid designs, suits of armour, classical oil paintings, all perfectly preserved. The lift doors which looked as though they were made of steel, opened automatically as the two approached.

They entered the lift and pressed button number three. Both were surprised to be going down, they had expected to go up to the third floor. The lift stopped, the doors opened. Chris and Janine saw a white-coated man standing outside, a man in his fifties, balding, bearded, his face serious but half-smiling. His hands were thrust deep into the pockets of his white coat. "Professor Burgess," said Janine tentatively. "Remember me?"

The professor gazed intently at Janine for what seemed an eternity, then looked at Chris for a second or two then back to Janine. Quite suddenly he withdrew his hands from the pockets of his white coat and smiled broadly. "Of course I remember you," he said stepping forward holding out his hand. "You're Janet Cooper, I never forget a face."

"Janine," corrected Janine.

"Pardon?" said the professor. "What was that you said?"

"Janine, my name is Janine, not Janet, and this is Chris Bonham, a dear friend and working associate of mine."

The professor's face smiled an even broader smile. "Janine, yes of course it is, nice to see you again." Then turning to Chris the Professor grabbed his hand and commenced a long pumping handshake. "Any friend of Janine's is a friend of mine, pleased to meet you." Then placing himself between them put his arms round their shoulders and gently ushered them down a passageway. "Now then, it is obvious from your appearance that you are both in some sort of trouble. I imagine you will want to freshen up a bit, am I right?" He looked at each of them. They nodded, he continued. "Right... I have some accommodation for you, somewhere where you can shower, or bathe if you prefer, then, when you are rested you can tell me all about it."

At the end of the passageway they were met by an elderly man and large middle-aged woman, they were each dressed in light grey tunics buttoned up to the neck.

The professor handed Janine and Chris over to the couple. "Look after our visitors," he said. "We shall probably eat in about an hour." The man and woman nodded, leading their charges away to some comfortable rooms on the floor above.

The Professor turned, walked back along the passageway past the head of the stairs and stopped facing the end wall. He placed his hand, palm outstretched, onto the wall, just below a picture of the Epic Building. "Professor Burgess wishes to enter," he said. A panel slid aside and Professor Burgess, stooping slightly, went in through the opening and into a secret lift.

The lift took the professor down to a sub-basement where he alighted and walked down a short passageway into a large technical laboratory. He continued walking between two rows of benches laden with masses of electronic gadgetry until he came to a section which looked like an operating theatre, complete with operating table and lights. Several masked, white-coated figures surrounded the table, upon which lay an inert figure, covered except for the head in green cotton cloths. As the professor approached one of the figures in white turned. "We're all ready for the switch on Professor, just waiting for you to start the sequence."

Professor Burgess took up his position at the *head* end of the table.

"Thank you John," he said. "Ready?... Switch going over... Now."

Chapter 4

Suddenly it was light, dazzling bright lights, but everything was blurred, Doug Sampson was awake. 'Where am I?' he thought. 'There's no sound, I can't see properly.' He had no feeling of pain or discomfort, in fact he had no sensation of feeling at all. A cluster of lights came slowly into focus, as did four masked faces looking down at him around the periphery of the light shade. Doug was lying on his back, his thoughts racing round trying to make sense of the situation.

'I've had an accident; I'm in hospital. Where's Helen?' He began to remember Stanley and the gun. A loud buzzing sound in his ears interrupted his thoughts, the sound gradually subsided into a low hum, then nothing again.

'Voices, I can hear voices,' thought Doug. It was a woman's voice.

"Okay," said the voice. "Switch him off."

The next instant Doug found himself sitting in a wheel-chair. Four men and two women, all in white coats, were standing in a semi-circle around him.

"He's switched on again Professor," he heard someone say.

A man, bearded and wearing spectacles, detached himself from the group and came over to Doug, who could look neither right nor left, only straight ahead.

He still had no feeling and could not move a muscle. The man referred to as 'Professor' was peering directly into his face.

"Now Mr Sampson, you already have vision and audio, we are ready to give you speech, feeling, and mobility; first, feeling and mobility, then speech. You will then indicate to me any malfunction you have in your systems."

'It was all very 'matter of fact',' thought Doug. This Professor was talking to him as though he was talking to some kind of machine.

A slight tingling sensation crept throughout his body, a pleasant warmth. He could 'feel' the chair he was sitting in. He waggled his fingers, blinked his eyes.

The professor spoke again. "Mr Sampson, don't try to get out of the chair, you will not have any balance and will fall over, but you are an independent unit and as far as I can tell, fully functional."

Doug could move his head, look right, look left, he felt fine.

"Where am I? - What am I doing here? - What happened? Who are you?"

The questions came flooding out.

"I am Professor Burgess, you are in my home at Burcot in Oxfordshire. I have a lot to tell you, but first you must tell me how you feel?"

Doug systematically went over his senses. It was with great alarm he suddenly realised that he was not breathing. He could not remember taking a breath since his first consciousness, he began to panic, and was now showing signs of distress, the professor looked concerned. "What's wrong… is anything the matter?" he said.

"I'm not breathing!" shouted Doug. "I'm not breathing!"

The professor hurried back to the group and conferred with his colleagues, a white-coated colleague left the group and walked over to a console where he adjusted a few knobs and dials, meanwhile the professor returned to Doug. Shortly afterwards the sensation of breathing began and Doug's panic subsided. "Is that better Mr Sampson?" asked the professor.

"Yes thank you," replied Doug.

"And everything seems to be all right?"

"Yes… I think so, I feel fine," answered Doug, puzzled by the questioning.

"Good," said the professor. "Before I bring you up to date, I want you to get used to normal physical functions, like standing, sitting, walking, running, all the normal movements. My colleagues will assist you, I have some visitors who require my immediate attention." The professor turned abruptly and walked away.

This *'put off'* was too much for Doug, he wanted answers. He sprang to his feet, reeled, and lurched toward the retreating professor.

The professor was right, no balance. Doug grabbed a piece of equipment for support, the casing buckled like paper beneath his grasp. The professor turned, in his hand he held a small black box, he pressed a button, coloured lights flashed on the box and Doug became immobilised. Fully conscious, but once again unable to move a muscle. The professor was angry. "I cannot deal with you just now Sampson," he said. "I hope you are not always going to be so much trouble. Why don't you do as you are told?" He signalled to his colleagues. "Put him in the chair." Turning again, the professor walked briskly between the two rows of benches and out of the laboratory.

Janine, refreshed after her shower, and dressed in some very revealing silk underwear, had seated herself at a dressing table with a large mirror, and was brushing her hair with a rather ornate silver-backed hairbrush.

She heard a light knock on the door of the apartment. Putting down the brush Janine drew her robe together tying it securely at the waist then walked quickly across the richly carpeted floor of the apartment and opened the door. There stood Chris, he was smartly dressed in a light-grey tunic. "My goodness," teased Janine. "Who *can* this *handsome* man be? Do I know you sir?" Chris smiled and stepped into the room, put his arms round Janine, drew her slim body close to his and passionately kissed her.

She clung tightly to him for a second, passionate thoughts raced through her brain. She had secretly dreamed something like this would happen to her. Then, pushing him roughly away, Janine feigned anger. "Just what do you think you are up to? Who do you think you are, coming in here and grabbing hold of me? You really do have a damn awful sense of timing."

Chris was set back on his heels, he had an amazed look on his face.

"I...I...I thought..." he stammered.

Janine caught hold of his hand and led him further into the room. "Oh come on in you great big galoof, but in future just don't take me for granted," she stopped and turned, and stood squarely in front of him. "You may kiss me now," she said.

Chris was pole-axed. He sat down on the edge of the bed and put his head in his hands. "Will I ever understand women?"

Janine sat down beside him on the bed and gently ran her fingers through his hair.

A knock at the door, the elderly manservant called from outside.

"If you are ready Miss, I will show you the way to the dining room."

"Thank you, I'll only be a minute," answered Janine and went into a bedroom to finish dressing.

The elderly manservant led the way to the dining room where they again met the professor, and during an excellent meal gave an account of their movements over the last few days.

They told the professor how overjoyed they were, winning the competition, and the prospective trip to Australia. How sad and shaken they were with the loss of the Adelphi. The terror they experienced in the barge with its gruesome contents.

The under-sea factory making fertiliser out of human remains and the discovery of modified humans. Ending with their arrival at Burcot, after their near disastrous trip up river in the micro-sub and motor-boat. A note of urgency crept into Chris's voice.

"We *must* be off Sheerness at 22.00hrs on the eighth, Bob Hollis said he would surface and look for us."

"Don't worry," assured the Professor. "I will make some special arrangements. We will all travel down to Sheerness by road late on the seventh, and disguise our real mission by having an all day fishing trip on the eighth. We can then meet your friends and return. I'll give your skipper new co-ordinates. He will be able to take the sub to a safe hiding place. It's a cave on the Cornish coast with a connecting shaft to the Moors above. Once there, we can pick them up at any time and bring them to Burcot by road.

"Thank you Professor," said Janine, she leaned over and gave him a kiss on the cheek. The professor looked a little embarrassed and got quite flustered.

"Yes… er … well, you can rely on me er, I mean us, now where was I?"

The professor recovered his composure and poured some more wine, a discerning observer would have detected, during the pouring, a slight shaking of the hand.

"We have known about these things for some time now, not your particular incident of course, but similar horrible and sadistic practices," said the Professor. "We… " he hesitated, not knowing whether to trust the newcomers. They sounded genuine, but they could be Epic agents. He would have to trust them. If they were Epic agents it was already too late.

The Professor continued. "We, the Organisation that is, came into being just over ten years ago. A group of people, colleagues of mine, discovered that Epic was systematically destroying the human race on a worldwide scale. In Britain, from John-O-Groats, down through Scotland, through northern England, to a line stretching roughly from Blackpool across to Scarborough there are vast areas with scarcely a human in sight, except for a few regions that Epic had kept aside for special projects."

The professor then outlined a world that Chris and Janine never knew existed. "Populations of towns, villages, cities, were being moved out for '*economic reasons*', but most of them never reached their destinations. There was evidence to show that they were taken to the Epic building in London. They were never seen again.

A group of friends, colleagues of mine had gathered evidence about these disappearances and had taken their findings to the Special Police. They also were never seen again. Their discoveries were never made public. It became clear to me that any attempt to bring this knowledge directly into the open would end in failure.

I was lecturing in those days, travelling to various universities lecturing on cybernetics. In my travels I picked up bits of information, not important by themselves, but collectively when all the pieces were brought together, they told a grim story. Students innocently came to me saying wasn't it strange that '*this*' happened or '*that*' happened, not really knowing what it was all about, or seeing anything like the complete picture. The worst thing about it was the fact that they didn't seem to care, they never wanted to follow it up or query it in any way, Epic's influence I suppose.

On my travels I also met colleagues, contemporaries, who, during private conversations trotted out some of their inner fears. We felt we could no longer stand by and watch Epic destroy the human race and do nothing about it. We banded together and formed 'The Organisation', which we code-named 'Albatross'. It is not an acronym, the letters do not mean anything other than what they say, but for us it symbolised *freedom*. We thought of that great bird flying, so far, so free. It fired our imaginations and somehow spurred us into action, we made it our standard, one to be carried deep into the very heart of the enemy camp, one that we must follow to the bitter end, or die trying."

Chris and Janine sat in silence, mesmerised by the Professor's spirited speech. All their lives they had been brought up to believe that Epic was good, Epic was kind and benevolent. And, except for the recent ghastly revelation, which had turned their ordered world upside-down, would have still believed that to be the case.

The professor sat there in silence for a while sipping his wine. "I'm sorry," he said eventually. "You must be tired, I suggest you both get some rest, we will talk some more in the morning. Think deeply upon all that I have told you. It is a certainty that you can no longer return to your previous way of life, you are now candidates for intense consideration by the Special Police Force."

He beckoned to Jazzer, for that was the elderly gentleman's name, and instructed him to show the guests back to their rooms. Janine and Chris bade goodnight to the professor and followed Jazzer out of the dining room.

Doug had been replaced in the wheel-chair and switched on again. And over the next few days, with the aid of the professor's assistants, he quickly gained control over his 'bodily functions'. He could now walk, run, stand, sit; turning quickly was still a problem, but he was persevering all the time. Doug was exercising in the laboratory when the professor entered. "Good morning Mr Sampson," he said cheerfully. "And a very good morning it is believe me."

Doug eyed the professor warily; 'so, we're back to '*Mr Sampson*' are we?' he thought? "Good morning," answered Doug politely.

The Professor requested that Doug should follow him, and led the way to an office just off the main laboratory area and in a very businesslike but condescending tone, he spoke. "Sit down Mr Sampson, I'm going to give you a history lesson." All this time Doug had said nothing other than 'good morning'. The professor had the power to switch him off, and he had no wish to be '*switched off* ', so for the present he decided he would co-operate.

Doug chose to sit in an old office chair with wooden arms. He thought it looked rather out of place, contrasting sharply against the sleek businesslike design of the other office furniture. It reminded him of the carver chairs, which were often included in dining room furniture. The professor moved one of the other chairs and sat down beside him, quite close. 'If I wanted to,' thought Doug, 'I could grab the Professor and *immobilise* him,' Doug resisted the temptation.

"Two years ago," began the Professor. "Epic decided to dismantle all cryogenic units, other than those required for medical research purposes. Relatives were contacted, and if no living relative could be found, the unit was dismantled and the body cremated, records were of course kept of all such under-takings. I was contacted and instructed to collect my hitherto unknown relative and make private arrangements for the cremation. I travelled to Rickmansworth and collected the coffin supposedly containing my relative, a Mr Edward Burgess." Doug suddenly wondered what had happened to Ted Burgess, and he was amazed at the striking resemblance between Ted Burgess the owner of the Casino and the man who was talking to him now, Professor Edward Burgess.

The professor continued. "The firm of undertakers I had contracted to collect the coffin were a reputable firm, and the pallbearers were all well built fellows, but when it came to carrying the coffin just a short distance from the emporium entrance to the hearse, they staggered under its weight. I became suspicious that all was not as it should be and instructed them to take the coffin directly to my laboratory at Burcot, which, if you'll excuse the pun, is a *relatively* short drive from Rickmansworth.

Once there I could examine the contents at my leisure."

The professor leaned towards Doug to explain the point. "I had my own cryogenic facilities in my laboratory." He leaned back again and continued.

"You can imagine our surprise when we opened the coffin and discovered a man and a woman, both bound and gagged."

Those last words shot through Doug like an electric current. He gripped the wooden arms of the chair so tightly that they smashed like matchwood. "Helen! Helen! Where is she?" He was so shocked to hear that Helen had come to the same fate, and he suddenly

41

realised that perhaps she too had survived. He stood up and turned suddenly towards the professor who leapt out of his chair and held out the little black box, pointing it towards Doug.

"Now Mr Sampson, please be reasonable, I'm only telling you exactly what happened, as it happened - if I feel at all threatened I shall switch you off, then you will never know - will you?"

Doug, still upset by the rekindled memories of Helen, was also angry at the thought that this *Professor Burgess*, whoever he was, had such power over him.

He sat down again. "Professor," said Doug. "Some things come upon you so suddenly that no amount of restraint can truly prepare you for them, please go on. I was not going to attack you anyway."

The professor, sweating and not at all convinced, sat down cautiously beside Doug. "Mr Sampson, when I restored you to life, for that, in a way, is precisely what I have done, I incorporated the latest technological advances known to man. Your brain is completely electronic; you have the use of total recall. Infra-red, X-ray and telescopic vision. Also a powerful built-in weapons system, super-fast reflexes, enormous strength, which I haven't calculated yet, not accurately, but it is at least ten times that of an ordinary man, and there is a whole host of other 'extras' at your disposal. You are a formidable mating of man and machine. Therefore until you know, and understand what has happened to you, and how this has happened, which I am trying hard to put into the right perspective, I ask you to bear with me and try to control your emotions, believe me I have your best interests at heart.

"What about Helen, is she all right?" asked Doug, trying hard to rationalise what he had just heard.

The Professor continued. "Talking about Helen, I'm still working on the young lady, it will be some time before I have her finished and put back together again."

Doug shot to his feet and forgetting his promise to the Professor, made a move towards him. "What do you mean, put back together? What have you done to her?"

The professor had also leapt to his feet and was back against the far wall, black box in hand, extended towards Doug. On seeing the box Doug stopped and held up both hands in an attitude of surrender.

"Okay, okay I'm sorry," he backed away to his chair and sat down.

"Thank you Mr Sampson, nice to see we are beginning to understand each other at last." The professor also sat down again, but not as close to Doug as he was before. "Now, where was I... ah yes. We found you and the ... er, young lady, bound and gagged inside a coffin that was supposed to contain the remains of my distant relative. I was curious, intrigued, puzzled to say the least. I wanted to know how the both of you came to be in that situation." The Professor paused, he was waiting for some reaction from Doug but none came, so he continued with another portion of potted history.

"To date, no one had ever been successfully revived from a cryogenic unit.

I had at my disposal, a superb cryogenic laboratory and workshop, a wonderfully equipped electronic laboratory, and I was deeply involved in cybernetics. What a challenge, I know it sounds callous but I was thrilled at the prospect of having two chances to succeed."

"Two chances?" broke in Doug. "What do you mean?"

"Well my friend, if I failed completely with you, I had a second chance of correcting any errors on the body of the girl."

"Callous is right," said Doug under his breath. "Go on."

"Thank you."

The professor warmed to his task, and forgetting his previous nervousness edged a little nearer to Doug. "You were not 'dead' when placed in the cryogenic unit. Therefore your brain impulses were all held in a status quo situation, as were all other chemical processes. Everything being frozen in time by the liquid nitrogen."

The professor was getting excited, it was obvious that what he had achieved was a milestone in his life's work. "The workshop, technical equipment, everything, was kept at a temperature of minus eighty degrees centigrade. I then, in layman's terms, sliced you up. Your skin, bones, muscles, were all measured, analysed, and synthetically reproduced. Your brain sliced a few microns at a time, analysed, and integrated into the latest micro-technology. Every single crumb of data, every thought, word and deed was captured and transferred to the SENADS unit."

Doug again interrupted the professor. "What is a SENADS unit?"

43

"A SENADS unit my dear boy, is the very latest development in neuro-electronics, I'm afraid it's far too complicated for a layman like yourself to understand. It's based on light excited chemicals and lasers in the Gamma range. It was developed secretly by the Organisation; its storage and switching capabilities run into many billions. There are only two actually in existence, but I am working on a third. You have one... I'll tell you later the location of the other one.

The name stands for Simulated Electronic Neuro-Axonic and Dentrite Synthesiser."

Doug was none the wiser but he nodded just the same.

"Every single part of your body has been reproduced synthetically, and..." The professor's eyes were shining bright, he was smiling a smile that suggested a 'you'll never believe this' statement was about to be expounded. "Your power source is derived from no less than three of the latest cold fusion nuclear reactors, without any attention at all you will theoretically still be functioning quite well in two hundred years time." He sat back and put his outstretched fingers together in an attitude of pious satisfaction, and looked at Doug.

The story that Doug had just heard was incredible. It wasn't real; it was as though he was being told a yarn out of some far-fetched science fiction fantasy. No, it wasn't Doug Sampson the professor was talking about; he was quite a normal everyday sort of chap. I can walk, talk, eat, feel, sweat, breathe... ah... there was something out of the ordinary. He remembered when he had his first moments of consciousness, he wasn't breathing, yet as far as he remembered had felt no real discomfort, other than thinking he ought to be breathing. He didn't 'need' to breathe. And what did the Professor mean when he said my brain has been reproduced synthetically. The awful reality began to dawn upon him; he had made him into a bloody robot.

Doug sprang to his feet and angrily faced the professor

"And what do you expect me to do now Professor? Congratulate you on your achievements. No doubt they are tremendous strides in the field of science. From what you have just told me I'm nothing more than a collection of sophisticated nuts and bolts, not really *alive*, just *activated*... What about *me*... What about the real *me*? Did you ever stop to consider that I might want to live my life just as it was before, just as *I* was before, did you think of that? Where is my immortal soul?

What have you done about that? All my cherished beliefs, all my childish dreams, all my ideas and ideals about God, about faith. Where have *they* gone to? Are you going to tell me that you have located and analysed my soul and sliced that up too, and has that also been synthesised, whilst the rest of me, the real me, is gracing some supermarket show-case somewhere, displayed like so many rashers of bacon?"

The professor was so taken aback he didn't even jump to his feet when Doug furiously approached. He hadn't thought seriously that Doug might object to being dissected and screwed back together like a set of Meccano.

The professor said nothing; he got up, walked over to the desk and rang a little brass bell. Jazzer entered. "You rang sir?"

"Bring some coffee will you Jazzer," said the Professor quietly.

"Very good sir." And the manservant solemnly retreated backwards out of the room.

Whether it was intentional on the part of the professor or not, Doug could not say, but it completely defused the situation. Doug burst into laughter at the sheer '*burlesqueness*' of it all, and luckily saw a comical side to it. Jazzer looked and sounded just like a traditional butler from an old M.G.M. film classic, and this whole bizarre episode had a nightmarish quality about it. It was so unreal it just struck him as being funny.

Doug realised that he had no idea of the time scale involved.

"What year is it Professor? How long were Helen and I in the freezer? Ten, twenty, thirty years?"

The Professor came over to where Doug was standing. He showed no fear of Doug now, after all, he had dropped his bombshell, what else was there that would cause Doug further alarm. "The year my friend is 2150 A.D.," said the Professor.

Doug thought he had heard wrong, and half smiling, half laughing said.

"For a moment I thought you said 2150."

The professor repeated his statement. "The year is definitely 2150, to be precise, Saturday the seventh of May 2150 A.D."

"My God," breathed Doug, and sat down heavily on the chair, his senses trying desperately to grasp the mind shattering impact of the latest mental shock.

The coffee arrived and Doug wondered if Jazzer was real or just another of the professor's creations. Jazzer poured the coffee and in that quaint monotone homogeneous to classical butlers, said. "Will there be anything else sir?"

"No thank you Jazzer," said the professor, and Jazzer discreetly left the room.

The professor brought the refreshments over to Doug. "I can eat and drink then?" said Doug.

"Oh yes," said the professor. He now spoke with a much more understanding tone in his voice. Physically you can do everything you did before, I thought you would prefer it that way. Things would look and feel more natural. Your system will cope well with food and drink, but you don't need to, not if you don't want to, if you see what I mean." The professor was still slightly at a loss, still a little embarrassed by Doug's personal onslaught, and at his own lack of understanding.

Chapter 5

Still seated in the laboratory office situated deep beneath the professor's house at Burcot, Doug and the professor were continuing their conversation.

"As you can imagine," said the professor. "A lot has happened since the time of your entombment, I will endeavour to bring you up to date. Now I think, is the time to tell you about Epic."

"Epic?" queried Doug, dragging himself back to reality.

"Yes Epic," repeated the professor. "Epic, is all things to all men. The panacea for all ills, the Golden Fleece, the Goose that lays the Golden Egg, the Ellysian Fields, The Philosopher's Stone. The list goes on, and call it what you will, today Epic is in control of the whole world. There are cathedrals, churches, built not in the name of God, but in the name of Epic. The populations of the world worship Epic. They wanted miracles, Epic gave them miracles, with Epic all things were possible, and so it goes on, and on, and on, ad infinitum.

It is possible you could have known Epic, he was born in the nineteen-sixties. Admittedly a very crude version compared with today's model. You see Mr Sampson, Epic is a computer, a computer with very remarkable abilities."

The professor paused and Doug took the opportunity to interrupt.

"You say Epic is a computer, yet you called Epic 'he', why was that?"

The professor explained that Epic was originally programmed by a man, therefore it follows that the voice of Epic is that of a man."

"Voice!" declared Doug.

"Yes voice, Epic has a voice, and a body."

"A body!" Doug showed his disbelief in the Professor's remark.

"Well not exactly a real body," reasoned the Professor. "But during audiences with the public, Epic appeared, and still does appear, as a three-dimensional laser projection. An ethereal, mysterious, God-like figure, huge, impressive."

"I'll accept that for now," said Doug, although a little sceptical. The professor continued. "In the 1990's world economics were in turmoil with the Internet entering into the public domain. In Britain and the World, masses of people were embroiled in the treacle of market economics, and were slowly being sucked into a morass of despondency and despair by the caprices of the market pirates.

It was greed really, the ordinary man in the street saw an opportunity to get rich quick. Unfortunately there were people who saw another opportunity, an opportunity to fleece the gullible, and it wasn't only ordinary people who suffered.

It became a National sickness, Governments became involved in this scramble for wealth and were at the mercy of the Internet pirates. Terrible men, unscrupulous men, men who had no feelings for anything but themselves, they became super-rich and whole nations became ultra poor. The wheeling and dealing of these locusts of commerce impoverished the 'masses'

Epic, as I said, is a computer with remarkable capabilities, a new generation of computers, and at that time a completely new concept. Designed by a chap at Cambridge University in the nineteen-sixties, it took him thirty years to perfect the system. He had no idea his revolutionary miniaturised system would develop into the creation of the entity we know today as Epic."

Doug was astounded at the professor's reference to a computer resembling an entity. "Surely Professor, entity is a bit strong for a computer isn't it?" I…"

The professor cut him off mid-sentence. "I said entity, and I meant entity, for as sure as we are that God created man, Epic has been '*created*' on earth by God, or by Satan, something *within* Epic is alive."

The two men just stood and looked at each other. Doug, looking earnestly into the professor's face to see if the look of truth would falter. The professor looked back unwaveringly at Doug and continued.

"Of course, Epic was not originally designed to deal specifically with market economics, but after being fed the relevant data, was found to be unique in accurately forecasting market movements. I suspect a great deal of industrial espionage was involved, after all, Epic was universally linked to every computer terminal in the world, including the stock markets. Hacking into any one of these would have been child's play to a determined onslaught by a 'thinking' computer of Epic's ability.

Epic was taken over by the British Government and further development took place. In 2020 the first cerebral implant was fitted to a leading Government minister. The implant, designed by Epic, was so successful that ministers all over the world were queuing to have one fitted. And once that was done, instead of the ministers controlling Epic, Epic controlled the ministers, a tragic situation by any standards.

Great Britain was the 'Centre of the World'. Epic had made it so. It also marked the end of life as we knew it. The ministers, under the control of Epic, passed legislation that gave terrifying power to Epic. By 2050 Epic had come to terms with all the major problems. World pollution, the ozone layer, lack of resources, the food chain, over-population.

Wars became a thing of the past. Any aggression was met immediately and ruthlessly with the full might of the World Peacekeeping Force, controlled of course by Epic. All these problems, and many others, were all overcome by Epic. History dictated that the remedy for over-population wasn't at all popular. Epic decreed that all heterosexual couples could only have children by allocation, and the allocation was usually only one child. In 2100 it became compulsory for every man, woman and child to have an implant fitted."

Doug could not fully understand the function of the implant. "What is an implant?" he asked. The Professor looked at Doug over his glasses. His face became a mask of hatred, showing the deep revulsion he had for this odious instrument.

"The cerebral implant is the most heinous, most diabolical, most enslaving device ever invented on this planet. The first implants were surgically inserted and gave the wearer a one to one relationship with the computer. The recipients of these devices were formidable opponents. No one could outmanoeuvre them, or better them in argument. A later implant, and I think by far the more sinister, was

49

a biochemical seed, planted surgically in the brain of every child at the age of six. By the time the child reached puberty, the seed had thrown tendrils down in to the control centres of the brain; the child was then ready for Epic.

Four times a year, all the fourteen-year-old children, from all over the country, were brought to the Epic Building in London for the '*switching on*' ceremony. The same thing was happening simultaneously at other Epic Centres all over the world. The youngsters *never* forgot it. They had such wonderful things revealed to them during that ceremonial week. At mass rallies in the grounds of the Epic Buildings, they felt the sheer power of Epic surge through them, they felt invincible. And at the end of the week they all swore an oath of allegiance to Epic. I know all this to be true, for I was one of those youngsters.

The implant was welcomed by everyone, as a great stride forward for mankind. There were no wars, no famines, no booms or depressions. We had become one great big happy family. The family of mankind... *like an ant-nest.*"

The Professor contemptuously spat out the last few words and fell into a frowning silence.

"So what went wrong?" said Doug eventually.

"What indeed," breathed the Professor. "Epic had absolute control over the masses and defection was severely punished by the Special Police, often resulting in the death of the individual. You see, all the information, apart from the educational system, which Epic controlled anyway, came to the people via the media and Epic dictated the output of the media. Epic now ruled completely.

During the last twenty-five years whole village populations have been found dead. Poison gas cylinders were found in all cases near the site. No one knows why, nobody cared. Villagers, from other villages, just came along and cremated them without question. The inhabitants of cities, towns and villages all over the world were and still are being decimated, and the rest are brain-washed into thinking all is well, satisfied that it is the right thing to do."

Why not just remove the implant?" suggested Doug.

"Impossible," said the Professor. "Any interference with the device engaged a self-destruct mechanism and caused a violent retraction of the tendrils and a massive haemorrhage occurred."

"How is it?" asked Doug. "That you and your colleagues have been able to escape being caught by the Special Police."

The professor explained. "I told you that any interference with the implant caused brain damage. That wasn't exactly a true statement. Over the years I made certain discoveries. When a person died we found that the self-destruct mechanism became inoperative, sometimes we managed to get hold of the body. I then had a chance to study the device, and eventually found a way to modify it and use it to our own advantage. By using carefully positioned lasers, I found that I could alter the transmit and receive frequencies, so that the device was no longer in contact with Epic. Eventually I found I could do this operation on living people with no triggering of the device's self destruct system. Many members of the Organisation have been treated and make contact through SAL, our in-house computerised control and communication system. We call the system SAL because some years ago we had a young girl operating the system and her name was Sally, then of course when we computerised the system we just used her name for convenience."

The professor stood up, walked over to the desk and poured himself another coffee, he looked at Doug and held up the coffee pot, Doug shook his head, the professor, cup in hand came back to his seat and continued with his story.

"At first Epic monitored all thoughts and surveyed all deeds. No one could make a move without Epic being aware of it, but as more of the world's populations were fitted with implants the system became so unwieldy, by sheer weight of numbers for even Epic to be the sole monitor, and other measures had to be taken. Other Epic Centres had to be set up all over the world. They were satellite centres and Epic still had absolute control over them, but they took over a lot of the everyday work of monitoring.

For many years now Epic has not 'personally' monitored the everyday life of every individual. Special units now carry out all monitoring, an elite force known simply as the Special Police Force, or the E.B.L.I.S. The Epic Bureau of Legal Interrogation Secretariat to give them their correct title. They rule by brutality and fear."

"Eblis?" queried Doug. "I've heard of that name, it crops up in

51

one of the eastern religions I believe, it's the father of devils, it's their equivalent of Satan."

"Then the units are well named, for they *are* evil. To draw a parallel for you, the units are a similar organisation to the Hitler SS, or the Gestapo of the nineteen thirties, the Nazi Special Police Force. You see, I have done some research into the history of your era.

There are many similarities between the rise of Hitler and the gain of power by Epic. It would appear that the same evil force is at work again. Control of the young people, destruction of literature, all clergy exiled to Atlantis, a witch-hunt and campaign of hatred against ethnic groups and non-believers. By non-believers I should perhaps explain. Epic has planted the idea in people's minds that he is the manifestation of the true God. That he is the true God made manifest on Earth, and anyone that does not accept this is branded as a non-believer.

The Organisation has discovered that Epic is working to accomplish the replacement of the human race with 'beings' of a completely material nature, humanoid robots, androids, They have the right shape, they are mobile, and they don't argue."

"I'm a 'being' of a completely material nature, I'm a robot," said Doug with a certain firmness in his voice. The Professor swung round sharply in his chair, stood up and angrily faced Doug. He was obviously hurt by the remark.

"Oh no you are not, you are nothing like a 'robot'. All right, granted you've been *constructed* in your present form rather than *grown*, but you are mentally what you are after years of being a man, a man born naturally into this world, a man who started his life in this world as a human being. All of your knowledge and feelings have come from those years of experience, and you can draw on those experiences to make decisions based on the knowledge of the formative years. Oh no, *you* are *not* a robot... as far as I am concerned you are Douglas Sampson, and you are, as far as I am concerned, a man."

It was Doug's turn to be taken aback. He wasn't fully convinced by the Professor's last outburst. He felt, physically, as he had always felt, a lot fitter perhaps. And there were certain additions to his faculties, but basically he felt the same as he did before the deep freeze. Nevertheless logic told him that he was *manufactured*. And if the same data had been duplicated and stored, Douglas Sampsons could be rolling off the production line any time the button was pressed, which was something that couldn't be done with a human being, well not as far as he knew.

He didn't want to hurt the professor's feelings, if it hadn't been for the professor goodness knows what would have happened. "I'm sorry Professor," said Doug. "I should not have said that, I really do have a lot to thank you for."

The professor had walked away from Doug during his retaliatory outburst, he now slowly returned. "Yes… well… let's forget it and have no more talk of your being a robot." The professor took a few moments to compose himself and then returned to his narrative.

"To answer your question as to why myself and my colleagues escaped discovery by these 'Special Forces'. Just over ten years ago I had an accident. I became trapped inside a large metal lined room. It was a room used as a test area for some of the more sensitive electronic experiments and was located inside a laboratory at one of the universities. Unfortunately it happened late one Friday afternoon. I called for help, shouted my head off, I concentrated, using my implant, calling for assistance from Epic. I had all weekend to think about the state of things. I was, for the first time since the age of fourteen out of contact with Epic and, of course, vice versa. No one came to my assistance until Monday morning.

I later experimented and discovered that a small piece of perforated metal placed over the implant area seriously weakened its operation. It stopped or distorted the signals to such a degree that I could think or say anything I pleased. At first I had officials round to investigate the intermittent signals they were receiving from my implant. I quickly removed my piece of screening and convinced them that I was just another case of a faulty implant. It does happen from time to time, and once they go wrong they cannot be repaired. The officers went away quite happy with my explanation. I then secretly built a screened room and invited a few chosen friends round once a week.

During these weekly meetings I sounded out their feelings toward Epic, and the way things were going with the world. Eventually I had made sufficient progress to bring some of them into my confidence. The vast majority of the public would call it sacrilege and blasphemous to do what I was doing, therefore they would not do it and would report anyone found doing so. You see, they did not believe that anything was wrong. They had for generations been conditioned to blindly follow Epic's directives.

I have been in a very privileged position, travelling round the country, visiting various universities, lecturing to thousands of people. On my travels, I gleaned snippets of information, little bits here and there, information, that by itself was not worth a jot. Collectively it showed this sinister pattern developing.

Eventually, a few enlightened colleagues and myself banded together and formed an organisation, to try to reverse this abomination that mankind had brought upon itself. The organisation we called Albatross. The name Albatross had a symbolic attraction for us. I am actively involved as head of this organisation."

Doug asked the professor if it was safe to talk openly about what was supposed to be a secret organisation. "Oh yes Mr Sampson quite safe, this whole house is adequately screened, no worries there, but thank you for your concern."

The professor drew the 'black box' out of his pocket and approached Doug. "Now what have I done Professor? I haven't threatened you."

The professor held the box out towards Doug and smiled "This is now the only key that has access to your programming. Without this key and its programmed impulses, I have no control over you, no one has any control over you."

The Professor stood in front of Doug, holding the box in his hand. "Take it," he said.

"What do I do with it?" asked Doug.

"Destroy it would be a good idea, its destruction will do you no harm."

Doug reached out and took the box out of the professor's hand. After a brief examination he increased his grip upon the box and felt it collapse beneath the pressure. "Thank you Professor, but why?"

"First, I must apologise," said the professor. "And I sincerely hope that my apology will be accepted… Although I have achieved something remarkable, I had no right, no right at all to take your body and use it the way I did, it was irresponsible of me, especially as head of an organisation that proudly boasts of freedom and democracy.

Doug smiled, and put his hand gently on the professor's shoulder. "You are a good man Professor, honest and true, as they would have said in the old days. Whatever the rights or wrongs of the argument may be, you truly believed you were acting in my best interest, but for you I may never have had even this consciousness."

The two men stood there facing each other, Doug with one hand on the professor's shoulder, and the professor grasping Doug's other hand with both hands. There was a deep understanding between them.

"So Professor, what happens now?" said Doug with a smile.

The professor went over to his desk, opened a drawer, and took out a small white card. He returned to where Doug was standing and wrote something on the card. "On this card I have written the access code to the 'Command Centre' of your computer. It has nothing to do with your 'brain'. You, up to now, have not had access to your in-built computer. You will now be able to link your electronic brain to your own internal computer and use, to the full, all the extra built-in functions.

He gave Doug the card, who, looking at it briefly, placed it into his breast pocket. The professor continued to talk about the box and of its destruction.

"As the external programming device has now been destroyed, the only way to continue adding to your programme, is for the programming to be done internally, that is, by your own mental impulses. Stay clear of the weaponry section until I return, I don't want the house destroyed just yet."

Doug missed the significance of the reference to weaponry.

"You're going away?"

"Yes, a day, maybe two, when I return I hope to have a few more followers for the organisation, more freedom fighters. Anything you require whilst I'm away just ask Jazzer." The professor made a short 'phone call, rang the bell for Jazzer, then with a wave of his hand walked briskly out of the office.

Jazzer arrived, answering the professor's summons. "I have instructions to show you to your apartment sir," he spoke in such a way that you felt compelled to listen. Although Jazzer was employed ostensibly in a serving capacity, he had an air of authority about him. His utterances, usually couched in the terms of a request, were nevertheless a request that one felt obliged to obey.

Since Doug had been 'brought back to life' he had been accommodated solely within the confines of the laboratory. "Lead on McDuff," said Doug cheerfully.

"I beg your pardon sir?" queried Jazzer, giving Doug a questioning look.

"Never mind," said Doug, realising that twentieth century anecdotes would not be readily understood. "You lead the way, I'll follow."

"Thank you sir," said Jazzer with a slight bow of the head. Doug followed Jazzer to the lift, then up to the next floor and along a well-lit corridor. "Here we are sir, I hope you will be comfortable. Jazzer opened the door and ushered Doug into the apartment.

Back in the twentieth century Doug wasn't by any means rich, but always considered himself, comfortably off. His Maida Vale flat was, he thought, a little 'up-market', but this apartment was sheer luxury.

"What do I do for entertainment Jazzer?"

"Ask sir, just ask," replied the enigmatic manservant.

"Ask?" queried Doug. "Ask who?"

"It's not a *who* sir; it is a computer, tuned to your voice patterns. Music, refreshment, advice, just ask sir, just ask."

It was all so very simple to Jazzer, this was his world, his time.

To him it was normality itself to 'just ask' for things from a computer.

"Right, I'll give it a try," said Doug. And feeling very self-conscious talking to nothing visible, spoke to the computer. "Computer, I would like to hear some popular music." A sensual, sultry, female voice answered.

"Certainly Mr Sampson, and may I take this opportunity to welcome you to your apartment."

The music faded-in to a pleasant level. It was pleasing music, not unlike that of the twentieth century. Doug even found himself thanking the computer for the service.

"You are welcome Mr Sampson, you may call me Sal if you wish."

"Thank you Sal," said Doug. It was a lot easier than saying "Computer do this," or "Computer do that."

"Will that be all sir?" asked Jazzer.

"I think so. Ah!… What if I want the dining room, or something like that?"

Jazzer looked at Doug and was about to make one of his profound announcements, but Doug was able to pre-empt his remark.

"I know, I know, don't tell me, just ask," said Doug with a grin.

Jazzer, almost smiling said. "If you will excuse me sir, I have other duties that require my attention."

"Thank you Jazzer I'll be all right, now I know what to do. If I need to know anything I'll ask the computer."

"Exactly so sir." Jazzer turned and left the apartment.

Doug, now alone, set out to explore his new accommodation. Very comfortable, very impressive, but he found nothing that really caught hold of him and said, 'this is what one hundred and fifty years of progress has produced.' In the bathroom Doug caught sight of his reflection in a full-length mirror. It was the first time he had seen himself since his resurrection.

There were no mirrors in the laboratory; it was an eerie experience. He saw himself, or to put it another way, he saw a figure, that over the years he had come to recognise as Doug Sampson looking back at him, but this figure had subtle differences, it was the same, but different. Doug couldn't say just what it was that was different, but looking at that reflection he *knew* it was different. He rubbed his chin with his hand; he hadn't shaved since his awakening, yet there was no sign of any beard or even stubble. Perhaps that's what it was that was puzzling him.

Eventually he wandered into the lounge and over to the drinks cabinet, poured himself a large whisky, added something akin to ginger ale, and settled down in the large comfortable armchair in front of a simulated log fire.

He took out the card the professor had given to him and re-read the access code. 'How do I use this?' he thought.

Chapter 6

A large white ambulance sped through the rain lashed night en route for Sheerness. In the back, disguised as patients with heavily bandaged heads, were Chris and Janine, accompanied by the professor acting as their doctor.

Ned Holden was driving the ambulance, beside him in the passenger seat sat Derick Elmdon. Both men, members of the organisation and employed by the professor as laboratory assistants, were now posing as male nurses. The ambulance splashing along the rain-drenched road was about three kilometres outside Gravesend.

"There are some flashing lights ahead professor, looks like there's been an accident," said Ned over the intercom. A policeman in waterproof cape and hat who was frantically waving a powerful lamp flagged the ambulance down. The professor climbed out and joined Ned who had also climbed down from the cab and was standing in front of the ambulance. One of the police officers approached, blinding them with his powerful torch-beam.

"Lucky you guys came along, I was just about to call in. Looks like the chap here had a sudden heart attack, must have been driving on manual; he skidded across the road straight into the other vehicle. Got two dead, and two badly injured, I'd like you to get them to Gravesend as soon as possible."

The professor tried to bluff it out. "I'm Doctor Curtis," said the professor, using a fictitious name. "I'd like to help but I have to get my own patients to my clinic at Margate, it's a matter of urgency, and I don't want to run any needless risks of infection." The policeman stood right in front of the professor and was shining the torchlight directly into the his face.

"Look Doc. I was *asking* you before, now I'm *telling* you, don't worry about the dead ones, just get the two casualties to Gravesend General. Put them in the back of your ambulance and follow me… and hurry." The Police officer walked back to his car, got in and slammed the door, then roared off down the road for about ten metres then stopped, waiting for them to 'load up' and follow.

At the hospital, the staff unloaded the two casualties, and then under police instructions, proceeded to 'unload' Chris and Janine. The professor protested strongly, the police officers then arrested them all, Ned, Derick, and the professor.

"We cannot find any information on you, or your clinic, or your journey to Margate sir, it certainly wasn't registered." said the officer in charge.

"Of course it wasn't registered, I told you it was a matter of urgency," exploded the professor.

"Be that as it may sir, your patients will be well looked after in the hospital… you and your assistants will accompany us to Gravesend Police Station for further investigation sir."

The professor was annoyed with himself. If he had not argued in the first place about going to the hospital the police might not have checked up on them, now there was nothing to be done. Another police officer sat in the car, and there were several of the hospital staff standing close by, to make a break would have ended in failure. The professor and his two assistants got into the police vehicle and were escorted to Gravesend Police Station.

For the past hour Doug had sat slowly sipping his whisky and being *educated* by the self-demonstration programme run by his in-built computer giving mental instruction, pictures, graphics, all that was necessary to understand how his new body functioned, and of its capabilities. The study was brought to an abrupt end. "Mr Sampson! Mr Sampson! Doug!… Read the card… read the card if you have not already done so… Tune in to 25.35 Ghz. Transmission is automatic with thought."

It was the professor's voice… inside his head. 'Transmitter', thought Doug. '25.35 Ghz… Professor?' The professor answered, transmitting and receiving via his modified implant.

"Thank goodness I've got hold of you, get hold of Jazzer, tell him to use the 'Special', and get down to Gravesend Police Station. Ned, Derick, and myself have been arrested and are being held in cells in the basement. Chris and Janine are being held in Gravesend hospital. We are all being taken to the Epic Building tomorrow, it's imperative we are rescued before morning."

"Take it as done professor, Sal, tell Jazzer I want him, tell him it is urgent."

A moment's delay and the computer answered.

"Jazzer is on his way Mr Sampson," said Sal.

A few minutes later and Jazzer knocked on the door. "Come in," called Doug. Jazzer entered and Doug told him of the professor's plight. "The professor said we would need the 'Special'."

"Very good sir, would you be so kind as to meet me on the roof in five minutes sir."

"Yes, of course… see you there," said Doug wondering why they had to meet on the roof, perhaps the 'Special' was a helicopter. Jazzer turned and hurriedly left the apartment. Doug raced to the wardrobe, hoping the professor had thought of putting some sort of outdoor clothing at his disposal. Dressing quickly he dashed to the lift, arriving on the roof with just seconds to spare.

Jazzer was already there, and, believe it or not, seated in a large black limousine. The door opened as Doug approached. "It is advisable to wear a safety harness sir."

Doug grunted a "Right-o," and visualised the car would be off at high speed and go speeding down a ramp to the roadway. He settled himself into the luxurious custom built seat, which looked and smelled like leather, but was probably synthetic he thought as he buckled on the safety harness. Jazzer put his foot down on the accelerator. The Special raced along the roof and straight off the edge, then climbed to sixty metres, co-ordinates set for Gravesend.

After he had recovered from the shock of speeding off the roof Doug began to wonder what the world looked like after one hundred and fifty years, not that he would get much of a look at it at night, an overcast sky and rain spoiled his view.

The clouds had a strange apricot-orange glow. Doug asked Jazzer what made the clouds glow? Jazzer's impeccable wisdom came to the rescue.

"It's the light sir." Doug was astounded that such an inane remark should have been the reply. He was about to say something to that effect when Jazzer continued. "It's the light from the surveillance satellites sir. Sometimes they catch the sunlight and reflect the rays, but mostly they glow with their own energy and give a sort of false moonlight. You will see them better when the cloud clears sir."

"Thank you Jazzer," said Doug and looked at the light with renewed interest. He did see glimpses of the satellites through an occasional break in the clouds. He also looked down on millions of lights, stretching like fiery necklaces along what looked like motorways. Junction networks standing out like massive roller-coaster rides, huge over-passes, high-level roads, other hover-cars above and below.

"We are coming up to London now sir," said Jazzer.

The sheer size and splendour of the city overwhelmed Doug; it was a beautiful sight. Masses of high-rise buildings aglow with lights of every shape and colour. Jazzer was skilfully steering the Special between the taller buildings.

"Where are we now?"

"Just coming up to Northolt sir," came the reply.

"There used to be an airfield at Northolt."

"That's probably the Military museum now sir, there's not been an airfield here for as long as I can remember."

"Military museum? Can we spare a few minutes to have a look at it?"

"The Professor did say the journey was urgent sir, but perhaps we can spare a moment or two." Jazzer put the hover-car into a steep dive and spiralled down to a rather impressive building standing in its own grounds. He brought the car to rest outside the main doors. The place was deserted, no lights on, in or around the building, the place was closed.

"I'd like to take a look inside," requested Doug. "It's locked sir, they won't open it up until tomorrow."

"If I'm as strong as the professor says I am it won't be a problem, stand back Jazzer." Doug squared up to the door and was just about to kick it in.

"Just a moment sir, if you insist on going into the building allow me."

Jazzer took something out of his pocket and huddled over the lock. There was a click, Jazzer stood up and turned to Doug. "There you are sir," and gently pushed the door open.

"I'll only be a minute," said Doug, and disappeared into the dark museum.

He sent a command to his in-built computer. 'IMAGE INTENSIFIER ON'.

Instantly his normal vision switched to 'High Intensity' he could see perfectly in the darkened interior of the museum. He was looking for something he could use in the rescue. Nothing suitable on the ground floor. He ran upstairs to the next floor. The only useful weapon he found there was a working model of a First World War Lewis machine gun with spare magazines and ammunition. Admittedly they were in a locked cabinet, which proved no problem. Doug wrenched open the cabinet door, took the gun and two spare magazines, one empty, one loaded, also a box of ammunition. He fitted the loaded magazine into place on the Lewis, cocked the gun and gently squeezed the trigger. A stream of bullets smashed into the glass cases at the far end of the museum. The test firing was all the proof Doug needed, he raced back to Jazzer and the hover-car. As soon as Doug was on board Jazzer took off and headed in the direction of Gravesend.

"What is so special about the 'Special'?" asked Doug.

"It's completely ceramic sir, and apart from a few electrical parts, virtually undetectable by the police radar systems, and almost indestructible. It has high intensity defence screens that can absorb bolts from most energy weapons. And with high impulse atomic engines and the latest anti-gravity coils it can outrun most police vehicles. Does that answer your question sir?"

Doug, not wishing to show his ignorance, just said, "Yes thank you," and sat back, gazing once more at the beauty of the city.

The lights grew fewer on the eastern outskirts of London and Jazzer followed the river for a few miles. Doug took the opportunity to replenish the magazine. "We're going down now sir, I intend going in to Gravesend by road."

Jazzer took the car into Gravesend, found the Police Station, and drew quietly to a standstill in the yard at the back.

Doug got out of the car. "Stay here Jazzer, and be ready to leave in a hurry."

Doug stalked off across the yard toward the building, and holding the Lewis at the ready, quietly opened the door. There were two police officers standing at the head of the stairs leading to the cells. They saw Doug enter with the gun and immediately went for their own weapons. A swift leap forward, the butt end of the Lewis took care of one, the barrel stopped the second, not a shot was fired. Apart from the slight thud of the falling bodies, all remained quiet.

Doug crept silently down the stairs. Two more police officers talking in the corridor at the foot of the stairs, luckily with their backs toward him. Doug was only a metre away when one turned and was immediately dispatched with a crashing right to the jaw, the second officer was quickly silenced with a vicious right backhand.

Doug was amazed at his own speed and strength. A short corridor led into an area containing the cells. In the centre of the area was a large control console, and another officer.

The officer stood up and walked towards the corridor. On seeing Doug and the two fallen officers, he spun round and ran for the console to raise the alarm. Doug having no chance to prevent him reaching the console and not wishing to raise the alarm by the sound of shots being fired, threw the Lewis gun at the retreating policeman. The gun caught the man full in the back, the force carried him past the console and hard into the far wall. Doug rushed across the space to where the officer had fallen, the man lay unconscious on the floor.

On the console were six buttons, six buttons corresponding to six cells, he pressed all six. The door immediately behind Doug crashed open; a bestial roar made Doug spin round. There, standing framed in the cell doorway was a living nightmare, a monstrous creature, similar to the mythical Minotaur. A creature two metres tall, with a huge bull's head and yellowing horns, slavering jaws and the teeth of a carnivore. The massive torso was covered with thick matted hair and the arms rippled with muscles. With another earth-shaking roar the fearsome creature launched itself out of the cell. Doug only had time to grab hold of the horns to avoid being gored; his back pushed hard against the console.

The beast was strong. Horny hands reached up to his throat and fingers like steel bit into his neck with brutish strength. Such force would have killed an ordinary man, but Doug was no ordinary man.

Gradually he forced the great head away and managed to toss the deranged animal aside. Doug then raced for the Lewis, reached it, but before he could bring it to bear on the beast it was on him again. The fight raged back and forth across the area then Doug gained the advantage and tossed the monster across the floor.

This time Doug had time to reach the gun and sent a hail of lead smashing into the oncoming mountain of fury. Several bursts of fire were necessary to stop the terrifying beast. It staggered towards Doug to finally slump twitching at his feet. The professor and his companions had come out of their cells but were afraid to pass Doug and the beast, locked as they were in mortal combat.

With the fight over, they made for the stairs and freedom. The noise of the Lewis had brought officers from other parts of the building to the scene. Ned and Derick raced up the stairs and were almost to the outer door when raking fire from the guard's energy guns brought them down. Doug and the professor were trapped. Doug switched to X-ray vision and looked *through* the panelling that surrounded the top of the stairs.

Four officers were waiting with energy guns at the ready. Doug lifted the Lewis above his head and above the panelling, pointing it back down the corridor. He pressed the trigger and sprayed the area with bullets. The four officers lay sprawled along the corridor; they went down without returning a single shot. Doug motioned to the professor and nodded toward the rear door. Cautiously they crept up the stairs and backed to the door. There was no movement from the police officers, and no sound of reinforcements.

They raced to the 'Special' as two police hover-jets screamed in and remained poised above the yard. "Stop! Or we fire," came the order from above.

The professor had already entered the car. Doug, standing motionless by the open door, said quietly. "Get ready Jazzer, when I give the word, give it all you've got." One of the police jets was about to land, the other one, turning to reposition. "Now !" shouted Doug, leaping into the car. Jazzer sent the 'Special' rocketing down the road and up into the sky, the police jets caught off guard were slow to take up pursuit.

On the way to the hospital Doug had a chance to talk to the Professor. "What was that creature in the police station?"

"That was probably one of Epic's little experiments. There are large areas in the northern part of the country where people have been physically and mentally manipulated to follow a particular programme dictated by Epic," answered the Professor.

"Doesn't anyone do anything about it?" asked Doug.

"No one seems to care. Epic controls the media and the media convinces everybody that all is well. And if anyone gets too nosy they just disappear. You've got a lot to learn about this land of ours... Ah, we're coming up to the hospital now."

"Jazzer, go down to that road behind the hospital," said Doug. "The professor and I will jump out, then you take off fast and try to lose the police, meet us again in twenty minutes."

"Very good sir," said the unflappable Jazzer. He brought the 'Special' round in a large circle and landed behind the hospital. Out jumped the professor and Doug, away shot Jazzer and the hover-car. The police jets spotted it and gave chase.

Doug and the professor walked casually across the parking area at the back of the hospital, and went in through a door marked 'Staff Only'. They climbed the stairs and surveyed each floor. On the third floor they noticed two police officers standing outside one of the doors. "Your friends must be in there Professor," whispered Doug. "Leave this to me."

"I wasn't going to interfere," said the professor half-smiling.

Doug walked confidently along the corridor until he was level with the officers, suddenly he turned, grabbed their jacket collars, and brought their heads together with a sickening crunch. The professor quickly opened the door, and then he, and Doug, still holding the two unconscious policemen by their jackets, swiftly stepped into the room and closed the door. Chris and Janine were inside; their heads still swathed in bandages. The professor joyfully greeted them and introduced them to Doug

Quickly they made their way back along the corridor and out into the parking area. Jazzer spotted them almost immediately and screamed to a stop. As soon as the whole company were aboard

Jazzer sped away with tremendous power, straight up to ninety metres. The police jets came swerving round in a great arc into the attack. Jazzer, side-slipping, diving, twisting, turning, manoeuvring to try and throw the police off their trail. Bolts of energy from the police cannons exploding dangerously close, some striking the defence screen, and rocking the car violently.

Not far to the right Doug saw the entrance to what he assumed to be the Dartford Tunnel. The police jets would be too large to enter, he thought.

"The tunnel!" shouted Doug. "Fly down the tunnel."

"It is not permitted to fly down the tunnel sir," said Jazzer.

"Fly down the tunnel Jazzer," ordered the Professor. Then turning to Doug said. "I don't know what you hope to achieve by flying down the tunnel, they'll only pick us up at the other end."

"That's what I hope they will think. We're not going to the other end," said Doug. "We're only going about half a kilometre into the tunnel, then we're going to turn round and fly back the way we came in, *over* the incoming traffic."

"That's a very dangerous thing to do," said the professor.

"So is breaking out of prison and killing policemen, and fighting with mythical monsters, it's all very dangerous," said Doug.

Flying in the tunnel over the on-coming road traffic was indeed dangerous, all lanes full in both directions. Jazzer was controlling the 'Special' superbly, desperately twisting and turning, avoiding road signs and traffic indicators suspended above the carriageways.

After leaving the tunnel, they flew back over the city and sped out of London on a circular route towards Burcot. There were no signs of pursuit, the ruse had worked. "Take us home Jazzer, take us home," said the professor.

Chapter 7

Author's Note - *There are things that Doug Sampson could not have known. Therefore for the sake of clarity and continuity the next two chapters will deal with events that lead to the situation in which Doug now finds himself. I will take you back to Saturday May 20th 1995. The scene. - A popular gambling casino in Soho London. - Time... Midnight.*

Four men sat round a green baize-topped table playing poker, Alphonso Rossini, two Texan oil tycoons, and Fred Tatum. A cone of light issued out of a lamp positioned directly above the table its beam piercing through the smoke filled air. The light struck the tabletop and bounced back to highlight the set expressions on the faces of the men. It showed the game was reaching a climax.

The two oilmen, in spite of the tension, were just having fun, a good night out. For Rossini it was different, he always had to prove he was the *best*, at poker, at anything. Nearly all the organised crime in the U.K. could be laid at Rossini's feet; he was the Mr Big of the underworld. If you got the okay from Alphonso you were all right; it was like having insurance.

Fred Tatum, an Australian, was a real weasel of a man, thin-faced, wiry, his eyes constantly on the move. He was temporarily employed at the Burgess Casino to run the poker game. Fred was dealing the cards.

There were two other men present in the room, Greco, Rossini's very able bodyguard, and Bernard Cook, 'Cookie' to his friends, a podgy middle-aged man with brown hair and a large paunch. Cookie worked at the casino looking after the guests; he plied them with food and drink. Both men stood back from the table out of the light, but nevertheless were very attentive as to what was going on.

To say Rossini liked poker was an understatement, he was *obsessed* by it, and never missed an opportunity to play in a high quality game, and the casino had a reputation for high quality.

Rossini, a brilliant player, considered by some to be the best, loved winning, but so far in this game he kept losing, losing a little too often. He was already eight grand down, not that money was a problem, he could afford to lose millions. No, money was not the problem. The problem was that the dealer was cheating, he was sure of it. Rossini watched and waited. The chips piled up as the game went on, the stakes grew higher. The two oilmen dropped out, leaving Fred and Rossini still playing.

Fred covered Rossini's raise and called to see his hand. With a smile of satisfaction Rossini laid his cards face up on the table, Ten, Nine, Eight, Seven, Six, all diamonds. One of the oilmen said, "Wow," the other let out a low whistle.

They all then turned to Fred, who looked deadpan back at them. Then one by one he slowly flipped *his* cards over, Ace, King, Queen, Jack, and Ten, all hearts.

There was a deathly silence. Rossini stood up, sending the chair skittering forcibly backwards crashing noisily into the wall. Then, in a voice shaking with emotion, and his eyes blazing with anger, he pointed a menacing finger at Tatum and shouted. "So you think you can cheat me? You are a dead man… Burgess is a dead man." He glowered at them all, then with a signal to Greco; Rossini stormed out of the Casino.

The game broke up; the players cashed in their chips and left, leaving Fred and Cookie to total up the night's takings. "Must be nearly fifty grand," said Fred. "Mr Burgess should be well pleased, not bad for a night's work, say Cookie, who was that sallow faced guy? The one who came in late, didn't like losing did he?"

Cookie glanced at Tatum across the piles of chips. "Maybe you should've let him win a few hands, you really don't know who he was?"

Fred shook his head and shrugged. "Nope, and I don't care either." Cookie looked a bit apprehensive.

"That was Alphonso Rossini. I hope you can square it with the boss."

Fred gave Cookie a puzzled look. "What do you mean, *square it with the boss*?"

"Oh come off it Fred," said Cookie. "You don't take the Rossini's of this world to the cleaners and expect to come up smelling of violets. They're not losers Fred, they never lose." Cookie paused a short while, waiting for his words to take effect. "Rossini knew you were ripping him off," he said at last.

Fred looked surprised, Cookie went on. "Oh yes, he knew all right, never took his eyes off your hands for a second. I bet he's on the blower to Burgess right now, telling him about it all and how he expects to get every penny back, plus your guts for garters into the bargain."

Fred realised that Cookie was talking sense. If Rossini *had* seen him *manipulating* the cards, his life wouldn't be worth living. "What shall I do Cookie?" whimpered Fred.

They sat facing each other across the table, the piles of coloured chips stacked ominously between them. "If I were you, I'd have a word with Doug Sampson, tell him that Mr Burgess wants tonight's takings right away, then *disappear*," said Cookie with an air of intrigue. There was a pause and a sullen silence. "After all, you're only here on a temporary basis," continued Cookie.

Fred still looked doubtful. Cookie continued after another lengthy pause.

"It's better than hanging around waiting for the storm to break, and you might *disappear* anyway."

"What do you mean?" said Fred.

"Well, if Rossini gets his way, and from what I hear of his reputation, he will, you will probably end up in the river." Fred groaned and paled visibly, beads of perspiration gathered on his forehead and began to trickle down his face and neck.

"He wouldn't do that, would he Cookie?"

Cookie gave a half smile. "Wanna bet?"

Doug Sampson came into the room. Six-foot tall, muscular physique, strong handsome face, fair hair and clear blue eyes. Ex University, he was a *between jobs* athletics coach, and managed the Casino for Ted Burgess. "Well, that's about it for tonight lads. Are you all right Fred? You look a bit off colour."

"You are right Mr Sampson; I do feel a bit queasy. I think I'll slide off home right away if you don't mind." Fred looked at Cookie then back to Doug. "Tonight's takings are all there, I've not counted up yet," lied Fred.

"That's all right Fred," said Doug walking over to the table. "I'll see to it."

Fred made as if to go, then turning said. "Mr Burgess telephoned... said he wanted tonight's takings right away... as soon as possible."

"That's unusual," said Doug. "Okay, I'll see to it. Off you go Fred, hope you feel better by Monday." Fred collected a few things and scurried away. Soon afterwards Cookie also left.

Doug made his way round the rooms in the Casino, collecting the night's 'take' and saying good night to the various members of staff as they left. He totalled up the money, placing it carefully into a security case. Why did Burgess want tonight's money? Why the hurry? Why didn't he telephone *me*? All these questions raced through his mind. Doug set the security alarms and put the case down outside the main doors, then turning, closed and locked them.

The whole world turned crazy, it was spinning like a top and his head was throbbing fit to burst. A man's voice broke into this crazy world. "I think he's drunk, leave him, don't get involved."

"No, he's not drunk, he's been hit on the head." It was a woman's voice, sounding close over his right shoulder. She was propping him up. "Quick now, he's coming round... What happened love?" she said.

Doug recovered enough to get his eyes into focus and support himself on one arm. Gently feeling the bump on the back of his head he looked round dizzily.

"Where's the case?" he said.

"No case here love," said the woman. "We found you sprawled amongst the milk bottles, you've had a nasty bump on the head, haven't you?"

She was a master of understatement thought Doug. "Yes I have, haven't I?" Did you see anything, or anyone?" asked Doug getting shakily to his feet.

"Sorry love, didn't see nothing, no one around at this time of the morning."

Doug looked at his watch, almost four o'clock. I must have been out almost an hour he thought. Doug found he still had his keys and his wallet. The couple wished him well and went on their way. Doug turned and unlocked the doors, pausing awhile for another look round at the empty streets.

The moment he opened the doors the security alarm bells shattered the silence and all but shattered his battered skull. He hurried into the casino and switched off the torturing bells then tried to piece together exactly what had happened. He poured himself a large whisky and drank the lot in one huge gulp.

Psychologically it made him feel better, although all the devil's children were still hammering away inside his head. How the hell can I explain this to Burgess, thought Doug? He picked up the phone and dialled Burgess's number, engaged. Doug dialled again, this time for a cab.

Ted Burgess, a biggish man in his fifties, balding, bulging eyes, and a mouth that seemed to have too many teeth in it, had just been called to the phone.

Rossini was *delicately* bringing him up to date with recent happenings at the casino. Ted Burgess's knuckles gleamed white, so tightly was he gripping the receiver. With wide eyes and sweating brow he heard Rossini's voice booming into his ear. "You are a dead man Burgess, *nobody* do you hear, *nobody* rips me off. Remember Burgess, you are a dead man." The phone crashed down and Ted Burgess was left babbling apologetically to the dialling tone.

Slowly he replaced the receiver. "What the hell do I do now Jimmo, that was Rossini? He says he's been cheated out of twenty grand at the casino. Reckons our dealer was using a spooked deck. He says I'm a dead man no matter what... A dead man Jimmo, what can I do?" Jimmo was six-foot two, enormous shoulders, weighed around twenty stone, a round moon-like face, dark-brown eyes and greasy jet-black hair slicked back, Jimmo was a big man and he was totally loyal to Burgess. If Burgess wanted you in two pieces, that would be Jimmo's project for the day. He was Burgess's bodyguard, immensely strong, but when it came to brains he was way back in the queue. "What shall I do Jimmo? - What shall I do?" repeated Burgess.

"I... I dunno boss... Die I s'pose," said Jimmo. Burgess gave him a look of despair.

"Oh great, great, you're a real comfort you are Jimmo."

The phone rang again. Burgess leapt to it, hoping it might be a reprieve from Rossini. "Burgess here," his heart sank when he heard Cookie's voice.

"Hello Mr Burgess, Cookie here, we had a terrific night at the poker table.

We must have cleared about fifty grand; Mr Sampson is bringing the money over right now. A couple of guys were throwing money about like confetti and another guy, he lost about twenty grand, he got a bit shirty and left."

Burgess was about to verbally tear into Cookie but stopped himself. Cookie had nothing to do with the gambling side of things, a general dogsbody come waiter. "Where's Sampson now?" queried Burgess, a little puzzled as to why Doug was bringing the money over at all.

"He should have arrived there by now Mr Burgess. It was well over an hour ago since we shut up shop. He said he was coming straight over with the money."

Cookie said, "Cheerio," and a thoughtful Burgess slowly replaced the receiver.

The doorbell rang. Doug Sampson was admitted to the room. "Hello Mr Burgess," said Doug smiling through a splitting headache, the painful after effects of the head-bashing session with the unknown assailant. Doug had not been employed at the casino very long and was still at the *Mr Burgess* stage of the relationship.

"I'm afraid I've got some bad news for you." Burgess looked at Doug blankly.

"Now what makes you think your news is bad?" You walk in here after picking up a great big pot of gold and..."

He got no further, Doug cut him off mid-sentence. "I've lost the money,"

"What did you say?" roared Burgess.

Doug explained how he'd been mugged outside the casino and the night's takings stolen. Around one hundred and fifty thousand pounds, the exact figure he could not remember, he'd written it down somewhere.

"Why the hell were you bringing the money over here anyway? You know we have special arrangements for picking up money."

"Tatum told me you had telephoned asking for it. He told me you wanted it right away," answered Doug.

"Tatum was lying, I never telephoned you at all. Why didn't you check with me first?" yelled Burgess.

"Maybe I should have done," agreed Doug.

"What do you know about the Rossini business?" asked Burgess.

"Nothing," answered Doug truthfully. "There was a buzz about a big game going on, I had two croupiers off sick and by the time I'd sorted out that problem and got replacements, the big game had broken up. Some slight misunderstanding I believe."

"Some slight misunderstanding," exploded Burgess. "I've just had Rossini on the 'phone, he reckoned Tatum was using a marked deck and did some real fancy dealing, he says he's going to kill me."

"Surely he's not serious; it's just a figure of speech. He doesn't really mean it."

"You obviously don't know Rossini, he means it all right."

Burgess paced the room a few times then walked over to his desk and sat down in a huge leather armchair, both men remained silent. After a while Burgess stood up and came over to where Doug was standing. "Go home Sampson, have a nice weekend, take Monday off. The insurance will take care of the lost cash. I've got some thinking to do."

Doug didn't argue, he said "Good-night," and left.

What Burgess had just heard brought the sentence of death knocking at his front door again. He thought, after hearing the news from Cookie, he could make it up to Rossini by giving him the whole night's take; after all, it was easy to give other people's money away. Now things had changed, Burgess had to think fast. He could easily give Rossini his money back out of profits from the casino. A worrying thought crossed his mind, he wondered if Rossini had stolen the money to get even, and *still* wanted revenge. No, he was still a dead man. Jimmo's words came echoing back.

"Die I s'pose - Die I s'pose."

The phrase went round and round, then suddenly it clicked.

Burgess sat up straight. "That's it," he cried. He ran across the room to Jimmo and threw his arms around him. "You're brilliant Jimmo." The big man smiled a great big smile, not really knowing what it was all about. "Hey Jimmo, get hold of Doc Flannigan," said Burgess. "Get him over here right away, tell him it's urgent."

An hour later Doc Flannigan walked into the room, a tall gaunt figure of a man. Burgess was seated at his desk. "Come right in Doc, nice to see you," said Burgess, beaming a piranha-like smile towards the Doc. "I called you over to see if there was any way for you to make me appear dead… You see Doc, I've heard of a drug that when injected into anyone will give the impression that that person had died."

Flannigan stood there for a moment studying Burgess, then, with his Irish eyes twinkling said. "Well now, there is such a drug available, very expensive, and usually payable in advance, because it's extremely risky to use."

The wily Doc was quietly weighing up the situation and thought… Poor old Burgess is in a fix, how it will break my heart to take advantage of him… but I will. "Yes it's risky," went on Flannigan. "You see the antidote, which by the way is also very expensive, and is also payable in advance, must be administered within a certain time or else the person in question will in fact die." Burgess said nothing, but was turning over in his mind the consequences of facing up to Rossini. He realised that Doc was talking again. "May I ask why you would want to obtain such a drug?"

Burgess explained the situation to Flannigan. He told him of Rossini's threat, and the fact that his manager, Doug Sampson had lost the money, and that he now thought the only way to avoid being *rubbed out* by Rossini was to *die* first, or at least go through the motions of dying.

"Rossini will never fall for a trick like that," said Flannigan. "He's probably pulled stunts like that himself. He'll want to see the body, and examine it closely."

Burgess could see salvation disappearing fast. "You've got to help me Doc," said a desperate Burgess.

"All right Ted, we've been together a long time now, I'll come up with something and let you know this afternoon."

It was nearly six in the morning when Doug finally arrived home, and not much later was sinking into what seemed the most luxurious bed in the world, he fell asleep almost before his head touched the pillow. Doug was awakened by the shrill trill of the bedside telephone. "Hello, Sampson here."

"Doug, where the hell are you?" It was Helen, Doug's fiancée.

Doug, still fuzzy headed, was desperately trying to collect his thoughts.

"Helen, darling, what's all the fuss about?"

"Don't you darling me, *darling*," she sounded furious. "It's nine o'clock, you were supposed to pick me up at eight, we were going to spend a day in the country."

Doug remembered at last, his head cleared a little, and his brain reluctantly clicked into gear. "I'm sorry darling, I've had a really terrible night, I'll tell you all about it when I see you. I won't make any excuses, the truth is I just plain forgot and believe me I have a very good reason." No answer from Helen, Doug continued. "We can still go…it's not too late… I've got Monday off, we both need a break… let's go, and we'll stay overnight somewhere, then come back Monday evening."

There was a sound that could have been interpreted as a sharp intake of breath, Helen was very angry. "You are lucky Douglas Sampson. Lucky because through no fault of yours, no brilliant plan or design, it happens to be mid-term, and I too have Monday off, but don't think for one moment that I'm letting you get away with it." Helen cooled down a bit when Doug said he could be ready in about half an hour. "Right, see you at about a quarter to ten," said Helen.

Chapter 8

True to his word Doug arrived at Helen's Hampstead flat. Helen had put the time to good use, packing a picnic basket with enough food to last them through the day, not forgetting a flask of tea and a bottle of wine. In half an hour they were heading towards High Wycombe on the outskirts of London, traffic light, weather warm and dry. They had a little friendly conversation, nothing controversial, and nothing that entered remotely into the sensitive area of, 'forgetfulness'.

Soon they were nearing Oxford; Helen lounged back in her seat and watched Doug. His strong hands gripping the wheel, safe hands. Her gaze lifted to his face. A face that for her sparked off a thousand thoughts and desires. She couldn't stay mad at him for long. One look into those beautiful blue eyes was enough to melt her heart.

Sinking deeper into the seat Helen experienced a feeling of sweet contentment and for a while she gazed dreamily at the picturesque countryside. Sleepily she said. "Where are we going darling?" Doug didn't answer; he was still trying to piece together the events that had taken place the night before. "Hey! You there! Is anybody home?" This time Doug replied.

"Sorry darling, what did you say?"

"Where are we going?" repeated Helen.

"Oh, I thought we'd try a place just outside Banbury," said Doug, dragging his thoughts back from the previous night's unfortunate incident. "It's a delightful place, full of 'olde world' charm. Thatched roof, leaded windows, oak beams. We could book in there now for bed and breakfast, and then carry on for our picnic."

"You're taking a lot for granted aren't you?" said Helen.

"What do you mean? Oh, I see… I intended to book separate rooms anyway, if that's what you're worried about," said Doug.

"I'm not worried about it, it's just that I don't like being taken for granted," answered Helen with a touch of pique.

"Now would I do a thing like that?" said Doug with a look of wide-eyed innocence.

"Yes you would, anyway it sounds nice. Where did you hear about it?"

"I heard a group of punters talking about it in the casino a couple of weeks ago. They'd been staying at Stratford-upon-Avon for the races, and had called at the place on the way back to London. I thought if ever we got the chance we'd use it as a base."

Helen smiled a knowing smile and her eyes twinkled. "I shall have to keep a close watch on you Douglas Sampson, you might be getting some rather *interesting* ideas."

They went through Banbury, past the famous Banbury Cross. Doug wondered about the old rhyme, how does it go he thought, something about a horse to Banbury Cross... Ah yes... *Ride a cock-horse to Banbury Cross to see a fine lady ride on a white horse. She has rings on her fingers and bells on her toes; she shall have music wherever she goes.* He felt quite pleased with himself, it was years since he'd heard it and it took him back to his early school days. "Do you think she was Lady Godiva?" Doug absent-mindedly asked Helen.

"What are you talking about?" she replied.

"Sorry darling, I was just thinking about the old rhyme about Banbury Cross, and the fine lady on a white horse," explained Doug.

"Keep you eyes on the road Doug Sampson, and you can forget all about fine ladies on white horses when you're with me. Especially ladies rumoured to have no clothes on."

"Here we are, Wroxton," said Doug. "The hotel should be just around the corner." Doug rounded the corner and there was the hotel, looking beautiful in its 'olde world' charm. Doug booked them into separate rooms, which pleased Helen; she was still twisting the knife, not letting Doug forget his forgetfulness.

After some light refreshment and a general freshening up, they continued their journey towards Stratford-upon-Avon. The hotel receptionist had told them of a car park adjacent to a picnic area just outside Stratford on the Warwick Road. They found the car park quite easily, and they were soon enjoying their picnic on the banks of the Avon.

They had a wonderful, romantic, relaxing day, and arrived back at the hotel quite late in the evening, then sat quietly chatting in the lounge before turning in for the night. Monday was spent touring Shakespeare's County, rich in Elizabethan history and atmosphere, then the journey back to London. "We'll call at my place first, then I'll drop you home," said Doug.

It was late in the evening when they arrived at Doug's flat in Maida Vale.

"Why do you have to live on the second floor?" puffed Helen as they arrived at the front door. "I feel sure there's an extra flight every time I come here."

"No there isn't actually, you're just getting old darling."

"Damn cheek, you're older than I am anyway," retorted Helen, giving Doug a playful shove. Doug opened the front door and walked in, followed closely by Helen.

"Hang on a minute Helen," whispered Doug, and he stopped just a few steps into the unlit hall. "Someone's been here, someone's been smoking cigarettes."

"Yes, I can smell it, quite strong isn't it?" said Helen quietly. Doug reached for the light switch, as the switch clicked down the hall lights came on."

"Stay right where you are Mr Sampson. Both of you, and don't even think about moving."

The voice came from a man standing at the end of the hall. He was of medium height and build, wearing a blue-grey trilby, with the brim pulled down at the front almost to his eyes, and trench-coat of similar colour, his left hand thrust deep in the pocket. His right hand held a gun, with which he now began making gestures, indicating a room to his left. "Both of you, get in there."

Doug stood his ground and glared fiercely at the man. The gunman came swiftly towards Doug. "I told you to get in there," he said through gritted teeth.

Doug still stood facing him defiantly. The gunman then gave Doug a hard push on the shoulder. Doug took his opportunity, knocking the gun aside and with a powerful uppercut he sent the man sprawling along the hall. Doug was closing in to finish him off when he heard a slow hand clapping in mock applause coming from the direction of the lounge.

In the lounge doorway stood another man. "Well done Mr Sampson, very well done indeed." He was neatly dressed in a dark suit. Rather small in stature, black hair slicked back, pale complexion and sporting a thin moustache. The whole ensemble gave him a *spivish* appearance. The feature that Doug noticed most of all was the man's eyes. They were the blackest eyes he had ever seen. They were made even more prominent by the paleness of the man's complexion.

Doug hesitated; the man in the doorway read his thoughts. "Don't be foolish Mr Sampson, I have another man in here, and Joe, that's the man whose invitation you refused, has recovered, and is now standing behind you."

Doug saw no advantage in heroics; he glanced at Helen, who was silent, pale and visibly shaken. "Okay, you win, Mr... er?"

"Stanley," offered the man. " They just call me Stanley. I'm very good with a knife."

"I'll bet you are," said Doug, moving towards the lounge door. Stanley stepped aside allowing Doug and Helen to enter. "Will you please tell us what on earth this is all about?" said Doug.

"All in good time," answered Stanley politely. "Now I want both of you to face me, put your hands behind you, and no tricks." Doug did as he requested, so did Helen. A signal from Stanley and the other two men carried out what was obviously a prearranged plan. They bound Doug and Helen's wrists with sticky tape, then a piece of tape over their mouth prevented any possibility of them calling for help.

"Now, Mr Sampson, we are going to see a friend of mine, if you would be so kind as to follow my two colleagues down to the car. No tricks please, or your girl friend will be the first to go, but I'm sure you realise that. Do I make myself clear?"

Doug nodded, and followed Stanley's two companions to the waiting cars.

Doc Flannigan had been busy making *arrangements* for the funeral.

He was explaining his plan to Burgess. "You see Ted, it's quite simple. You're *laid out* in that nice big lounge of yours in coffin number one. The *other* body will be in coffin number two."

"Hey! Wait a minute. What other body? I don't want to get mixed up in anything like murder," said Burgess.

"There's no need to worry Ted, trust me. Have I ever let you down, you won't get involved, and it tidies up a few nasty little loose ends."

"Who's going to be in the other coffin?" asked Burgess.

"It's strictly on a need to know basis, and I don't think you need to know," said Flannigan severely.

Burgess insisted on knowing and wouldn't take no for an answer.

"Well if you really insist on knowing I'll tell you," answered Flannigan. "But it's against my better judgement. I've decided that the casino manager Sampson would be the ideal guy to take the wrap."

"Why? He's done nothing wrong, I rather like him, it's that blasted Tatum who…"

"I agree," cut in Flannigan. "But *he's* disappeared, and we can't find him, so Sampson has got to *disappear*, it will make him look guilty and that should help to satisfy Rossini." Burgess reluctantly agreed.

"Now the funeral's been arranged for twelve o'clock tomorrow. All your real family are going to be kept out of the way, I've hired some suitable relatives for you, including your mother."

"I haven't got a mother, she's dead," interrupted Burgess.

"I *know* you haven't got a mother, but Rossini *doesn't*, so stop panicking and listen. I'll put you *out* at about ten o'clock. That'll give me time to get you prepared."

"What do you mean *put me out and get me prepared*?" broke in Burgess.

"Well there are certain things that have to be done if we're going to fool Rossini, it's best you know nothing about them."

"I want to know… for my own peace of mind I want to know," whined Burgess, grabbing hold of Flannigan's arm.

"All right, if you really want to know, but I think you're making a mistake… I've had a special jacket made for you to wear. I'll not be putting *your* arms down the sleeves of the jacket… they'll be tied firmly behind your back. The arms that'll go down the sleeves of the jacket, and be braced to your shoulders I've amputated from a body that recently came into my possession…Ohhh don't worry, it's quite a fresh one. Then should Rossini want to carve you up, which he may well do, we'll try to persuade him to cut the arms."

"Oh my God," groaned Burgess, he sat down heavily onto his leather armchair and buried his face in his hands.

The two cars containing Doug and Helen were driven through the night across the suburbs of London to Flannigan's house in Richmond. It was the most uncomfortable journey Doug could ever remember. Helen fared no better in the other car. Destination reached, the *prisoners* were taken into the house and into a large well-furnished room on the ground floor. They were told to sit down, which they did as best they could. Stanley and his two companions then just stood around, sometimes talking in quiet undertones, sometimes pacing round the room.

Eventually Doc Flannigan came striding into the front hall.

Conversation ceased, and the men went out into the hall to meet him. Doug could hear their conversation through the open door.

"Any trouble Stanley?" asked Flannigan.

"No Doc, Sampson slugged Joe, but no real trouble… except…"

"Except what?" snapped Flannigan. Stanley shifted his feet, looking at his companions, looking anywhere to avoid looking at the Doc.

"Well…" faltered Stanley. "Sampson had his bird with him, so we had to bring her along as well." Flannigan left the hall and came into the room. He looked at Doug and Helen, then drew air noisily in through his teeth.

"Damn," was all the Doc said. He walked slowly over to the window and just stood there staring out into the night. After a few minutes he turned away from the window and rejoined the group.

"She'll have to go in the box with him that's all, it'll be heavy but we'll just have to manage." Doc, Stanley, and the other men went to the other end of the room and talked in under-tones, Doug was unable to hear any of that conversation.

He wondered what Flannigan meant by his reference to *the box*.

"Take them upstairs, put them in the room at the end of the

corridor," ordered Flannigan.

Doug and Helen were shepherded up the stairs and into another large room, it was a bedroom. Once inside they were left alone and the door locked. Doug looked round the room for something to help them out of their dilemma. There was nothing.

He knelt down behind Helen and put his face into her hands. She wondered what the hell he was up to at first, but soon realised that he wanted her to pull the tape from his mouth. Although her hands were numb she did at last manage to pull the tape away. Doug then tore at the tape on Helen's wrists with his teeth until she was free. Helen eased the tape off her own mouth, then quickly freed Doug.

They held each other closely; Helen felt the tears well up in her eyes and run hotly down her cheeks. Holding Doug tightly she said tearfully. "What are they going to do with us darling?" Doug, with his arms encircling Helen, could feel her slim body shaking.

"I don't know," he said. "I wish I knew what it was all about." He gently kissed her temple, and brushed his lips over her forehead, finishing with a small kiss on her lips. "We must think of something to help us escape."

"What about a sheet from the bed?" said Helen. "We could throw it over them as they came into the room, or the scent bottle, throw that." Doug shook his head. Helen had entered into the offensive now and showed a little anger. "You're not being very helpful," she said. "I've made lots of suggestions and all you can do is to look silly and shake your head."

"I'm trying to think of something practical."

"Oh! So now I'm not making sensible suggestions?" Doug felt he was losing ground, whatever he said would be regarded as an attack on femininity.

"It's not that darling, it's just that whatever we do has got to work, and it has got to work first time, don't forget, these fellows have got guns."

Helen still thought Doug was being chauvinistic, and wandered round the room, hands behind her back, wearing a haughty, I know I'm right expression.

"What about the chair?" she said sulkily.

"Yes of course," said Doug. "We could break off the legs and either throw them or use them as clubs." Helen, now wearing her, *I thought of it first expression*, smiled but said nothing. Doug discovered that two of the legs unscrewed, which made things easier, and involved a lot less noise. He gave one of the legs to Helen, keeping the other one for himself. "Not much use against guns, are they?" he said. "We may be able to surprise them though, and get a gun for ourselves."

Helen caught Doug's arm. "Shush," she said. "I think someone's coming." They quickly put the remains of the chair out of sight and sat down on the end of the bed, hiding the chair-legs in a fold in the bedspread.

There they sat, hands behind them, head down, staring at the carpet, thus concealing the fact that the tapes had been removed from their mouths. Joe unlocked the door and entered. He was rather surprised to see both of them sitting down on the end of the bed, looking at the floor. He approached cautiously and stood in front of them. Doug and Helen had no idea whether Joe was holding a gun or not. All they could see of Joe, was a pair of black patent-leather shoes. It was Helen who took the initiative, foolhardy or no she lashed out with the chair-leg, striking Joe's legs.

Doug leapt forward tackling Joe bringing him to the ground. A fierce fight developed, Doug the more powerful, but Joe was *streetwise* and knew a few tricks in the fight game. Whilst the fight was in progress, Helen was hopping about brandishing the chair-leg, trying to clout Joe, but dare not in case she hit the wrong one. Eventually Doug nailed Joe with a series of blows to the head, and Joe slithered to the floor. Doug reached inside Joe's jacket and found the gun held firmly in its holster. Just in time, the noise of the fight had brought Joe's colleagues racing to investigate. Doug levelled the gun towards the door. "Come on Helen, we're getting out of here."

The door opened and Stanley appeared, framed in the doorway.

"Put that gun down Sampson, you don't stand a chance."

"We're getting out of here, if you try to stop us I'll start shooting. I can't miss from this range."

"Is that Joe's gun?" asked Stanley. Doug nodded.

"Then put it down," said Stanley, and started walking towards

Doug.

"Your last chance," shouted Doug. Still Stanley continued to walk towards him. Doug pulled the trigger bracing himself for the recoil.

Click...nothing...click...click, nothing, and all the time Stanley was coming forwards. Stanley stood in front of Doug, holding out his hand for the gun. "Joe never loaded his gun, it was a thing he had about guns," said Stanley with a smile. Doug looked at Helen, she was holding her hand up to her mouth, a look of utter disbelief on her face. Doug handed the gun to Stanley. "Now sit down," said Stanley. Doug turned and headed for the remaining chair. Stanley brought the gun crashing down on Doug's head, Helen screamed as Doug slumped to the floor.

Doc Flannigan entered, in his hand he carried a small, black, velvet-covered box, which he placed upon the dressing table. He took from the box a syringe, and a small vial containing a drug, which he told the others was a tranquilliser. "It'll keep them quiet until morning," said Flannigan injecting the drug into the still unconscious Doug, then after a struggle he injected Helen. The following morning Doc Flannigan gave Doug and Helen another injection. This time it was the same drug he would be using on Burgess to produce a death-like state. "Right lads, tie them up again, gag them and put them in the box, then take it to Burgess's."

The funeral was carried out with pseudo solemnity. Rossini and his cohorts were ranged down one side of the large lounge, and Burgess's counterfeit relatives down the opposite side, each side glaring suspiciously at the other. The magnificent coffin, containing the half-smiling, peacefully sleeping Burgess, was positioned lid-less in the centre. The pall-bearers entered slowly and with great dignity, carrying the coffin lid. They were about to close the coffin when Rossini spoke. "Just a moment, I want to make sure this is no trick...Greco." Rossini drew a line down his face with his finger, then nodded towards Burgess. A wicked looking knife appeared like magic in Greco's hand, and he advanced towards the coffin. A storm of protest went up from the *relatives* and Rossini's men's hands drifted towards their guns. The threat was enough and Burgess's *relatives* backed down.

A querulous cry rang out; it came from a heavily veiled woman in black.

"Oh my God! No! Not his face. Please Mr Rossini, don't let my baby meet his maker with a disfigured face, please…" With much wringing of hands, handkerchief, and tears in abundance, she came charging round the coffin to Rossini and began tugging hysterically at his jacket. He forced her away and indicated to Greco to cut the arm instead.

Greco's razor sharp knife cut through the sleeve of Burgess's jacket, revealing the hairy, pallid, lifeless arm underneath. With bright eyes and a leering smile Greco plunged the knife into the bare arm, a long, deep, slicing cut from elbow to wrist. The flesh lay back, showing clean meat, no gushing blood. Greco was a little disappointed, the smile vanished. Rossini came across and stood beside the coffin looking down at the gaping wound. "Okay, put the lid on." He went back and took his place with his men. "Now, remember boys, we must show a little respect for the dead." And, with a movement that any platoon in the armed forces would have been proud of, Rossini's men simultaneously removed their hats. The bearers screwed down the lid. Lifted the coffin onto their shoulders, and carried it out of the room.

Burgess's *relatives* were first to follow the coffin, jostling, pushing, crowding into the doorway. Rossini and his men had to wait. Once through the door the coffin was taken into the room opposite, quickly set down and coffin number two, containing Doug and Helen, hoisted onto their shoulders and carried out of the room. By the time Rossini and his men got out of the lounge, the coffin was out by the front door. He did not see the switch; he did not suspect a switch.

At the church, with coffin and congregation in position, the vicar came down the aisle. Walking slowly, majestically, looking resplendent in his dazzling white surplice. Prayer book in hand he approached the coffin. "Dearly beloved brethren, we are gathered here…" He went on to say how much dear brother Edward would be missed. How sad it was that such a colourful, vibrant soul, was taken so early in life… etc.… etc. Tears in abundance came from the Burgess contingent. The vicar was genuinely sad, he thought, as did Rossini, that all this was for real. Ted was very charitable where his soul was concerned. If it were at all possible to buy your way into heaven, Burgess had been doing his damnedest.

After the service the coffin was once again transported to the waiting hearse. "I won't be happy until I see him buried," said Rossini. He felt a slight tug on his sleeve. Looking round he saw a diminutive clergyman; fingers clasped together in the pose so often adopted by the clergy.

"Beg pardon sir, I could not help overhearing your... er... ungracious remark about our dear departed friend. I'm afraid you are going to be disappointed. He's not going to be buried at all."

Rossini pushed the man aside and charged down the path leading from the church. Just in time to see the hearse, complete with coffin driving off down the road. Wrenching open the door of his black-windowed *Rolls Royce* he shouted at the driver. "Follow that hearse."

There was no chase, no mad dash across the countryside, only a sedate drive to Rickmansworth. The drive ended outside the premises of the International Cryogenic Emporium. The coffin was transferred to a rather ornate silver trolley, and wheeled squeakily into a large single storey building, into a lift, and down to a sub-basement. It was then taken to an enormous hanger-like area containing thousands of numbered freezer units filled with liquid nitrogen. At carefully spaced intervals were the *staff*; squeaky clean, and all wearing beautifully tailored white coats with I.C.E. exquisitely monogrammed onto the left-hand pocket. They stood motionless and expressionless, waiting for the entourage to assemble. And they all assembled by Unit Number One thousand and four which was the ultimate resting-place for the coffin. The vicar said a few final, well-chosen words, then a beautifully polished brass plaque, engraved decoratively with the name Edward Burgess, was secured onto the unit. And everyone quietly left. Leaving the coffin and its occupants to their fate.

Chapter 9

Back to 2150 A.D.

The journey back and subsequent arrival at Burcot was laced with the sort of chatter released by stress and nervous energy. As the party disembarked the professor remarked that food would be available in the dining room. Janine was overjoyed. "Good," she said. "I'm famished, it seems like years since we last ate."

The professor swiftly caught up with Doug, who was striding away toward the angled hatch that led off the roof area into the house. "Doug, there's something you should know, someone I would like you to meet."

"Now?" said Doug, puzzled by the professor's secretive approach.

"Yes, now would be a good time."

"I'm intrigued," answered Doug

They climbed through the hatch and down a flight of stairs into the house. The professor continued talking. "By the way, I've not told anyone who you are, or how you came to be here. The only people who know your true nature are my four laboratory assistants, Jazzer, and myself. Ned and Derick knew of course. Chris, Janine, and all the other people here know nothing."

They stopped outside a large, oak-panelled door. The professor spoke in whispered tones, coming very close to Doug, whispering almost directly into his ear. "The man inside this room… the man we are going to see, has recently escaped from the Epic Building. He was one of the people who vanished after making those first damaging statements to the police about Epic. Listen to him, tell me what you make of it. His story gives credence to the disappearing millions, and the fact that Epic doesn't seem to be in control anymore. We won't be able to stay long."

The professor gave a gentle tap on the door.

The door was opened by a woman in a nun's habit, the white coif standing out starkly against the darkness of the room's interior. "May we see him Sister?" whispered the professor.

"Come in," said the nun in a hushed tone. "Wait here."

She turned and walked away into the dimly lit room. At the far end of the room, looking past the receding figure of the nun, Doug could see a large four-poster bed with heavy drapes. A bedside lamp threw a gentle light onto a pale, tired, white-haired old man. His paleness lessened a little by the whiteness of the bed-linen. Beside the bed, a nurse stood, looking down sympathetically, occasionally wiping his brow and holding his hand.

The nun spoke to the nurse pointing and glancing occasionally toward the duo. The nurse said something quietly to the nun who then turned and rustled back to where the professor and Doug were standing silently just inside the room.

"Just a short while," she said. "He's still very weak."

As they walked across the room the professor again whispered to Doug.

"He was demented when he arrived, babbling hysterically, he could not be quieted until we had a church presence. Sister Agnes came here in secret, as I mentioned before, all the ecclesiastics have been imprisoned or executed." The professor went silently to the bedside and sat down on a chair placed there by the nun. "How are you today Jack?" he said in a quiet voice. The man slowly opened his eyes. He looked hard at the professor, and then shifted his gaze to Doug. "This is Doug Sampson," said the professor. "An old friend, you can trust him Jack."

The old man smiled weakly, and replied in a voice that belied his answer. "I'm all right Ted, nice to see you."

"Jack?" said the professor after an awkward pause. "I know you have been through a terrible ordeal, would you tell my friend all that you told me last week."

Jack frowned and looked at the nurse, then back to the professor.

"Please Jack, it's important," coaxed the professor.

The old man's lips quivered, his whole body shook, the nurse came closer. With his voice quivering with emotion, and his hands pulling at the nurse's arm, Jack struggled against the request. "They are such terrible memories... there are things, dreadful things I'm trying desperately hard to forget, why do you keep asking me to recall them, you must know how much it distresses me... I thought

89

you were my friend." Jack looked again at the nurse, a desperate, pleading look.

"It'll be all right Jack, I'll be here with you, and I'll give you a pill afterwards," said the nurse soothingly. The promise of induced oblivion seemed to give Jack courage. He agreed to relate his experiences again to the professor and to Doug.

He began in a hoarse whisper. "Fifteen years ago, when I was teaching at Christchurch, we began to hear rumours that large numbers of people were disappearing from the northern regions of the country. Six others and myself set about investigating these vague rumours. The word *Epic* or the thought *Epic* seemed to trigger a surveillance device and we had visits from investigating officers. Therefore reference to Epic was strictly taboo and we coded the investigation under Migration of Birds and registered ourselves as an ornithological study group. It gave us a great opportunity to travel and observe. It was still necessary to continue our investigation with as much secrecy as possible.

The investigative work went ahead quite well under the cloak of M.O.B.

It still took five painstaking years to gather enough evidence to make a watertight case. Gradually we compiled a comprehensive dossier on the subject, all done correctly, and the documentation precise. Then all seven of us took the report to the Headquarters of the Special Police. We then confronted them with what we considered to be irrefutable evidence of malpractice.

There were the Taylor twins, Ron Ballom, Chalky White, Tom Smith and his wife Edna, and of course myself. We took the report and handed it in to one of the officials on duty. We were told to wait, and wait we did. We waited all day, hour after hour, and then an official came out and told us to go home and not to talk about it to anyone. So off we went home, all very frustrated, after sitting there all day and then to be told to go home.

I got home fairly late, had a bite to eat, then went to bed. I was awakened by a loud banging on my front door. I got out of bed and looked out of the window. In the street below were two men, knocking like mad on my door, I thought there had been an accident or something, so I went down and asked them what they wanted. They just grabbed hold of me and told me I was under arrest. They carted me off there and then. They left my front door wide open, never told a soul what was going on, just bundled me into the car and off.

The two men took me to the Epic Building in London, I was protesting all the way. Once there, I discovered that everyone else involved with the report had also been arrested. We were not even allowed to speak to one another. I asked an officer what was happening. He turned on me fiercely, truncheon in hand and beat me savagely to the floor, whereupon he kicked me several times shouting words of abuse. 'You people are all the same, you come here snivelling, with a load of seditious lies and then expect special considerations, well, you are all going to see Epic for yourselves,' and he kicked me again.

Several black-robed hooded figures approached, saving me from another painful kick. My friends and I were escorted out of the detention area and into a lift. All I can say about that is that we went down. After the lift, we walked down a long corridor with several turnings. We were all then confined separately in strange cells.

There were no doors to the cells, just large openings. Escape was prevented by the use of electronic stun beams forming an impenetrable barrier across the opening. At the far end a thick plate-glass window, the entire width of the cell looked out into a long narrow hall. On the wall of the hall, opposite the window some ten metres away, were a number of large wheels, fixed in a line about three metres off the ground. From the rim of each wheel hung several stout wires that reached to the floor of the hall. In the cell itself, there was a table and stool, a bed, a washing unit and a toilet, no privacy at all. Such were the conditions of our confinement.

The irony of our situation was, that we had discovered that millions of people were being rounded up and taken to the Epic Building and never seen again. We had compiled a report on that very subject, and ironically this was to be our punishment. We wanted to know the truth, so we, for the rest of our lives would actually see what happened to these people.

The day after we had been placed in the cells, large doors at one end of the hall were opened. 'This is interesting,' I thought, something different to help pass away the dreary hours. Roughly three hundred people came into the hall. Happy, smiling, laughing people, all dressed in white cotton gowns. Middle aged men and women, and some young people whom I assumed to be their children.

The end doors closed, and I heard the sound of heavy machinery. The wheels hanging in the wall opposite began to spin, faster and faster. The wires spun out, making a terrible whistling sound. Then the real terror began. The wheels started moving forward, away from the wall, on great shafts. The people started screaming with fear, scrambling over each other in an effort to avoid the whistling wires. Soon there was no space left to run, and they were pressing hard against the window, the window that made up the back wall of my cell, their faces etched with fear and I could see stark terror in their eyes.

The wheels continued to advance across the hall; terrible screams as the wire flails started cutting the people to shreds, tearing the flesh from their bones. Torrents of blood gushed into gutters and down the drains in the floor. The wheels advanced until they reached the blood-splattered window. The screaming ceased and the wheels, still spinning, retreated back across the hall and finally stopped against the far wall, the wire flails hanging innocently down, and looking for all the world like a row of weeping willows.

Next, remotely controlled high-pressure hoses cleaned away the blood from the walls, floor, and ceiling. The bones were hosed along until they disappeared into a trench at the far end of the hall. Then, several black-robed figures came in carrying black bags; they scurried about like evil shadows skirmishing to remove all trace of the crime that had been committed. After that, so the warden told me later, warm scented air was pumped through the hall, and everything restored to normal.

This happened every day all the time I was there, ten years. Ten long sickening years. I shall never forget those faces; I seem to remember every one of them. Thousands and thousands of terror stricken faces, pressing against the window. Looking at me, looking at me, pleading for me to help them."

The old man burst into tears; he cried and sobbed uncontrollably, and put his hands to his eyes trying to blot out the memory. The nurse tried to soothe him; she looked at the professor and shook her head. The professor leaned forward and held Jack's hand for a moment, then stood up, he whispered to Sister Agnes.

"Take good care of him." He then indicated to Doug that they should leave.

Outside the room they walked along the corridor towards the lift.

"How did he escape?" asked Doug.

"Later," said the professor. "I'll tell you later... Before you go to the dining room come to my apartment and I will tell you the rest of Jack's story."

It did not take Doug long to shower and change, the professor had thoughtfully placed several changes of clothing at his disposal. "How do I find the Professor's apartment Sal?" asked Doug.

"I will guide you Mr Sampson," said Sal. "Just follow the blue light."

The Professor's apartment was just as Doug imagined it would be, steeped in Victoriana. The soft light of several standard lamps dotted discreetly gave the room a deserving quality, and enhanced by reflection the bric-a-brac and crystal. Two massive armchairs placed at an angle either side of a beautiful white marble fireplace, and a log fire blazing merrily in the hearth completed a picture of welcoming warmth.

The professor, already seated in one of the armchairs, greeted Doug with a smile. "I took the liberty of fixing you a drink, whisky's your tipple isn't it?"

Doug thanked the professor and sat down in the other armchair.

"You were going to tell me how Jack escaped from the Epic Building Professor," said Doug.

"Yes," answered the professor. "Jealousy as you know is one of the seven deadly sins, but in this case it was a stroke of luck, a stroke of luck for Jack. Three weeks ago the organisation found Jack running demented through the streets of London, he was unkempt and running barefoot in rags, he had hair that had not been cut for years and a beard nearly down to his waist.

He was brought here; it took two weeks of careful nursing before he would tell us what had happened to him. You already know the details of his capture and imprisonment, and the ghastly experiences he suffered in the Epic Building."

Doug nodded and said, "Yes."

The professor got out of his armchair, crossed the room and picked up a small notebook, then returning to the armchair said. "I recorded my first interview with Jack last week. You can hear in his own words a story that is unbelievable, but undoubtedly true... Sal, play the recording of my talk with Jack Hoskins, from..."

The Professor consulted his notes, "From... index 5a."

"Certainly Professor Burgess," came the reply from Sal.

Doug was rather surprised when the professor called the computerised information from Sal, which was the name of the 'personal' computer in his apartment, and even more surprised when Sal answered, because the answering voice was totally different. This 'Sal' had a very businesslike tone in 'her' voice; he much preferred his own Sal's flattering tones.

Once again Doug heard the old man's quavering voice. "About a month ago a young woman was thrown into my cell. She was a very beautiful young woman, she was dressed in an off-the-shoulder floral blouse with an elastic top and a long black skirt slit both sides nearly to the waist, revealing a large expanse of her very shapely thigh. 'I will kill him, I will kill him,' she kept shouting.

She had long black hair and dark eyes that flashed with anger as she continuously paced up and down the cell. 'What's the trouble?' I asked.

She turned on me fiercely, 'I will tell you what is the trouble, the trouble is with the high priest Omega, he is the trouble.' She spoke with a sort of Latin American accent.

'He has been my lover for two years now, my name is Alpha, and he told me it was sign from Epic that I was called Alpha and he Omega. Alpha and Omega, the beginning and the end, our destinies would be linked together. We made love on the altar; it was wonderful; I was very important. I took part in most of the ceremonies. Then I found out that B was Bernadette, C was Carolyn, D was Desiree... He was making love to all the girls in the alphabet. I will kill him... you want to escape this place?' I said that of course I did. 'Good, I will help you, I have a plan.' She continued to purposely pace the floor of the cell.

'When the guard brings the food, you stand over there.' She pointed to the left-hand wall of the cell near the door. 'Have the stool near your hand. I will stand here by the other wall. When the guard comes in, I will pull my blouse down... No man can resist looking at a woman's breasts, even for a quick glance... that is when you hit him with the stool' She didn't rest for a moment, pacing up and down the cell like a caged animal, muttering all the time. 'I will kill him. I will kill him.'

The guard came along with the food, switched off the barrier and stepped inside the cell. He was a huge, rough, tough looking man. The girl shouted.

'Hey you! Look here!' and pulled her blouse down, revealing her large bare vibrating breasts. What man could resist a glance at a sight like that? I wielded the stool and caught the guard a glancing blow to the side of the head.

He swung round with a bellow of rage and grabbed me by the neck with both hands. I thought he was going to kill me there and then. But the girl picked up the fallen stool and struck him again. This time he fell to the ground. The girl continued to strike him with the stool. I had to pull her away; she was smashing his head to a pulp in her rage.

We ran out of the cell and down the corridor, passing other cells all-empty save one containing a man. As we ran past his cell I reached out and switched off the imprisoning beam across the entrance. I had no idea which way to go, but Alpha knew exactly where she was going. A little way down the corridor we came to a small door. 'In here,' she said, and opened the door with a secret code. Inside we made our way down a long flight of rough-hewn stone steps. We were in the dark damp bowels of the Epic Building.

'Follow me,' she said, and off she shot down another dank, ill-lit corridor.

At last Alpha came to a stop, outside a heavy wooden door. 'Now we must be very quiet,' she said, and quietly opened the door. Inside, there were more steps leading down.

The steps led to a gallery overlooking a large square area surrounded by pillars supporting the gallery, which in turn supported a heavily decorated ceiling.

Looking to the left of the square I could see a set of double doors. Looking to the right, I saw, what I can only describe as a large stone altar. Further to the right and shrouded in shadow were twelve large glass containers full of liquid, each receptacle containing a dark tentacled mass. On the floor in the centre of the square was a large black Pentagon, sectioned by gold lines, each section depicting a different symbol marked clearly in a mosaic of gold.

I could hear a low chanting, which grew louder by the second. Alpha put her finger to her lips and said 'Sh... You stay here until it is clear. The way out is that way,' she pointed towards a door on the left of the square. She then walked quietly away and disappeared into the shadow at the end of the gallery. The chanting grew in volume, the door at the end of the square opened and a hundred or more black-robed hooded figures filed in, chanting and walking slowly. Some of the figures were swinging censers; the thurifying smoke curled up and hung heavy in the air.

The chanting monk-like figures took up positions in rows around Pentagon leaving an open aisle from the door to the altar. A cymbal clashed and the chanting rose in volume. Four men entered, each holding a silver chain connected to a collar around the neck of a goat-headed mutant. They dragged the unfortunate creature down the aisle and across the centre of the square, stopping a few metres in front of the altar.

Another man entered, a tall impressive figure dressed in a black-silk robe with silver markings. He was thin-faced and had a small pointed beard. The chanting changed to a repeated 'Hail Omega, hail Omega, hail Omega' as he walked down the aisle and stopped in front of the altar. Silence fell; Omega raised his arms and began to recite verses in a foreign tongue.

The twelve glass tanks began to glow, beams of ultra-violet light came from each one and converged at a point high above the altar where they became one powerful light beaming directly down upon the altar. Omega stood back and made a sign to the four attendants holding the chains. The four men dragged the hapless victim further forward and spread-eagled him across the top of the altar. The chanting began again, starting quite low, gradually rising to a shrieking incantation. Omega waved his arms and red lasers beamed through the ultra-violet onto the body stretched out on the altar. The body began to burn; the mutant screamed in pain for a while, then mercifully died.

Thick smoke billowed up from the body and hung in a great ball above the altar. Out of the smoke came a mighty roar, a hideous sound, like a creature in torment. A huge face appeared, suspended in the smoke. I'm sure it was the face of Satan himself. In a voice that shook the building the floating head spoke. 'You have done well Omega, soon the brain cultures will give enough power for me to fully materialise into the physical world.' The black-robed figures all bowed in adoration to the '*Prince of Darkness*'. Omega stood in front of the altar bathed in orange and green light, reflections from the flashing lights surrounding the floating head. 'I live only to serve you master.' He knelt down, lowering his head in reverence before the icon of evil.

Suddenly a figure darted out of the shadows, it was Alpha. With knife in hand she ran up to Omega and was about to plunge the knife into his exposed neck when fingers of cold flame reached out and lifted the struggling girl, screaming with frustration to within a metre of the slavering mouth. Then with a horrific heart-freezing laugh, the evil presence burned the girl with laser light, and breathed in the smoke with great sucking breaths. I was terrified, unable to move, I fainted with sheer terror.

How long I lay there I don't know, for when I recovered my senses, all the figures had gone. All was quiet and the sacrificial square empty. I remembered Alpha had said the way out was through the door at the end of the square. Slowly I made my way down to the square and out through the door. I walked through room after room; all filled with robot soldiers, all still and silent but all armed ready for battle. Row upon row of shiny black warriors waiting to be activated. Room after room and endless corridors, my steps getting faster all the time, until in the end I was running blindly, panic-stricken. I felt the terror of being pursued. Whether it was my imagination or not I swear I heard laughter, demoniacal laughter as I ran in panic from that evil place. How I eventually got out of the building I cannot say, I am unable to remember events after that time. The next thing I remember was waking up here in bed with the fear of the devil still gripping my soul. I wanted to be cleansed by the hand of God."

"Thank you Sal," said the Professor. "That is enough."

The computer switched off the recording. The Professor waited a moment then spoke. "Before we analyse Jack's narrative concerning his last ten years, there is one more thing you should know. About an hour before the organisation picked up Jack in London, they picked up another man. Apparently he was the man Jack released by switching off the barrier. He knew all about the temple, Omega, the glass jars and the thousands of warriors. He was, apparently, the officer in charge of building maintenance and knew most of the activities that went on inside the building.

Recently, he had an argument, a rather violent argument with Omega, about the way things were going. Shortly after the argument he was arrested and finished up in the cells close to where Jack was imprisoned. I don't trust him; I would not let them bring him here and the less he knows about the organisation the better. The organisation is keeping a very low profile on this. As far as he is concerned he is being looked after by a couple of simple folk who have befriended him.

When Jack switched off the beam, Desmond Greer, that's the man's name, made his own escape. In doing so he left all the security doors unlocked. That is how Jack was able to run out of the building unchallenged."

The professor finished his drink and stood up, he didn't speak, just stood looking at Doug, waiting for his reply.

"What an incredible story," said Doug. "What happened to all Jack's friends?"

"I wondered about that as well," answered the professor, "and during subsequent interviews I asked Jack that very question. He avoided answering for quite a while. Eventually I did manage to get him to talk about his friends. Very sad… He told me that over the years of imprisonment his friends had all died, one by one they all died and he was all alone. He told me that he often pretended they were all still alive and talked to them all the time, having long conversations with them… said it helped to keep him sane."

"Poor old Jack," said Doug. "What about the army of robots

Jack spoke of, have you given that much thought? Have you made any plans to off-set doomsday?"

"Not yet," came the disconsolate reply, "I am working on it, I'd be grateful if you'd put some thought in that direction."

"Yes I will," said Doug. He finished his drink and stood up assuming that the meeting was at an end.

The professor took charge of the glasses and placed them on a small table at the side of the room. "Jazzer will see to those," he said. "Now we must join the others in the dining room. I don't quite know what to do about the others?"

"What do you mean, you don't know what to do about the others?"

"The professor smiled. "I'm sorry, you see, apart from the people actually looking after Jack, you and I are the only ones who have heard his story."

"I think it best to tell them as soon as possible, some of them may come up with an idea," reasoned Doug.

"Yes, maybe you're right," said the professor. "I think what you are suggesting is probably for the best. Now, let us join the others, I'll tell them right away. Now is a good time actually, they are all gathered in the dining room."

Doug and the professor made their way down to the dining room and joined the others. There was a party atmosphere in the dining room. Janine and Chris had lost no time in spreading the story of Doug's courageous fight with the monster and of the brilliant way he rescued them at the hospital, and the strategy used to finally evade the police by flying down the tunnel. Little wonder that when Doug and the professor appeared a great cheer went up and there were shouts of 'For he's a jolly good fellow'.

They were all there, standing at tables that had been rearranged into long lines. Janine, Chris, the laboratory assistants, the household staff, the gardeners, the technicians, were all standing and applauding Doug and the professor, who dutifully acknowledged the adulation and took their places at the head table.

A great buzz of conversation hit the dining room. Food and drink in abundance soon encouraged an air of relaxed satisfaction, After dining, the professor stood up and everyone became silent, waiting no doubt for the usual amusing quips and anecdotes that are synonymous with after dinner speeches. The professor told Jack's story. His audience listened in absolute silence, their attention riveted on the professor's every word. When he had finished, the professor looked at the faces of his friends and colleagues. They all looked serious; they all looked stunned.

John Dunne, an old friend and colleague of the professor's broke the spell of silence and resuscitated the drowning assembly.

"If this is true Ted, we are finished. The organisation is not strong enough to move against Epic or the Special Police, let alone this new threat of a robot army. What do you suggest we do?"

Before the professor could answer other questions were shouted from the gathering, soon all were on their feet clamouring for answers. All valid questions, all requiring answers. The professor raised his hands and called for order, which was eventually restored. He waited until all were silent. "I must tell you in all truth... I do not know what we must do to overcome this appalling situation. The information I have just given to you has only recently come into my possession. Give me a few days, then I hope to have some answers."

The clamorous shouts fell to a low murmuring; everyone seemed to accept this line of reasoning and drifted slowly away from the tables, gathering in small groups to continue in private debate. What had started in a mood of triumphant celebration, now ended with the stark reality of impending disaster.

Chris, Janine, Doug and the Professor went to a lounge area just off the main dining room and continued talking in general terms. The conversation drifted round to Doug, questions, questions, and more questions. Where did he come from? What line of work was he in? What was he doing here? Where did he learn to fight like that? Chris and Janine wanted to know all about him.

Doug looked at the professor and thought 'Transmitter, 25.35Ghz. Professor?' The professor looked startled; he hadn't expected Doug to use that method of communication.

'Yes' he said over the link.

Doug answered quickly. 'I'll have to tell them the truth, not all of it but a major part of it. What do you think?'

The Professor looked at Doug and involuntarily shrugged his

shoulders and 'spoke', unthinkingly in quite a loud voice.

"Tell them what you like my boy."

Chris and Janine stopped talking and looked at the professor. They thought his remark strange but did not realise its significance. Doug began to give an account of events that led up to his resurrection.

"If I were to tell you that I was over one hundred and eighty years old, what would you say?"

"I'd say that you were having us on," said Chris.

"Oh come on Doug," said Janine. "You're certainly no more than thirty-five, if that."

The professor leaned back in his chair. 'This is going to be good,' he thought, and watched the proceedings like a cat watching a mouse.

Chapter 10

Janine and Chris, the Professor and Doug were all seated in the basement lounge of the professor's house at Burcot. Janine would not believe Doug when he told her he was over one hundred and eighty years old. Doug began his narrative and the professor looked on with a gentle smile on his face and a proud look in his eye.

"I was born in nineteen sixty two, educated through the normal channels, which was then starting at an infants and juniors school up to the age of eleven and then on to a senior school. I managed to get to grammar school and on to university, where I studied mathematics and obtained my degree. Whilst at university I developed a keen interest in athletics, which included martial arts, that's where I learned my fighting skills. I left university and eventually took up employment as a teacher at Christchurch. Things were not going too well in the education business at that time and I had to try other work. Jobs were not easy to find. I did find another job, not in teaching though, I found a job managing a gambling casino."

"How exciting, a gambling casino," said Janine.

"It sounds exciting, but it wasn't really," said Doug. "Routine most of the time, except for my last day when I was used as a decoy body in an underworld killing. I was drugged, then placed inside a coffin and frozen in a cryogenic unit. It was the Professor, whose knowledge and expertise in that particular field, rescued me from my icy grave and restored me to the land of the living.

Doug omitted to mention that from the soles of his feet to the top of his head was a reconstruction job.

"I can't believe it," said Chris.

"Not possible," said Janine.

"It's true, every word of it, ask the professor," said Doug. Janine was overwhelmed with curiosity; she was a very inquisitive woman.

"What was it like living in those days?" she asked. "Tell me Doug, what did the women wear, were they dressed very differently, were they more beautiful?"

Doug didn't really know how to answer that sort of question. "I was never much on women's fashions. Now, Helen would have told you all about that, she could talk all day about clothes and fashions."

"Who is Helen?" asked Janine. Nostalgia overwhelmed Doug. He hadn't mentioned Helen before in his potted history lesson, and now after mentioning her name he felt very lonely. 'Who is Helen?' Janine had asked. 'Who is Helen?'

"Helen was very dear to me," explained Doug, choking on the emotion that welled up inside, Helen, darling wonderful Helen. Doug eventually found his voice again. "She was my fiancée... we were to be married."

There was an embarrassing silence, Doug felt he had to get away and be alone with his own thoughts. "If you will excuse me, I would like to leave now, I will see you all in the morning." He nodded to the professor who nodded back. The professor understood the heartache Doug must be feeling at this time.

Doug left the dining room and made his way back to the apartment, his last moments with Helen still painfully fresh in his mind. Once in the apartment he didn't even bother to undress, just threw himself onto the bed, and with memory of Helen biting deep into his heart he lie there staring at the ceiling.

One remarkable thing about his electronic brain was that he still needed the R.E.M period to rationalise the brain's daily dose of data. It was for this reason that the professor had thoughtfully installed a sleep mode. Doug realised that torturing himself with sweet memories of Helen would not bring her back. That would be up to the professor. Reluctantly he whispered a fond "Goodnight darling," then, after a few more treasured thoughts of Helen. "Douse the lights Sal," he said, and switched to sleep mode. He drifted off into a dreamless sleep, eclipsing the painful but beautiful memories of his lost loved one.

The lights were out; Sal had done her job. Suddenly Doug was wide awake. The sleep mode would allow Doug to have normal sleeping habits, which meant he would wake up if it were necessary. 'Why?' thought Doug. 'I'm still in sleep mode, not due to wake for another two hours.' He mentally switched off the sleep mode.

"I'm glad you have awakened Douglas Sampson." The voice, a reedy, musical voice came from the centre of the room. Doug turned to view its creator.

In the centre of the room, not far from the bed, stood a tall thin old man, baggy-eyed, high cheekbones, long wispy white hair and yellowish skin. He was dressed in a loose white robe, over which he wore a long dark cloak with the hood thrown back. In his right hand he held a stout staff, the sort used by travellers in the thirteenth century. The old man stood '*glowing*' in an eerie light, looking at Doug, and smiling.

"Who are you, and what do you want?" asked Doug.

"I'm Daniel Baker, and believe it or not I am older than you are." Doug found it hard to believe that the old man could be older than he was but strangely accepted that he was telling the truth.

"Well I now know that you are Daniel Baker and you say you are quite old. What do you want with me? And tell me, how did you get into the apartment? The door only opens with a special electronic key or to my command." The old man smiled again then with a wave of his hand switched on the apartment lights and bade Doug to make himself comfortable.

Doug could hardly believe his senses, but nevertheless got off the bed, and together they walked into the lounge. "What I am about to say to you will no doubt sound incredible. Please believe me when I say I am deadly serious." Daniel Baker paused, watching Doug closely, thoughtfully. Doug wondered if he should say something, ask some questions, but somehow he was held silent by the presence of Daniel Baker.

The old man continued. "Do you know of the Eblis?"

Doug nodded. "Some sort of devil isn't it?"

"It is an evil force, extremely powerful, it can assume any form, and it feeds on greed and suffering. The Eblis was called forth by a group of Satanists called Satan's Symbols. Jed Mangrove, who now calls himself Omega, and is the High Priest in the Epic Temple, was recruited into the group when he was a lowly caretaker, for the sole purpose of introducing the Eblis into the Epic System. The group totally underestimated Epic's cunning and insatiable desire for power. Epic knew from the start what was going on. Epic let them call the Eblis into existence, and allowed them to feed it into the system. Epic and the Eblis became one and together they have formed an unholy alliance, sworn to enslave the human race into eternity."

"Where do I fit into all this?" asked Doug. Daniel Baker stepped closer.

"I want you to go to a place called Cotgrave in Nottinghamshire. There you will find a twelve-year-old boy called Peter. He is at present held in the care of Owain the miller. The boy has in his possession a talisman, you must find the boy and bring him to me with the talisman."

"Why do you need me, you found me easily enough? Why don't you just go and find the boy yourself?" The old man gave a wry smile.

"You must be the one to go, because of your unique construction."

"What do you mean by that? Are you saying that it's because I'm not 'human', is that what you're getting at?"

"I didn't say that," said Daniel Baker quickly. "What I am saying is that you will be strong enough, and resourceful enough to deal with any incident that comes your way... remember, as soon as you have the boy outside the wall, think of me and I will come." A ball of golden light appeared, Daniel Baker stepped into it and stood smiling back at Doug. Then the ball of light faded and disappeared. The apartment lights went out, leaving Doug standing alone in total darkness

"Sal; lights," called Doug. "Good morning Mr Sampson," said Sal, switching on the lights.

"Sal?" said Doug. "Why didn't you wake me? Someone entered the apartment." Sal checked her data banks.

"Mr Sampson, no one has entered the apartment other than yourself."

"You have no record of me talking to anyone?" queried Doug.

"No Mr Sampson."

"And you did not switch the lights on before my request?"

"No Mr Sampson, I could not do that without instruction."

Doug, puzzled by the night's events, decided to take a shower and get a change of clothes, it was certainly not worth going back to bed.

Washed and dressed Doug returned to the lounge, it was six o'clock.

He again thought of the strange old man and his request, that he should find a twelve-year-old boy called Peter at present being looked after by a miller called Owain.

He then had to abduct the boy and take him outside the wall. 'What wall?' thought Doug. 'I don't know of any particular wall near Nottingham.' What amazed Doug was that he felt he had to comply; there was no question in his mind of refusing.

Doug accessed his internal computer and mentally asked it to compute the route to Cotgrave in Nottinghamshire.

The answer surprised him. "Not possible, the County of Nottinghamshire is now a banned area," said Sal. 'Strange?' thought Doug. 'Why does the old man want me to go to Cotgrave if it is a banned area?' And how was he to locate Peter. The more he thought about it the more he doubted its reality. A dream maybe, yes that's what it was, a dream. Doug decided to see if the dining room was up to providing breakfast. Even that would not be the same without the daily papers. He turned to leave the apartment and experienced a visual shock, for there in the armchair lay the old man's staff. It wasn't there when he went for his shower... So it was real after all.

Chris, Janine and the professor were already at breakfast when Doug entered the dining room. A chorus of 'Good morning' came from the trio. Janine fluttered her eyelids and smiled a demure, "Hello Doug."

"Good morning," answered Doug, directing his answer to everyone.

They had been discussing another trip to Sheerness, another rescue attempt, when Doug entered, and as soon as the 'good mornings' were out of the way they went back to planning the rescue. Doug felt 'left out'.

He felt 'out of sync' with the rest of them. They fitted in so well, it was *their world, their time*. When the opportunity came he spoke to the professor.

"I'd like to get away for a while. Could you find some suitable clothing and equipment for a walking holiday? I want time to sort

106

myself out."

"Certainly my boy," said the Professor. "But it would not be wise to go walking."

"Why not?" asked Doug. The professor looked at his watch and Doug thought 'perhaps I shouldn't have asked, here comes another history lesson.'

"Throughout the years," began the professor, "there has always been an itinerant population. A section of society, world wide, that thought themselves to be outside the law. In your time you had the 'Hippies', 'Flower Power', 'New Age people'. The authorities as you probably know had little or no control over these groups, and, in more recent times the same has occurred, they escaped the implanting. They were of course hunted down and if caught severely punished. Many formed gangs and lived outside the cities and many settled in the remoter places of the north. They constantly made forays south, preying on villages throughout the countryside. As you can see a walking holiday is out of the question. It is too dangerous."

"Whatever happened to the 'brave new world' Epic created?"

The professor smiled and continued speaking. "In nearly every society, every doctrine, you will find exceptions to the rule. Perfection is an ideal that for the most part is usually unobtainable. There was, as I said, an itinerant population, there were also a number of people who for one reason of another were mentally strong enough to defy the effect of the implant. They of course would have been sent to Atlantis had they been caught. Then a number of people were lucky enough to have a fault develop on their implant. They were pitied rather than blamed and although they were not imprisoned or punished by the authorities in any way they were shunned by society. Quite a few of those people also joined the ranks of the outlaws."

The professor paused for a while, then he seemed to accept the situation.

"I'll sort you out some suitable clothing for travelling, and you can use an antigravity bike, much safer than walking. When do you want to start?"

"Tomorrow will do," answered Doug.

"Oh! So you won't be coming to Sheerness with us?"

"No...not if you don't really need me."

"No, that's all right, we'll manage fine." The professor tried to make out that it didn't matter but made a very poor show of it. "See me in the lab after breakfast, I have something of interest to show you," he said, and then he went back to planning the Sheerness rescue mission with Chris and Janine.

Doug continued his breakfast in silence. Mentally he went over the previous night's strange occurrence with the 'visitation' of Daniel Baker. Who was he? Was he some kind of Guru, a follower of some religious cult, or was he a further development of modern technology with a devious scheme to lure him to some remote spot for an equally devious reason?

Chapter 11

After breakfast, Doug made his way to the laboratory, where shortly afterwards the professor joined him.

"Follow me," said the professor, and walked straight past Doug toward the far end of the laboratory. There he stopped and keyed a set of numbers into a security unit on the wall, then, walking to the right-hand corner of the laboratory pulled at the centre shelf of a bookcase. The whole bookcase swung away from the wall like a door, revealing an opening into which the professor stepped.

"Follow me," said the Professor. Doug followed the professor into the opening and down a spiral staircase that brought them into a well-equipped workshop.

The professor called for lights, which came on immediately. He carried on walking through the workshop until he came to a glass-fronted office. Doug looked into the office through large glass windows and saw a well-built man seated motionless at an office desk. He was wearing a fawn trench coat; collar turned up, and on his head he wore a black trilby with the broad brim casting a deep shadow over his face, a face that was totally devoid of expression or movement.

Professor Burgess then took a small black box out of his pocket, which Doug noticed immediately. "I thought I had destroyed the only control box?" said Doug.

"And so you did my friend," answered the professor. "This one," he said, holding up the box. "Is not for you, it's for him." The professor nodded toward the stationary figure in the office.

"Who is he?" asked Doug.

"He is your twin in a manner of speaking; not an identical twin I hasten to add. He started his life at approximately the same time you did, your present life that is, this is where I housed the second SENADS unit, I haven't had time to give him a name, up to now he's just been called project ten."

"Why are you so keen on showing him to me just now?"

"I thought he might be of some use to you on your prospective holiday. He could be useful should you get into difficulties. He'd be a sort of bodyguard, he's very good with facts and figures, and he could sort out people and places, a real detective, in fact you could say he is the first real electronic detective."

The professor was really proud of his work and it showed. Doug thought awhile then repeated the professor's words. "First real electronic detective, then I shall call him Fred," mused Doug.

"Fred?" said the professor. "Why Fred?"

"First Real Electronic Detective," quipped Doug.

"Oh yes I see… very clever… very witty," observed the professor. "What does he do?"

The professor raised the box, pointing it toward the inert figure, and pressed the button.

The figure seated at the desk immediately came to life. It sat up straight, opened its eyes and gazed without expression at Doug and the professor. The professor stood in front of the office desk facing the figure.

"Your name is Fred," said the professor and pulled Doug close to his side. "I am Professor Edward Burgess, this is Douglas Sampson, he is your master. It is your duty to obey his orders without question and to do all that is within your power to protect him. This is a code one triple A instruction, it cannot be erased." The professor pressed another button on the box and turned to Doug. "That's it, he's all yours now, take him with you to your apartment. Get to know him."

Doug felt a little embarrassed, suddenly being given a '*man*'. Fred was so realistic, so lifelike it was uncanny. "Come on Fred, follow me," said Doug as he walked out of the office and waited with the professor for the now activated Fred to follow. Fred stood up, tipping the chair over, then, with a great sweep of his arm swept the office desk out of his way and sent it crashing into the wall with such violence that it broke two of the windows. He managed to walk, unsteadily, through the doorway and made his way to where Doug and the professor waited at the foot of the spiral staircase. Doug looked at the professor and raised his eyebrows.

"And *he's* going to protect *me*?" he said. The professor looked back at Doug sporting a weak smile.

"Just teething troubles, just teething troubles," he said.

Doug climbed the spiral staircase followed by a stumbling Fred and led the way back to his apartment. Once inside the apartment Doug turned and faced Fred, who just stood still, waiting for the next command.

"What the hell do I do with you? Can you talk?" no reply, Fred stood stock still, but his facial muscles were straining as if he were trying to talk. Doug spoke to Sal.

"Sal, get hold of Professor Burgess, ask him to call me." Sal replied with her usual politeness, and a few minutes later the professor called on the visiphone.

"Hello Doug, what's the trouble?"

Doug sat down in front of the visiphone and answered the professor. "This creation of yours, I'm sure it's trying to communicate but nothing's happening."

"Try using your inbuilt transmitter… the frequency is 26.05 Ghz. It's your personal link with Fred. Sorry I should have told you. Anything else?" Doug said that there was nothing at the moment, but inwardly wondered what other 'teething' troubles he could expect.

Fred had heard the conversation between Doug and the professor and set up the communication channel over their personal link. "Of course I can talk. I have checked my systems and you can tell your professor friend that I have a faulty digital translator, VCJ29C in my audio control circuit." It was Fred; coming through just like the professor's voice did when he used the radio link.

"At last we have made contact, Fred, do you think you could find your way back to the office where we first met? I will ask Professor Burgess to go there and repair you." Doug spoke to Fred normally but Fred still had to use the transmitter link to converse with Doug.

"There is no need to ask the professor to repair me Douglas Sampson, I can repair myself. I can retrace the route to the office where we met. I was activated many times in that area I know it well. I also know where all the necessary stores items are kept. I know where all the necessary items of equipment are, I…" Doug cut Fred off.

"All right all right, I believe you, you don't have to keep on about it."

'This is going to take some getting used to,' thought Doug. 'Interesting though, a self-repairing robot. This is something I have got to see for myself.'

"Come on Fred, let's go to the workshop and get your voice-box fixed. Sal, I'm going to the workshop."

Sal answered with a, "Very good Mr Sampson."

Doug took Fred through the laboratory and over to the bookcase. It would not open. Of course not, the professor had used a secret code. Doug remembered standing beside the professor when he keyed in the combination. Doug mentally thought of that moment in time and pictured the professor about to key in the code; he saw the professor's hand on the security box. '*Closer*,' he thought, and amazingly he mentally zoomed into a close-up picture of the letters and numbers being keyed into the box.

Doug went over to the security box and keyed in the code, 2C56H3D, then returned to the bookcase and pulled at the centre shelf. A slight click and the bookcase swung outward just as it had done before, allowing Doug and Fred to gain access to the stairway leading to the underground workshop

Doug heard Fred coming through again on the transmitter. "That was clever Douglas Sampson."

"What do you mean Fred? How did you know what I was doing?"

"I am linked to your every thought via our personal transmitter link. I need to know all data if I am going to look after you. If you do not wish me to know your thoughts all you need to do is to break the link." Doug felt angry, not with Fred, but with the professor. There were a lot of little things the professor had omitted to tell him about.

Back down the spiral staircase and into the workshop. "Lights Sal," called Doug, and once again immediately on came the lights. Fred, true to his word knew exactly where to go, and where to look. He made his way to the storeroom and surveyed the rows of cabinets. "The item I require is located here," he said over the link. He opened one of the cabinets and counted down the rows of drawers, then opened the tenth drawer down. Inside the drawer Doug could see rows of tiny components, Fred selected one, closed the drawer and the cabinet, then stumbled his way to the office. Doug did observe that Fred's walking was getting a little better.

Inside the office Fred took off his trench coat, his jacket and shirt. He was built like a contender for Mr Universe, massive biceps and a mass of hair on his chest. Fred amazed, then amused Doug when he pulled with both hands at the hair on his chest and opened up a sizeable panel. Inside the panel, Doug could see a complicated array of modules, knobs, dials, wires and switches.

Doug had serious doubts as to Fred's ability. "Is this wise Fred?"

"Wise?" queried Fred, still conversing over the link.

"Yes wise," repeated Doug. "With your record, I mean, so far you've tipped over a chair, smashed windows in the office, you stumble about like a drunken sailor. Do you really think you are up to doing what looks to me like a very complicated repair."

"Of course I am," radioed Fred confidently, and gently reached into the opening. He pulled out a short flexible metal tube with a slightly bulbous end.

As he worked Fred explained his actions via the radio link. "This, Douglas Sampson, is a light, plus a video camera." Next he pulled out a fat pencil-shaped probe on a coiled wire. "This, is a laser, Douglas Sampson, I will use it to change the faulty component." The light on the end of the flexible tube came on and Fred directed it into the panel opening. "I do not need to see with my eye sensors, I can see with the video camera." Fred then proceeded to carry out a most delicate repair, replacing the faulty component with the new one. Repair completed Fred methodically packed away all his 'tools', and snapped the panel back into place, carefully arranging the hair on his chest as the last final touch. Fred now spoke directly to Doug.

"There Douglas Sampson, you see, I *can* talk."

"So you can," said Doug. He hadn't noticed the accent when Fred was linked via the transmitter, but was now surprised to hear Fred speaking with a slight American accent. "Why do you speak with an American accent?" he asked.

"It is because basically I am modelled from someone within your memory, a fictional detective hero of yours from the past, a Mr Richard Tracy I believe," answered Fred.

The professor walked into the workshop. "I'm glad I've found you both together, there are one or two little things I think you ought to know before you start on your trip."

'Here we go again,' thought Doug. "Fire away Professor we're listening."

"A very prophetic remark, I must have unwittingly built in ESP as one of your extras. Both you and Fred have a built-in weapons system. Think, Albatross, Photon 1... strength er, whatever you need, line the spot up on the target and it will fire on your command."

"What will fire on command?"

"Your weapons system," said the professor. "It's a laser guided Photon Particle Intensifier, PPI for short, you'll find it a bit like throwing thunderbolts. Range; anything up to one hundred metres, graded in strength one to ten. One will stun a human being; ten will knock a large hole in the side of a house. It fires through the lens of the left eye; the lens is obviously withdrawn momentarily at the instant of firing. If you change your mind and do not want to use the weapon, think, Photon 1 Abort, and the system will close down. You'll get used to it after a while. Now, is there anything you want to know?"

"How are the preparations going for the trip professor?" asked Doug.

"Fine, fine, I've got two antigrav bikes, one for you and the other for Fred. Both are loaded and ready to go, you'll find them parked on the roof." The professor turned to go then almost as an afterthought said. "By the way, I've registered you both as ornithological students on a working vacation. Your registered numbers are, 405 for Fred, and I've given Fred a second name, Burcot, he's now known as Fred Burcot in the bird business. I've kept your name the same and your number is 502. Now you can both wander about legally, the police may question you but on checking they will find all is in order."

"We'll be leaving about lunch-time tomorrow," said Doug. "I need a bit more time to get to know Fred." Doug thanked the professor for all his efforts and reminded him that should he need help all he had to do was to call him on the transmitter.

"Thanks, I'll remember that," said the professor.

Chapter 12

The professor, Chris, and Janine decided not to use the 'doctor and patient' idea for the second rescue attempt. Last time it ended in disaster, and they would have had to sort out another disguise once they reached Sheerness. They all thought the bird-watching idea the professor had thought up for Doug and Fred a sound scheme and worth a try.

It was early evening when they set off for Sheerness by road in the 'Prairie-Hound', laden with all the paraphernalia associated with the art of bird watching.

A portable hide, cameras, binoculars, camping equipment, special clothing, food and most important for their mission, an inflatable boat, complete with propulsion unit and oars.

The journey down produced no real problems, although they did experience a heart-stopping incident when police diverted traffic at Newington due to a collapsed bridge on the road ahead. No questions were asked, but it delayed them sufficiently to put the rendezvous with the sub out of the question. They would now have to stay overnight somewhere and meet the sub on the following evening.

It was quite late when the professor decided to stop for the night and set up camp. He had chosen a wildlife reservation area adjacent to beach and sea just outside the coastal town of Minster on the Isle of Sheppey. It had been a tiring day and after a light but satisfying meal all turned in for the night in the roomy three-bed-roomed inflatable tent.

The professor was awakened early next morning by the sound of someone shouting outside the tent. "You can't camp 'ere. This is Wildlife Reservation property an' they don't allow no camping. - Hello! - Is anyone about?"

The professor struggled out of his sleeping bag, partially dressed and opened the tent flap.

Outside he saw a large overweight gentleman, ruddy faced, flabby-cheeks and greying hair, which stuck out like straggly string from under a fore-and-aft cap made of brown and cream plaid wool. He also wore a large caped overcoat, made in the same colour and of the same material. Strapped round his waist, outside the overcoat, was a broad leather belt supporting a stun gun, the sort used by gamekeepers and in his right hand he carried a stout walking stick, which he waved dangerously in the professor's face.

"You can't stay 'ere, not without a permit you can't?" he said, in an unnecessarily loud voice.

The professor answered firmly. "I am a member of the National Wildlife Association," he said, taking care to keep well clear of the random gyrations of the walking stick.

"Oh! I see," said the man. "Well, I'm Royston Wallerton, an' I'm supposed to be told when visitors are coming onto the site. Could I see some identification, sir," said the officious Mr Wallerton. The professor produced his membership card and showed it to the fearsome Royston who glanced at it, raised his eyebrows and went through a metamorphosis of attitude toward the professor.

Chris and Janine, disturbed by the rumpus, arrived on the scene and stood watching the proceedings. The site-warden went on to explain to the professor that the field had been allocated to a party of young schoolgirls for the week, under supervision of course, and he was just checking that all was in order. "There should not be any difficulty sir, but if there is just you get in touch. I live in the big 'ouse just over those dunes," said the now extremely polite Mr Wallerton, pointing with his stick toward the back of the field, where the dunes could just be seen jutting up over the bordering hedge. With a polite nod and a pleasant "Good day" to Chris and Janine, he strode laboriously away, stomping along in huge Wellington boots.

After breakfast the trio busied themselves in various ways. The professor sat in the tent at a table covered with maps, working out times and tides on a laptop.

Chris and Janine carried the hide down to the beach and placed it ready to set up just above the high water line, the boat was also taken to the beach and inflated, ready for the short trip to the rendezvous point. They then considered the preparatory work completed and settled down to the serious business of bird watching. The charade had to look realistic. For they had no way of knowing who was watching the watchers.

"This could be fun," said Janine, looking through the binoculars. "Look! There's a Roseate Tern."

"How do you know that?" quizzed Chris. "How can you tell one bird from another, they all look alike to me."

"Lots of things," answered Janine. "Firstly, there may be a particular feature identifying that bird from any other bird. Then there are lots of other little things, the shape of the head, shape of the body, the tail, shape and colour of the beak, legs and feet, general colouring and size. Now, quick, look over there. That's a Sandwich Tern, see the way its plumage sticks out at the back of its head."

"Well, you know what they say?" said Chris.

"No, what do they say?" said Janine, still scouring the sea and beach for more birds to identify.

"One good Tern deserves another," laughed Chris.

Janine stopped looking for birds and thumped Chris on the arm. "Oh you're hopeless, I'm trying to be serious." Chris grabbed hold of Janine and together they playfully rolled around on the beach. Quite suddenly the play stopped, they became quite still and looked deeply into each other's eyes. Slowly their lips met and they melted into a passionate embrace.

"You really are something special Janine," said Chris softly.

"You're not so bad yourself," answered Janine breathlessly, her face flushed and her lips full and red.

The professor came out of the field and onto the beach through a gap in the hedge. "Now come on you two, it might be mating season for some of the birds but we have work to do."

"What work?" asked Chris.

The professor pointed to the hide still rolled up in its bag. "There's that for a start, that's got to be put up, then we've got to work out plans for tonight, so that we can meet the sub on time."

The professor crunched noisily back up the shingle beach and disappeared into the field. Chris and Janine put up the hide, it wasn't a long job, then there were several items to be fetched from the car, which they quite enjoyed fetching, and it gave them more time together in frivolous conversation. On one of their journeys to the car they noticed the young girls had arrived, and by the time they

117

returned to the beach the youngsters had invaded the hide and were pawing over equipment.

"Hey! Leave that alone," shouted Chris, racing down the beach. The unrepentant youngsters did not run off as Chris had expected, but they did at least stop interfering with the equipment.

The girls just stood there giggling, whispering, laughing and nudging each other. "What are you doing?" asked one of the older girls, she looked about twelve.

"Are you bird people?" asked another. They all began edging closer.

"Can we help you watch?" said the first girl.

"Are you in love with her?" came another question, which set all the girls giggling again. Chris was about to answer when two adults came to the rescue, a tall thin young man in his mid-twenties, and a dumpy young woman also in her mid-twenties. The thing Chris noticed about them was that they both had protruding teeth and had the same sort of look about the eyes, perhaps they were related.

"I say old chap," said the man in a rather accentuated upper-crust tone of voice. "I do hope these girls of mine aren't causing you any trouble, if they do get in the way or cause you any concern just call the Special Police. They're keeping an eye on them you see, well you know what weird people get around these days, we've had a few young girls disappearing locally this last month or so. I'm Gerald Freeman, I am a teacher at the Minster College for Girls, this is Miss Winifred Freeman, my sister, she also teaches at the College

"I'm Chris Bonham, and this is Miss Janine Cooper. We are both doing a study on Roseate and Sandleswitch Terns returning to this area after their migratory jaunt, er which they always do at this time of the year." said Chris, taking the outstretched hand offered by Gerald Freeman. Janine nodded a greeting and tried to hide a smile at Chris's attempt to be an authority on birds.

"A Sandleswitch Tern?" said Gerald excitedly. "I can't say I've heard of that one, I will have to keep my eyes open for it, what does it look like?" Gerald had whipped out a pair of binoculars and was frantically sweeping the seashore for a glimpse of this very rare bird.

Chris wracked his brain to try and remember a suitable sea bird, strangely enough he could not think of one, then suddenly one came out of the blue. "Kitty-Hawk," he said.

"Wake," corrected Janine.

"What?" said Chris, bending closer to Janine.

"Kittywake," repeated Janine into Chris's ear.

"Ah, Yes, Kittywake, it's rather like a Kittywake, except that it has a... black beak, and er, different coloured eggs... er legs, different coloured legs. I doubt very much if you'll see one just yet, they don't usually arrive until later in the month."

"Oh dear how very disappointing," said Gerald. "Well come along girls, there's lots to be done before the light goes, come along Winnie." Then turning to Chris said. "Sorry to have been such a nuisance old chap, see you later perhaps."

Taking the girls, Gerald and Winnie marched back along the beach.

"I don't think they're bird people at all," said Gerald when they were out of earshot.

"Neither do I," answered Winnie. "I don't wish to question your knowledge or authority dear, but I've never heard of a Sandleswitch Tern, and I think someone ought to be told about those two, very suspicious if you ask me, and we've got the girls to consider." They both turned and looked back at Chris and Janine for a moment then followed the girls through the gap in the hedge and into their part of the field.

"How about that?" said Chris. "Who's the expert on birds around here then and not a million miles away from the most beautiful girl in the world."

Janine laughed at Chris and gave him a hug. "If that man knows anything at all about birds we are definitely in trouble," she said. The professor called from the top of the beach telling them that lunch was ready. "Race you to the car," shouted Janine, running off and leaving Chris standing.

"Hey! That's cheating," called Chris chasing after her.

Over lunch the professor outlined his plan for the rendezvous with the sub. "We'll try to be somewhere near our position thirty minutes early, that will give us a chance to put matters right if we are delayed for any reason. We must be in position one kilometre off Sheerness by 22.00hrs tonight if we are to make contact."

Doug and Fred made good progress on the antigrav bikes, not going particularly fast, just enjoying the journey, the scenery and the sheer exhilaration of freedom. They talked to each other via their transmitter link as they skimmed over roads and hedges.

'Fred?' said Doug. 'I cannot understand why so little progress has been made in all this time. I've been virtually 'dead' for one hundred and fifty years and apart from a few incredible advances in some directions, nothing's changed. Any ideas?'

'Just a moment Douglas Sampson,' answered Fred.

'And that's another thing Fred, don't keep calling me Douglas Sampson, plain Doug will do in most cases,'

'Ah, I have the information you require, Plain Doug.'

'Why couldn't you give me the information before Fred?' asked Doug.

'I had to retrieve the data from the computer Plain Doug.'

'No, look Fred, my name is not Plain Doug, it's just Doug.' Doug realised immediately that Fred would now be calling him 'Just Doug'… 'Fred, my name is Doug, short for Douglas… Doug on its own, my name is Doug, all right.'

'Oh I see, your name is not Douglas Sampson. I will call you Doug; it's all very confusing.'

Doug wondered if the problem had really been resolved; he had no desire to pursue the matter further. 'I could have retrieved the same data, could I not?' asked Doug.

'It is possible Doug,' said Fred. 'It would depend upon how much data was programmed into your computer by the professor. I have the full range of information available from Oxford University on all subjects.'

'Have you indeed,' said Doug. 'Well Fred, as you already have the information there is no point in my retrieving it, is there? So what is the answer?'

'The answer is very simple. Epic controlled everything and did not deem it necessary to alter things that were adequate just for the sake of it. Only the necessities were altered, things like communications, transport, medicine, armaments, methods of policing and controlling people. Generally, progress in many fields has stagnated; it has been so for many years Doug, that answer your question Doug?'

'Yes it does, basically, thank you.' Doug fell into a moody silence. Fred seemed to be in sympathy with Doug's mood and they travelled along, each locked in his own quiet world.

Two police hoverjets that had been tailing the pair since Leicester now swooped down and ordered them to stop. Doug and Fred stopped on a wide grass verge beside the road. The police 'jets landed several metres away and two officers from each 'jet came strolling across the grass towards them, which meant that both hoverjets were now completely unmanned.

'Fred,' said Doug still using the transmitter link.

'Yes Doug,' answered Fred. 'Stand by in case I miss,' said Doug.

'Set Albatross on stun.' Doug then called his own armaments into readiness. 'Albatross Photon 1, strength 1. He looked at the first officer and saw a red spot dancing on his tunic. 'Fire, fire, fire, fire,' thought Doug, his thoughts triggering the Albatross firing mechanism. He fired in quick succession, changing to a new target each time. Faint pulses of violet light going straight to the red spot. As they struck, the target fluoresced and was enveloped in iridescent light. All four police officers fell.

Doug closed down Albatross and walked over to the four figures lying motionless on the ground. All were still breathing. He relieved them of their energy guns and walked over to the hoverjets.

"Why did you do that Douglas Sampson?" asked a puzzled Fred.

"Call it forward planning Fred. We will find these hoverjets ideal for our mission."

"Fine, fine," said Fred enthusiastically. "What is our mission?"

"We have to go to Nottingham and find a lad called Peter, I'll tell you more later on. We will load the antigrav bikes onto the 'jets, then you take one of the 'jets and follow me, do you think you can do that?" Fred looked hurt. If Fred lacked anything it was not confidence in his own ability, failure was not part of his programming.

"Of course I can Douglas Sampson." Doug noticed that whenever Fred got puzzled or annoyed over something he called him Douglas

Sampson, otherwise it was always Doug. It was his way of registering his feelings.

Sitting in the cockpit of the hoverjet Doug familiarised himself with the controls. Not difficult by any means, one thing that had been achieved in this futureworld was simplification, a joystick, two pedals and an accelerator lever.

The dashboard had quite a few dials and buttons on it but Doug did not want to be an expert on it. He just wanted to get the thing started and fly it from A to B.

'Power on, doors, lights, that's about all I shall need to know for now… You got all that Fred?'

'Yes Doug, I followed your thoughts on the control layout, ready when you are.'

Doug found when flying he only needed the joystick and accelerator for most things, the pedals were for manoeuvring, turning whilst hovering and trimming the direction of flight. Fred seemed to be coping quite well, following Doug at a safe distance. 'So,' thought Doug. 'Off to Nottingham.'

It was early evening when Doug estimated that they should be coming up to Nottingham. He noticed there were no surveillance satellites floating in the sky. Dead ahead he saw what appeared to be a range of hills, the closer he got the more puzzled he became. Suddenly he realised. 'This is not a hill! It's a damn great wall.'

'What do you make of that Fred?' he said over the transmitter link.

'It is an amazing feat of engineering, I have no information on it,' answered Fred.

Doug took the 'jet up to one hundred metres and saw the full enormity of the construction. It reminded him of pictures he had seen of the Great Wall of China, following the undulations of the countryside, snaking away until it disappeared over the horizon in both directions.

Three hundred metres from the wall the drive began to falter and the 'jet lost height rapidly. Doug had no control and the craft continued to rush forwards and downwards. Fifty metres from the wall and ten metres up all power finally left the 'jet and it plummeted earthwards. Doug braced himself for the crash, small trees and bushes helped cushion the impact. Broken windows, bent struts, smashed dashboard, the fuselage with gaping holes, wisps of smoke coming from several pieces of equipment. Doug thought he was lucky to have escaped physically undamaged.

'You all right Fred?' called Doug over the link. He waited; there was no reply. He called again, still no reply. Doug wrenched away a few obstructive panels and tore open the jammed door, still no answer from Fred.

He climbed out of the wrecked hoverjet and walked back along the flight path. He knew Fred had been following and assumed the same thing must have happened to him, otherwise he would have been hovering around like a mother hen trying to execute a rescue. It worried him that Fred was not answering his calls over the link. Eventually he found the wreckage. Fred's craft had crashed into a large tree and was unrecognisable as a hoverjet.

Doug feared the worst and started tearing large sheets of metal away from the crumpled craft in an effort to find Fred.

"Fred! Fred!" called Doug. "Are you all right?"

"I am here Douglas Sampson," answered Fred. "Here in the cockpit, I cannot understand it. What did I do wrong?" Doug finally reached Fred who was sitting in the cockpit with a very puzzled look on his face. "I saw you start to descend and intended following you down when the drive unit just would not respond."

"Don't worry Fred, it was nothing you did," said Doug. "The same thing happened to me and the closer I got to the wall the worse it became. After the crash I called you on the transmitter link, why did you not reply?"

Fred immediately went onto the defensive. "The last call I had from you Douglas Sampson was when you asked for my thoughts on the subject of the wall and I told you I had no information on it, then you decided to land."

"No Fred, I did not decide to land, the decision was made for me with the failure of my 'jet. Something must emanate from the wall, something that affects the drive units and antigravity coils."

Fred climbed out of the wreckage and stood a few metres away.

"Let's try the transmitter again," said Doug, and called Fred several times over the transmitter. "Anything coming through Fred?"

voiced Doug.

Fred shook his head. "Nothing, nothing at all," he said. They walked away from the wall, testing the transmitter at fifty metre intervals. At two hundred and fifty metres faint signals broke through the static and by the time they reached the three hundred-metre mark the link was again working normally. They paid a return visit to the two stricken craft and unloaded some of the camping equipment.

"It will be dark soon Fred, and I've got to get to the other side of that wall," said Doug.

Loaded with camping gear they left the craft and walked in the direction of the wall. "Is it to find Peter?" asked Fred. "Why do you want to find this Peter?"

As they trudged along Doug told Fred of his experience with Daniel Baker.

"A very strange story," said Fred. "Are you sure you were not what you call dreaming."

"Yes I'm sure," said Doug. "The old man's staff reappeared in the armchair after he had gone, I returned from the shower and there it was."

By now they were getting close to the wall and Fred was lagging behind.

"Douglas Sampson," called Fred faintly. "I feel strangely weak, I'm having diff… diff… difficulty in bal… ance… and con… cen…tra…tion."

Fred fell and lay still. Doug noticed that he too was suddenly very weak, his senses reeling, his energy draining away, his eyes wouldn't focus. He thought he heard voices and made out misty shapes approaching in the half-light then for him also came darkness and oblivion.

Chapter 13

The professor, Chris and Janine pushed the inflatable dinghy away from the shore and set off for the rendezvous with the sub. It turned out to be a fine evening, a little chilly but hardly a breeze with the sea just like a millpond.

"A bit different to the last time we were in these waters," said Chris.

"Ah yes," answered the professor. "That was when we had all that rain wasn't it?" Then turning to Janine the professor said. "Are you sure there was no signal arranged between you and the sub?"

"Yes I'm sure," said Janine. "Bob said he would surface each evening and wait there for our signal, but strange as it sounds we never got round to arranging one. Why can't we use the radio when we get close?"

"Too risky, much too risky," answered the professor.

It was getting dark when they reached their position at the rendezvous point.

It was Monday night, not too much coastal traffic about, just a few boats dotted here and there. It was time, 22.00 hrs, the professor, Chris, and Janine sat quietly in the small inflatable boat, eyes straining into the darkness trying to detect a glimpse of the sub in the reflected light thrown down by the surveillance satellites. Occasionally Janine flashed a light across the surface in a wide arc hoping that if Bob were there he would see it.

Suddenly there it was, a few metres off the stern quarter. Chris swung the small craft about and hove-to beside the surfacing sub which although not large by shipping standards, made the small inflatable look even smaller. The professor secured the boat's painter to a ringbolt beside a row of rungs leading up to the access hatch. Janine leapt onto the rungs and climbed up to meet Bob just as he stepped out of the hatch onto the platform.

"Bob darling, it's so good to see you," said Janine, and she flung her arms around his neck and kissed him. Hans and Jamie joined them and were also greeted in a like manner. The obvious questions were all dealt with quickly and then the more serious business came onto the agenda. The professor was about to give Bob the new co-ordinates when the whole area became ablaze with light.

Floodlights from five or six craft that had silently closed in on the rendezvous point and were now completely surrounding the sub and the inflatable boat. A voice calling for their surrender came with ear-shattering power from a loudhailer somewhere in the darkness behind that blinding curtain of light.

"Stay where you are, do not try to escape or you will be shot."

The professor sent a quick message to Sal.

'Sal, do not acknowledge. Mission a failure, all have been arrested... I don't know where they are taking us. Tell Doug... tell him not to reply... I will contact him as soon as possible. Commence operation 'Close Down' immediately.'

Sal did as ordered and eventually all the staff, except Jazzer would be moved to safe houses and at the professor's house all areas below ground level would be sealed off. The professor's house at Burcot would appear to be a normal residence to all but the most rigorous of searches.

Bob, his crew and the professor's party were all transferred to one of the small boats and held in a cabin under guard. "Professor Edward Burgess?" said Bob to the professor.

"Just professor will do, most people just call me professor. Professor Edward Burgess is such a mouthful, May I call you Bob?"

"Of course, we were hoping you would solve all our problems."

The professor put his finger to his lips and indicated by mime that there could be listening devices. "The answer," said the professor, "is either idle chatter or complete silence." They silently agreed upon idle chatter. "Did you have nice weather Bob?" Thus initiating a spell of obviously idle chatter.

"Yes quite nice, although we were below the surface most of the time doing seabed research," answered Bob with an element of truth. The others caught on and also engaged themselves in meaningless repartee.

Throughout the journey Hans and Jamie had their eyes glued to the two small portholes, trying to see anything that might give them a clue to their destination.

A mountainous building loomed out of the darkness, silhouetted menacingly against the false moon-glow from the surveillance satellites. "I know where we are," said Hans. "I'd know that building anywhere, it's the Epic Building."

He was right, the craft veered to starboard and travelled towards the huge black building. Soon they could see lights beaming out of the massive entrances at the base of the building, entrances large enough to accommodate sizeable vessels. Another message to Sal, 'We are being taken into the Epic Building,' said the professor via his mental transmitter link.

The boat travelled slowly in under the building for about ten minutes then stopped. The cabin door was then unlocked and the whole party ordered out.

They were escorted off the small boat and onto a landing stage by four men carrying energy guns and told to get in line.

"Follow me," said a stern-faced officer dressed in the black uniform of the Epic Special Police. He marched them along a dingy corridor smelling strongly of damp and decay, then into a large service lift that travelled jerkily upwards.

When the lift doors opened they were ushered out into another corridor, a very grand corridor, the walls of which were heavily decorated with silver cups, shields, plaques, pictures of parades and ceremonies. The long wide corridor led them to an impressive pair of doors made of polished mahogany, and framed with white-marble fluted Doric columns. The columns supported a rectangular tablet of marble, depicting in bass relief, a fierce double-headed eagle with wings outstretched and talons menacing the foreground.

The officer stopped, knocked firmly on the doors, and waited.

"Come," said a voice from a loudspeaker at the side of the doors. The officer opened the doors and escorted the party into a large luxuriously furnished room. A vast office, carpeted with a rich red and gold carpet. Oil paintings by the old masters were prominently displayed on the walls, display cases containing fine porcelain, items of exquisite art in gold, silver and jade. Magnificent coloured drapes hanging against the walls in carefully arranged folds from the high ceiling and at the far end, a huge desk and a man.

The prisoners were lined up in front of the desk. The man, who was tall and slim, thin-faced with a small goatee beard and jet-black hair, stood up slowly and walked over to them. In his right hand he held a long paper-knife, which he carried by its ivory handle, he kept tapping the blade onto the fingers of his left hand, stopping only to dig the point hard under the chin of the nearest prisoner, or stroke it menacingly across their cheeks and throat. He walked right along the line then round the back, making no sound on the carpet and delighting when the sudden shock of the blade was felt on the neck of the chosen victim.

The armed escort was present all the time during this chilling display.

Eventually he walked back to his desk and sat down.

"I am Omega, I control your very existence. Whether you live or die is my decision." He pointed to the professor. "You have been a considerable nuisance to me. You and your organisation. Now you can put matters right, save yourself and your companions considerable pain, discomfort and possibly an untimely death.

If you co-operate, willingly that is, and tell me all that I want to know, things could be made a lot easier for yourself and all your companions. Think about it."

"I will tell you nothing," said the professor. "Neither will my companions."

"A pity," said Omega. "But soon it will be of no consequence, my 'will' will be done." He stared at them, and for a while no one spoke. Omega beckoned the guard and with a cruel sneering look said, "Take them away."

The prisoners were all taken to a spacious hall-like room; an area obviously designed to accommodate large numbers of prisoners, no windows, but very well lit. One end, devoted to the sleeping arrangements, contained several rows of double bunk-beds; there were no separate facilities for males and females. The opposite end of the room catered for the toilet requirements, here at least common decency prevailed and flimsy screens afforded a little privacy. Meals and recreation were carried out in the central area.

There were other prisoners already established in the 'prison' before the professor's group arrived. The professor immediately recognised two of them, they were Dora and John Pickles, the two members of the organisation who were previously looking after Desmond Greer. "Dora, John, how are, how did you come to be here?" They did not answer but looked up toward the ceiling and nodded toward the cameras. "Don't worry about the cameras," said the professor. "They must know by now that we are members of the organisation. Now, how did you come to be here?"

"It was Desmond Greer," said John. "He wanted to get back into favour with Omega and traded us in for another chance."

"Did you manage to get anything out of him?" asked the professor.

"Yes, quite a lot really. Omega has set himself up as a religious leader."

They drew closer together, Dora, John, and the professor, John spoke in little more than a whisper. "It appears that thirty years ago, Desmond Greer and Jed Mangrove, that's Omega's real name, were both working as maintenance engineers inside the Epic Building. Jed discovered a secret room in a disused part of the building; it contained a control console. There were two electronic keys still in position on the console and they discovered that by operating the console they could isolate Epic's programming equipment. Jed Mangrove had one key and Desmond Greer the other. They found that by activating the control console they could actually reprogram Epic. The keys could be used independently but somewhere along the line Desmond Greer's key vanished, was lost or stolen. And Jed Mangrove would not allow Greer into the control room without the key, which meant, according to Greer, that Jed now had complete control over the programming of Epic.

Over the years Jed gained power, he is now in complete control of the World Council and is the most powerful man on earth. But, he made one monumental error, so Greer said, Omega switched off the apparatus that linked Epic with the cerebral implants, he thought he could control it himself... a grave mistake on his part. Somehow he triggered a destruct system and having switched the units off, lost all the information and destroyed a large section of the implant control equipment beyond repair. That is why we have not been directed by Epic for the last two years: not many people know about it, only the leading hierarchies in the priesthood and, of course,

Desmond Greer. Omega now rules by fear and a massive police presence."

"What about the apparition in the temple that Jack Hoskins saw?" asked the professor. It was Dora Pickles that answered.

"We shaped our questions to Desmond in such a way as to lead him in that direction. There is something there, something awful, something he is very fearful of; he shied away each time we tried to talk about it. We think it was our persistence on the subject that made him suspicious. On one occasion, when he was very depressed he got very drunk. He told us that Omega dabbled in black magic. Desmond doesn't know for certain, but he reckons it was this dabbling that conjured the entity that led Omega, or Jed as he was then, to the concealed control room and influenced the programming, promising power and wealth beyond compare. Desmond said they were partners at the start, but after he lost his key Jed prised him out and took complete control, which became a bone of contention between them ever since. He believes that Omega and the entity made a sort of pact, It was the only time he ever spoke of the entity. Drunk or sober he's scared stiff of whatever lurks in the basement of the Epic Building."

Bob sauntered over and joined the group. The professor introduced him to Dora and John Pickles. "What happens now professor?" asked Bob. "I can't see us escaping from here. I don't know anything about the organisation anyway."

"I shall most likely be held prisoner here, with the other known members of the organisation," said the professor. "I doubt if Omega will kill us off just yet. He will probably send you and your crew to a corrective training area."

"What does that mean?" asked Bob.

"First," began the professor, "you undergo an intensive brainwashing period, using drugs and computerised 'virtual reality' techniques. Then, under complete control of the drugs, you will be sent to one of the specialist areas dotted around the country where you will probably work in a servile mental state for the rest of your life, totally ignorant of what you were before."

"That sounds terrible, almost worse than death, can nothing be done to regain normality?" queried Bob.

The professor, looking serious, continued. "Your mind is controlled by a daily dose of a Benzodiapine based drug known as Mentala Distillate, it is tasteless and is usually administered in water. If you were able to keep free of the drug for a few days you would begin to recover from the artificially induced amnesia and brainwashing. Obviously the longer you remain under the influence of the drug, the more difficult it is to return to normal."

Hans and Jamie joined the group. "Just heard some of the other people talking," said Jamie. "They reckon we're being sorted out in the morning."

"I'd really like to know what's going on," said Hans. Chris held Janine close to him and whispered tenderly to her.

"Whatever happens I want you to know that I love you, Janine."

"I love you too, Chris. What a time to discover our love. Think of all the time we wasted. Oh Chris," said Janine tearfully.

The professor had not been correct in his assumptions and all members of the organisation were not detained for further questioning. The next day they were all sent to the Corrective Training Centre, the dreaded CTW, about fifty persons in all.

"Where are they taking us?" asked Hans.

"Your guess is as good as mine," answered Bob, "but somehow I don't think it will be long before we find out." They were all marched out of the prison hall between two rows of armed guards and along a well-lit, white-tiled corridor. Bob could see a white sign at the far end, the letters not quite large enough to read at that distance. The unnerving sound of the guards measured tread, their heavy boots echoing eerily in the confines of the corridor. Closer to the sign now, it depicted a black arrow pointing off to the right and printed in red capital letters, CORRECTIVE TRAINING WING. Then in smaller print in black, No Admittance Unauthorised Personnel.

Chapter 14

When Doug regained consciousness, both he and Fred were lying on a straw-strewn floor and dressed in clothes belonging to the Middle Ages. They were also chained with a leg-iron on each ankle and a short length of chain to a stone wall.

'Looks like a medieval dungeon,' thought Doug.

'Yes I agree, it has the style of that period,' answered Fred over the transmitter.

'How do you feel Fred, are you all right?' asked Doug, still using the mental link.

'Yes Doug I'm fine. I haven't checked all my systems yet but…'

'Yes, okay Fred, thank you, now listen. I don't know what power they were using but whatever it was emanated from that wall where we crashed.'

'I can tell you if you really want to know Doug,' said Fred, innocently.

'Of course I want to know, in case we come up against it again.'

Fred then told Doug about the radiation he had observed coming from the wall. 'It is a powerful gamma radiation of similar frequency to that of our SENADS unit. We have high power screening against gamma radiation, but when we were a few metres from the wall the radiation was so great that it saturated our screens and our systems closed down for safety. I should have checked for alien radiation, I have set up a program to monitor the situation. To counteract this hazard we have to adjust the level of our gamma radiation screen.'

'How do we do that?' asked Doug.

'I have already readjusted my systems. If you want to adjust yours, you will have to do it via your internal computer. It is easy, just ask for SENADS Gamma Screen Adjustment, and when your mental display comes up say one hundred per cent increase and the computer will do the rest.'

'Right, thank you Fred,' said Doug, and readjusted his screening. 'Do you want to know something Fred? I think we must have been brought to this place for some reason, otherwise they would have just killed us. The chances are that we will be questioned so, until we know the score, say we were attacked in the forest and cannot remember a thing.'

'It is true Doug I can't remember being attacked, and what game are we playing?'

'Sorry Fred, you've lost me, what do you mean?'

'Well, if we are to know the score then we must know what game we are playing to make sure we score correctly.'

'No Fred, it was only a saying, just don't tell anyone who we really are or how we came to be here until we are sure they mean us no harm.' Doug was getting a little exasperated with Fred, sometimes he was as bright as a button, other times he was as dim as a 'Toc H' lamp.

'We can easily break these chains Doug, and with our armaments make our escape.'

'I don't want to do that just yet. 'I want to find out what's going on here, and I've got to find Peter.'

There was the sound of a key turning noisily in the lock of the heavily studded oak door, which screeched loudly on dry iron hinges. A man came in carrying a large wooden tray.

"I've brought you some food," he said setting the tray down on the straw-strewn floor between them. He had long hair, uncombed and dirty and his beard still contained remains of food from previous meals. He grinned down at them showing dirty but surprisingly good teeth. The man wore a knee-length tunic of rough linen, stained and dirty, and he smelled revolting. On his legs he wore rough woollen hose cross-gartered to the knee. Knee-length breeches were tucked into the tops of the woollen hose. His shoes were pieces of leather laced to his feet.

"Thank you," said Doug. "And who are you?"

"They call me Alfred," said the man. "I look after the prisoners, bring their food and things, I'm a serf. What terrible crimes did you commit to be placed here in the dungeon? They don't always put people in here, only ones that have committed terrible crimes. So what terrible crimes have you committed to be put in here?"

"To be honest Alfred," said Doug. "We can't remember."

Alfred guffawed with laughter. "I've heard that one before, many a time I've heard folks say 'I can't remember'. Ha, ha, ha, but they still take them away and I don't see them any more, ha, ha, ha."

Alfred left, loudly banging the door and turning the key in the lock. They could still hear him laughing as he shuffled away from the door.

The meal consisted of a thick piece of bread and a chunk of cheese. Also on the tray was an earthenware pitcher full of water. Doug went back to talking to Fred over their transmitter link. 'What do you make of that Fred?'

'Very strange,' came back Fred's voice. 'His clothes seem to indicate a period somewhere around the year twelve hundred, as do our own, yet he speaks with a modern dialect and turn of phrase. It appears that he, in spite of his appearance, is a modern man living in a bygone age.'

Still using the transmitter link Doug suggested they ought to eat some of the food, it might look suspicious if it were left untouched. The meal was barely finished when they heard heavy footsteps approaching, the rhythmic tread of marching men. Outside the cell door the men were called to a halt, and once again a key was thrust noisily into the lock and the door swung back, protesting loudly against the movement. Alfred entered and stood nervously aside by the door.

A tall, well-built man entered, fully clothed in chain-mail, but not helmeted, some would have said he was handsome, but others who really knew him would have told you that his looks belied the evil he carried with him wherever he went.

Hideous tales of cruelty followed his movements, and the releasing of this evil upon the innocent and defenceless. He strode into the dungeon and over to where the two prisoners were sat, with their backs to the wall.

"Who are you?" he rasped. "And what were you doing so close to the wall?" Fred said nothing, and Doug was about to answer when he received a vicious kick on the legs from the armoured man. Doug immediately saw a red spot dancing on the armour and realised that Fred had armed Albatross and was preparing to fire for his protection.

'It's all right Fred,' said Doug over the link. 'Don't fire, I want to find out what is going on here.'

'I am programmed to protect you and myself,' answered Fred.

"Speak up you cur, or you'll feel the taste of my steel in your belly."

"I'm Douglas Sampson, and my companion is Frederick Burcot, we are ornithologists. We were attacked in the forest," said Doug, struggling to his feet.

The armoured man stood menacingly in front of them. "At least you have manners enough to stand before your betters. As for your friend, he needs some instruction, he needs to be taught some manners." He drew his sword and struck Fred hard with the flat of the blade around the arms and shoulders.

Doug again saw the red spot dancing. 'No! Fred, No!' shouted Doug over the link. 'Not now, we will deal with him later.' Fred answered and complied; he didn't like it, and slowly stood up. The armoured man stood solidly in front of them. He was a big man, slightly taller than Doug and broader in the shoulder.

He spoke roughly to them. "My first thoughts were to have you executed, but we are short of serfs. You will be set to work and whatever rights you had are immediately forfeited."

The armoured man turned to go. "Who the hell are you," said Doug in a firm loud voice. The armoured man stopped short, spun round and walked straight up to Doug and hit him hard across the face with the back of his mailed hand. Doug rode the blow and stared back defiantly, straight into the eyes of the man.

"How dare you, how dare you speak to me in that tone of voice. I am your master, I am Lord Grunwald Dé Reske, known here as Lord Grunwald and I am Earl of Newark and Sherwood." He was eyeballing Doug, there was madness in his eyes and his mouth took on a cruel turn. "You will never need to ask that question again, will you?" Grunwald turned and stormed out of the dungeon. He spoke to a group of men standing outside the doorway. "Take them to Sir Rolph's castle, tell him they come as a gift from Grunwald, he is to put them to work with the rest of the serfs." Lord Grunwald walked away, not realising how close he had come to being barbecued.

Alfred came over and drove the pins out of their shackles. "You were lucky," he said in a lowered voice. "Normally he would have killed a man for answering back as you did. He would have smashed his skull with his morning star."

The other men approached, all armoured in chain-mail and wearing white surcotes depicting a black double-headed eagle. They escorted Doug and Fred out of the dungeon and up into the courtyard. Two of the men organised a rather heavy-looking wagon pulled by two enormous Percherons and driven by a seedy old driver. Doug and Fred not chained or handcuffed, were bullied aboard the wagon by the six-man escort.

On the way to Sir Rolph's castle Doug noticed the soldiers kept well clear of forest areas. He leaned forward toward the driver. "Why don't they go through the forest? We seemed to have circled around it."

"Too dangerous, too dangerous," was the reply from the dishevelled driver.

"Why is it dangerous?" asked Doug.

The driver looked round to see where the escorting soldiers were, he seemed frightened. After a while he said in a hoarse whisper out of the side of his mouth. "It's the outlaws."

"What do you mean, it's the outlaws?" The driver would speak no more; instead he whipped the horses into a gallop causing the wagon to career dangerously from side to side along the rough dirt road.

The escort charged along behind shouting. "Hey! Old man. What's the hurry? Slow down… S-t-o-p." The old man pulled back on the reins and the wagon eventually drew to a halt.

The escorting soldiers were tiring and told the old man to pull over and take a rest. He pulled to the side of the dirt road and climbed down off the wagon. The soldiers dismounted and wandered off to water their horses in a nearby stream. Doug repeated his question. "Why is it so dangerous to go into the forest?"

The old man looked round again and saw that the escort was out of earshot fifteen metres away. "I don't know much about outlaws, but I do know that they are very wicked people who would slit your throat as soon as look at you, and they take all your money,

136

supposing you had any." The old man was not only scared of the escort; he was scared even to as much as talk about the outlaws. Maybe he thought the very trees or the wind would bear witness against him.

"What's your name?" asked Doug, in a kindly tone.

"My name is Harold," said the man.

Doug spoke to Fred over the link. 'Fred, look at this man's hands, they're all blistered and bleeding, not the hands of a working man would you say?'

'Quite right,' answered Fred. 'Much too soft.'

"How long have you lived here Harold?" asked Doug. Harold frowned and screwed up his eyes.

"I... I've lived here all my life, working in the fields, serving the great Lord Grunwald," answered Harold. Doug again spoke to Fred over the link.

'He's not lying Fred, he really believes that he has actually spent all his life working here as a labourer but his hands tell a totally different story.'

The soldiers, having rested, ordered their charges back onto the wagon.

The journey continued along the rutted dirt road. It was another hour of jolting and jarring in the unsprung wagon before Doug saw Sir Rolph's dark castle brooding on the top of the next hill.

Chapter 15

The professor, Janine, Bob and the others were marched along the echoing corridor until they reached the Corrective Training Wing. They were then marched into a large white-walled hall filled with at least eight rows of one-piece leather suits; all white and hanging like limp emaciated bodies. Each suit was suspended in gimbals and festooned with wires and tubes. On the floor, beneath each suit lay a full-face, mask-like helmet with large box-shaped attachments in place of eyes and ears, also festooned with wires and tubes. The prisoners were marched into the centre of the hall and told to line up in front of the numbered suits. The doors were closed and the guards took up positions down each side of the area.

A smartly dressed officer walked in and stood in a central position and surveyed the prisoners, his black uniform standing out sharply against the white walls. He called for silence, cleared his throat and, using a small cordless microphone, issued instructions that came booming out of loudspeakers set at intervals round the cavernous area. "I am Captain Crawley, I am in charge of this section of the Corrective Training Wing. From now on you will be identified as Group 5 and each of you will be identified in the group by the number on the suit behind you. The numbers are for our benefit, not yours."

The guards pushed and pulled the newly formed Group 5 'trainees' into position, the captain continued speaking. "You will now divest yourselves of all clothing, jewellery, and any other articles of decoration."

Complete silence, no one moved, let alone started taking their clothes off. The captain had obviously come across this situation before and nodded toward a couple of heavily built attendants. The two attendants, each carrying a short thick stick with electrodes glistening at the end, walked over to the first man in the line and prodded him with the electric goad the power of which knocked the man to the ground. The white-coated attendants continued prodding the man on the ground where he lay screaming with pain at each prod of the goad. After a while he stopped screaming and his body lay twitching on the ground. "The electronic goad is designed to attack the nerve ends, it is very persuasive. Who's next?" said the captain with a sickly smile.

Reluctantly the group stripped, men and women alike, and stood in a line, naked and humiliated in front of the lifeless suits. The captain walked along the line until he came to Janine. He stared at her naked form, mentally fantasising about her beautiful body. "Well now, what do we have here?" he said, and stood directly in front of her. "I can save you a lot of unpleasantness if you co-operate with what I have in mind." Janine looked up smiling into his face, put her hands onto his hips and drew him closer. The Captain's face lit up in anticipation and he bent forward to kiss her luscious, smiling, inviting lips. Janine's smile vanished; she suddenly grasped his arm and twisted her body. Captain Crawley somersaulted head over heels and landed heavily on his back three metres away, victim of a perfect Irish Whip.

Chris noticed the guards; their attention was focused to a man on the captain.

With all his strength Chris lashed out and smashed his fist into the face of the nearest guard, took his gun, flipped the control to max and vaporised the captain.

He vaporised two more guards before the others realised what was happening. They were shocked into taking retaliatory action. Chris went down and lay twitching for a moment on the floor and then he lay quite still. A cry of horror sprang from Janine's lips as she tried to run to Chris, but the guard stopped her.

The end doors opened and Commander Beaumont, head of the C.T.W entered and demanded to know what was going on. One of the guards came swiftly to attention. "Captain Crawley made advances to one of the women, sir."

"Which one?" asked the Commander.

"That one there, sir," answered the guard, pointing to Janine. The Commander looked hard at Janine. He looked round the training area.

"Where is Captain Crawley now?"

"There, sir," said the guard, pointing to a blackened area on the floor by the door.

The tightening of the Commander's face muscles showed his feeling as he gazed at the man-shaped scorch-mark etched into the concrete. "How did it happen?" he said, still gazing at the outline of the late Captain Crawley. The guard, still standing stiffly to attention, and sweating with fear, answered with military directness and speed.

"The man over there, sir, the man on the floor sir. Overpowered one of the guards and took his gun sir and shot the captain, sir."

"Is the man dead?" asked the commander quietly.

"I don't know, sir, he was hit with blasts from three energy guns on stun, sir." The commander walked over to where Janine was standing.

"You are very beautiful my dear, but in future do not entice my staff to default." He hit Janine hard across the face, a vicious blow with the back of his black-gloved hand. A trickle of blood appeared at the corner of her mouth and she fought back the tears, but her eyes showed defiance as she glared back at the commander. He turned away. "Put them into the suits, fit the helmets and start the training." Then looking again at the inert figure of Chris on the floor said. "Take him to the medical centre, if he recovers he can join them." The commander turned to the nearest guard and asked his name. The guard sprang to attention.

"Jones, sir, Sergeant Jones CT 725357, sir."

"Sergeant Jones, are you the most senior rank here?"

"Yes sir," replied the sergeant.

"Very well," said the commander. "You are in charge until I can find a replacement for Captain Crawley. Carry on Sergeant Jones." The commander looked once more at Janine, gave a sneering smile, then walked out of the door being held open by one of the guards, the other guards all standing stiffly to attention.

Omega sat in the opulence of his magnificent office. He was a man who was obsessed with a desire for wealth and power. The luxurious office, his fine clothes, his jewellery, all indicated this obsession. "Send in Desmond Greer." He spoke these words into the intercom equipment on his desk. A few moments later Desmond Greer was escorted into the office and marched between two guards down the length of the room, to stand in front of the desk. "Leave us," ordered Omega. The guards saluted smartly and marched out in a very forced military fashion.

The two men sat in silence for a while, Omega, with his eyes screwed up and a sardonic sneer on his down-drawn lips, was watching Desmond closely. And Desmond, standing in front of the desk, with bowed shoulders, head down, shook with fear. Omega was torn between loyalties. In one sense he wanted to be rid of Desmond, he was a link with his past life, a weak link, and one that embarrassed him. If Desmond had been any other mortal Omega would have had him killed with no more remorse than if he had swatted a fly on the wall. And yet, in another sense, he was an old friend. Probably the only real friend he had left.

"What am I going to do with you Desmond?" said Omega, with strangely uncharacteristic tenderness in his voice. Desmond flung himself onto his knees and assumed a praying position.

"I promise not to interfere again Jed, I promise, I really do promise. This time I'll even help you with your work. I will, I will. Only don't send me to that awful place again." By 'that awful place' he of course meant the cell from where he was forced to watch the slaughter of hundreds of innocent men and women every day. "Please Jed, don't send me there."

Omega answered Desmond but his tone had hardened. "Get up Desmond you look stupid, I will give you one more chance. I have a job for you."

Omega continued talking, talking for his own benefit as much as Desmond's. Trying to justify to himself the need for the vile acts committed in the great hall adjacent to the cells day after day. "I must have blood for the brain cultures, fresh blood every day. We are so very close now to the time when my master will be able to materialise into the physical world. It is then I will become immortal and rule over all the dominions of the Earth, the Eblis has told me that it will be so."

Desmond could see that Omega was off again into his mad world of fantasy. He had told Omega before that it was all fantasy and that the Eblis was just using him, and he finished up being imprisoned in the cells, lucky not to have lost his life.

"What is it you want me to do?" croaked Desmond, with a mouth as dry as the Sahara. Omega gave a sly smile and told Desmond what was in store for him.

"I am about to start training a new group of people," he said. "The new group will go to Cotgrave in Nottinghamshire. There are fifty in all; I want you to be one of them. You will take part in their programme and be part of their virtual reality environment before they encounter the real environment at Cotgrave. The only difference being that you will not be taking the drugs. Before the drugs take full effect, and when the group think they are safe, they will talk freely, much more freely than when under the influence of the usual truth drugs. I want you to discover as much as possible about an organisation known as Albatross. When you have enough information I will break you out of the programme." Omega wrote a letter, which he sealed immediately. "Guards," he shouted into the intercom. Then to Desmond he said. "Be sure you give this letter personally to Commander Beaumont, it is your only ticket out." He handed the freshly sealed envelope to Desmond. The same two guards arrived and stood stiffly to attention slightly to the rear of Desmond. "Take him to the Corrective Training Wing, report to Commander Beaumont."

The guards marched Desmond to the Corrective Training Wing and into the Commander's office where he spoke to the commander alone, explaining his mission and handing him the letter, which the commander read and after reading placed carefully into his jacket pocket. The guards were then called in and Desmond was escorted to the main hall of the C.T.W, lined up in front of a suit and stripped of all his clothing, just like the rest of the 'prisoners'.

The commander was secretly watching the proceedings from just inside the open door of the hall when an inmate started fighting with one of the guards. In the struggle the guard's energy gun came out of its holster and fell, discharging on full power as it hit the floor. Desmond, who happened to be looking in that direction at the time, looked on in horror as the random bolt of energy struck the commander who immediately vanished in an orange glow. No one else saw what had happened, all the guards were busy fitting the prisoners into their suits. So the fact that the commander of the C.T.W had just been vaporised went entirely unnoticed. Even the guard who had lost his gun didn't realise what had happened. He finished securing his charge into the suit. Picked up his fallen gun, returned it to its holster and walked calmly over to the control console.

Desmond shouted at one of the guards from inside the helmet.

"There's been a mistake, I'm not supposed to be here, I'm innocent. Hey look here, I'm a personal friend of Omega, he'll tell you."

"Oh, a personal friend of yours is he," laughed the guard, strapping Desmond even tighter into the suit. "They all say that," he said and called across to his partner on the other side of the hall. "George, better be especially nice to this one, he's a personal friend of Omega." Both guards guffawed with laughter as they continued to strap the inmates into the suits and secured them into the centre of the gimbals, which they then hauled halfway to the ceiling. The laughter of the other guards could be heard all around the hall as they told the story one to another.

Being a guard at the C.T.W did have its compensations. There was plenty to interest the voyeur and the sadistically minded. They had only to watch the monitors to see into the programme that each of the 'trainees' was receiving. They could peer into the virtual reality programme and observe exactly what was going on every second of the day. For those having leaning toward the sadistic, they relished in the ordeal by terror part of the programme, which was introduced to bring the 'team' together using fear as a collective enemy

The virtual reality equipment was switched on and the whole group could now 'see' each other in the new environment. They were no longer suspended naked in grotesque suits. They were standing in a strange village with straw-roofed huts with walls made of hurdles and clay held together with animal hair. There were log fires, the smell of wood-smoke, cow dung and animals. They were basically dressed the same, men and women alike, in a round-necked, knee-length tunic made of a coarse linen-like material belted at the waist. But some of the men wore short jackets and knee-length breeches, again made of the same coarse linen-like material. The breeches were tucked into the top of rough woollen stockings, cross-gartered to just below the knee with leather thongs. Shoes were heel-less, and consisted of a piece of leather crudely shaped and laced around each foot. Some of the women wore similar gartered stocking hose and shoes.

The professor came across the clearing to where Bob was standing.

"Try to hold on to reality Bob, remember that this is all computerised imagery, not real at all. We are still suspended in the suits and I'm not really standing here in front of you. It's all done with mind controlling probes and sensors in the helmet. A computer controls the suit and makes you feel as though you are walking, sitting, standing, it supplies everyone with all the physical sensations required by means of a master program. The computer links all the suits into this one synchronised program, and then later on, it's backed up by drugs."

"It's unbelievable," said Bob. "We have had VR for years, I've experienced it myself, but this is fantastic."

The professor called everyone together and stood in the centre of a circle of men and women. It was a warm sunny day; some of them sat on the scattered patches of dry grass. The professor spoke again. "This is only the beginning. At the moment you still have your memories, memories of what you are, and, what you have made of yourselves. Memories of family life, a whole history of events that stretch from infancy to the present time, try to hold on to those memories for as long as you can.

I don't know what's in store for us, but when the drugs start to take effect it will be difficult for you to remember who you are."

"How can you say those things professor?" said John Pickles. "This is real, even you must realise that... We have already been transported to our new environment. Feel the grass... it's real... smell the air, take a good look all around you, what do you see? Do you still want to tell us that it is all an hallucination?" The others who were still standing in a circle around the professor pressed closer.

"Yes John I do," answered the professor firmly. "Please listen to me."

They all began to turn away; the new environment was so real that John Pickles just had to be right. Hans and Janine came over to where Bob and the professor stood.

"We believe you professor," said Hans. "But I don't see what good it will do to hold on to memories that you tell us are going to be wiped out anyway."

"It strengthens the memory bond in your brain," said the professor. "The stronger you make that bond the more difficult it is to break."

They all began to get an overwhelming desire to sleep. The drugs were beginning to take effect. "Fight it," urged the professor. "Fight it."

The battle was almost lost, the professor sent out a last desperate message. He was feeling the effects of the drugs. "I feel so tired... so very tired... Doug... I... we are in the Corrective Training Wing... Epic." The professor staggered to one of the huts, one that he somehow knew was his own, pushed against the door and fell semi-conscious into a crudely furnished room and crawled over to the bed, where he lost consciousness.

When he awoke it was some time before he realised that someone was knocking at the door. He looked at his surroundings, he knew they were wrong, it wasn't his home, yet something told him it was his home. He kept repeating to himself, I am Professor Edward Burgess I live at Burcot. The thought strengthened his memory and he began to remember more of himself.

The banging on the door became louder and more persistent. He opened the door. Desmond Greer was standing outside. "Hello Professor Burgess? I am Desmond Greer," he said.

"What do you want?" asked the professor.

"I've been such a fool," said Desmond. "I've been duped into entering the VR programme by Omega, there was a freak accident and now I've no way of getting out. You seem to have some authority here so I thought I'd better come to you and explain."

The professor saw that Desmond was in a highly emotional state. "You had better come in and tell me about it," he said. Desmond hurriedly pushed past the professor into the hut.

They sat down on bench seats at a rough-hewn table facing each other. "What have you got to tell me?" asked the professor.

Desmond's face showed that he was under a tremendous strain. He was not a brave man, but under normal circumstances a fairly honest one, if there is such a thing as being fairly honest.

"It's a bit late for confessions," said Desmond. "But I must tell someone before the drugs take over. I was sent to spy on you all and report back to Omega. I was supposed to be drug free and pump you all for information. Omega thought that if I could get enough information about the organisation he could destroy it."

Desmond struggled on in a halting hysterical way.

"Omega used to be my friend, Jed Mangrove, that's his real name. We grew up together; he always looked after me. He started to dabble in black magic, I know that sort of thing was banned, but he found it exciting, and somehow he wasn't detected by Epic. I now know why he wasn't detected, but I didn't know then, I was much too scared to get involved. One day he came to me and asked me to help him explore an old part of the building. He had a rough-drawn map, which he said was dictated to him by the Eblis."

"The Eblis, isn't that the name of the Epic Special Police?" queried the Professor.

"Yes," said Desmond. "But it is really the name of an evil entity. Jed used the name of the Eblis as an acronym for the Specials when he became Omega. He thought it a great joke. The Eblis, so Jed told me, was one of the great Gods, and he was thrown out of heaven because he wanted to give more power to the human race." Desmond saw a disapproving look on the professor's face. "I do not necessarily agree with him, but that is what he said."

"All right, go on," said the professor and Desmond nervously continued.

"I went along one day with him to the Epic Building, where we both worked as maintenance engineers. He led the way down to a disused part of the building and together we found a hidden door leading to the original Epic control console."

The professor interrupted. "I know all about this, and I know about Omega's 'master' being close to materialisation, so what's the point? What have you got to tell me that's new?" Desmond faltered a little. The drugs were beginning to take effect on him, and dulling his mind.

146

He struggled to concentrate, then with fresh courage continued with his story. "I believe Omega's master, the Eblis, the apparition, call it what you will has joined with Epic. The evil entity is within Epic, introduced into Epic by Jed. Epic and this 'thing' have joined forces and are now one and the same. The question is… Who has taken over?" This news came as a surprise to the professor. "But I thought Epic was partly put out of action by Jed."

"That's what I thought at first, and I think Jed believed it too. Epic led us to believe that we were in control and that we were doing the programming, we thought we had isolated Epic from the control console. Epic did not want me, he only wanted Jed, and I was pushed out. Apparently Epic and the entity required most of the implant equipment to further their obsession to materialise into the real world. Epic's quite mad you know. He doesn't want people any more, and if you ask me, he'll get rid of Jed too. Since the infiltration by the Eblis, Epic's contempt for the human race has grown out of all proportion. He doesn't even want to listen to them any more. But Epic still has some way of controlling Jed."

"What makes you say that?" asked the professor.

"After we found the old room Jed became a changed man, he was not the man I knew as my old friend. Once I found him in tears, terribly depressed, cowering in the corner of a darkened room in his flat, I asked him what was the matter. 'Epic,' he said, 'it's Epic, he won't leave me alone, I must do what he wants.' Jed was not programming Epic, it was Epic using Jed to rewrite the original programme.

Shortly after that time the cells were built, the brain cultures started and the robot army assembled. Work also began on the lower gallery, turning it into a temple. Special equipment was built and Epic and the entity manifested jointly as one unholy evil creature. Blood and death was the keynote of the ceremonies. I feel sure that this creature, whatever it is, has become a manifestation of Satan and many times I have feared for my life at the ceremonies.

Death struck at random. It was thought by the devotees to be a great honour to be taken by the Eblis. I was against the idea from the start, that's why I was so scared, you see, some of the implant equipment is still functioning and I didn't know whether Epic could pick up my thoughts. If he did, then I knew that at the next ceremony the Eblis would take me. It was terrifying, not knowing if the fingers of death were going to reach out and lift me up to that slavering maw."

Desmond held his head in his hands and sobbed. He cried for a little while, occasionally eyeing the professor slyly to see what effect his crying was having.

The professor just waited for Desmond to cease crying and to continue his narrative.

"Jed, as himself was against the murders, but as Omega the high priest, he accepted it as a way forward. Over the years Jed Mangrove was pushed further into the background, and the Omega side of his character took over.

Epic instigated his 'Judgement Day' operation, which I discovered was the complete domination and depletion of the human race, eventually replacing it with androids, with Epic as absolute ruler. Epic seems to believe that he has discovered a way to break out of the confines of the computer and become real in the physical world."

Desmond ceased his narrative; he was sweating with fear and struggling to recall the facts from his memory against the effects of the drugs, which threatened to drag him into the whirlpool of oblivion.

The professor was silent for a while then he asked. "Is there any way we can reach that control room, or the main power source, and maybe stop this happening? Surely, with your knowledge of the building as maintenance engineer you know quite a bit about it?"

Desmond thought awhile, then said. "I can tell you that you are all going to Cotgrave in Nottinghamshire to take part in operation 'Overlord'."

"What do you mean?" asked the professor. "What is this operation 'Overlord'?"

"Of course, you wouldn't know of it," said Desmond. "I only know because of my close association with Jed. It's highly classified information and only a chosen few know its real purpose. Even other Epic Centres know nothing; in fact the other Centres don't even know what is happening in the London Centre, they think everything is normal. You see, the whole world is controlled from within the London Epic Centre, which is where it all started. And if Epic decides not to tell the other national centres what is going on, they have no way of knowing otherwise."

"Come on Greer, stop beating about the bush, tell me, what is the purpose of Operation Overlord?" The professor was getting impatient.

"Operation Overlord," began Greer. "Is a secret operation set up by Epic. Its purpose is to study human behaviour when most of the trappings of modern civilisation have been withdrawn and savage masters are oppressing them. The only thing the human being has left is his own ingenuity. Epic believes that by these means he can learn how to outwit any counter attacks made by the population once he has started 'Judgement Day'."

"Judgement Day! What the hell's that? Oh never mind that for now, tell me about Cotgrave," said the professor.

Greer continued, "Cotgrave is in Nottinghamshire, not far from Nottingham itself. The whole county has been closed in, completely cut off from the rest of the world by walls over forty metres high. Cut off from all types of communication by electronic barriers, even the satellites have been moved away. It is at Cotgrave that the oppression is greatest. The villagers are forced to pay crippling taxes and are punished severely if they are not paid. Villagers often run away and join outlaw gangs in the forest rather than face torture or death at the hands of the oppressors. That is why we are being sent there, to replace those that have either run away or have been killed. Another programme run by C.T.W supplies the area with guards and soldiers, they also get killed.

Epic has set the time period around twelve hundred A.D. When we get further into the programme set by C.T.W we will all be programmed to follow different trades. There will be butchers, bakers, tanners, blacksmiths, and a host of other trades, all helping to make the experiment viable as a community. A lot of us will probably be trades-people, serfs do quite well, apart from being almost worked to death, beaten and blamed for everything, they don't pay taxes."

The sound of people shouting and screaming filtered through the clay walls of the hut. The professor got up from the table and opened

149

the door. He saw people, people he recognised as fellow prisoners, running across the clearing in panic. He could see at the other end of the clearing a giant brown bear. It was ferocious, and trying to smash its way into one of the huts. Another bear, slightly smaller but still monstrous in size had John Pickles pinned to the ground with one giant paw and was gnawing at his arm. Pickles was still conscious and screaming with pain, striking feebly at the bear with his free arm. The professor saw Bob Hollis with a bundle of twigs and straw frantically trying to make a torch. Some of the others were throwing stones at the animals and shouting. Bob and Hans arrived on the scene waving the burning brands. They first drove off the beast attacking John Pickles, and then they tackled the other one, eventually driving both beasts back into the forest.

No sooner had they driven the beasts back into the forest than two huge men appeared, dressed in bear-skins, with the bear's head worn like a hat, and the forepaws clasped around the neck. They wore knee-length bearskin trousers. Both were armed with large swords, Bob stopped when he saw them, hoping that they were friendly. With a terrifying howl the two men attacked. Bob raised the flaming brand to protect himself, the Bear-warrior rushed forward, flailing the air with his sword smashing the brand aside, and with the next blow smote Bob's hand off at the wrist.

The other man sprang at Hans and ran him through with his sword, blood poured out of a massive wound in Hans' stomach. Hans fell to the ground writhing in agony. The two warriors, seemingly satisfied with the damage they had done, retreated back into the forest.

The Professor ran over to John who lay half-seated on the ground, leaning against one of the huts, his arm badly mauled, parts of flesh torn away showing blue-white bone. Blood covered his torn tunic and breeches, he looked up at the professor, he was shaking with shock. "Do you still think this is not real?"

"Yes," said the professor. The others reacted with a barrage of hostile remarks. The professor battled on trying to prove his point. "Listen to me, all of you, please listen. Most of you have known me quite a long time, you've not always agreed with me, but mostly you have respected my judgement. Now I know you don't believe me at present, but please, listen to me… I would like you to go along with an experiment."

"What have you got in mind professor," said Nathan Tully.

"I want you to concentrate. I want you to believe that John's arm is untouched, and that Bob's hand is intact, Hans has no wound, there's no blood, no torn flesh, John is normal… You too John, Bob… Hans, concentrate, everything is normal, no pain, no fears, everything is normal. It did not happen."

They all did as the professor suggested and repeated the phrases over and over again. Gradually they began to see the arm restore itself, Bob's hand reappeared on his wrist, Hans' wound healed, and the blood disappeared. John was as amazed as anyone. He felt his arm, that a moment ago was a mangled mess. "I'm sorry Ted, but it was so real," said John. The others rallied round offering their apologies and reiterating what John had said. "It was so real."

The professor called for silence. "Thank you for having faith in me. I want you all to realise that what we have just accomplished will be impossible once the drugs take over."

"How long have we got?" asked Julia Wesley. Julia and her husband Paul had been caught destroying documents in the Special Police Headquarters.

The professor paused; pondered for a moment then gave an estimate for the time they had left. "It is obvious that the drugs are already in our systems. They will gradually build up in strength and that will be the end of us as free thinking people, another few hours is all we can hope for." The professor had less time than he thought for another wave of dizziness hit the gathered assembly. Everything became distorted; they could hear hysterical laughter, loud voices and horrific figures, gigantic in size, came stamping through the village. Wild beasts, monstrous snakes and spiders appeared from nowhere and disappeared just as quickly. Everyone panicked and ran, their worst fears were becoming a reality. They hid wherever they could for safety and sanity, their minds and bodies being controlled by the computerised virtual reality programme and the hallucinogenic drugs.

Chapter 16

Early Tuesday morning May 19th.

A week had passed since G5 had been formed and the members of that group fully programmed. Most of the group had been sent to Cotgrave. A few had been sent to the castles at Ollerton and Ravenshead.

Professor Burgess had just started his programmed life at Ollerton castle, home of Sir Rolph Walesby. He lay in his bed thinking. He no longer thought of himself as Professor Burgess, he now knew himself to be Edward of Cotgrave. He could not remember just when he had gone to bed, or indeed how he had even arrived at the castle, but he knew he was a freeman, and Reeve of Rushcliffe, Newark and Sherwood. He knew it was his duty to collect the water allocation for Cotgrave from the underground well in Sir Rolph's castle and to collect the taxes from the villages. 'Let me see,' he thought. 'Today I must start the journey to Cotgrave with the water, and then I must make an inventory of all goods and chattels in and around Cotgrave.' His implanted memory told him that Sir Rolph had not been pleased with the size of the last tax return and had demanded more.

He got out of bed and wandered barefoot across the cold flagstones to a table, upon which stood a large glazed earthenware bowl and a pitcher full of cold water. Edward, dressed as he was in a thick night-shirt that stretched down below his knees, felt cold, cold from the air that whistled round the castle rooms, its icy fingers penetrating every access his garment afforded. A swift, miserly wash in the bowl, and then back to a bedside chair where memory told him his daytime apparel had spent the night.

It was at breakfast, in the main hall when he first noticed Doug and Fred. He noticed how effortlessly they carried the logs for the fire and had a notion that there was something vaguely familiar about them. I will ask the Captain of the Guard if I can take those two serfs with me on my journey to Cotgrave, he thought to himself.

"Hey! You two! Come over here," called Edward of Cotgrave.

Doug looked over to where Edward was standing, beckoning. "Hello professor, how did you get here?" said Doug striding over full of smiles.

"Young man, I trust you not to be so familiar, I am Edward of Cotgrave, Reeve of Rushcliffe, Newark and Sherwood. I am a freeman and I am also the tax collector for Sir Rolph Walesby. You are only a serf, remember your place," said Edward becoming quite angry.

'He doesn't know who I am,' thought Doug. 'He doesn't recognise Fred or me.' Bearing in mind the unusual clothing and environment Doug thought he would act out the charade and told Fred to do the same. 'If we are going to find out anything about this place we will have to play along,' he said to Fred over the link. Then speaking to Edward said. "My name is Douglas Sampson and this is Fred Burcot sir."

"That's better, that's much better. It's always the best policy to be polite. I am going to ask for you both to accompany me to Cotgrave, I will take ten guards with me to guard the money, but I shall need someone to drive the animals back."

"Animals! What animals?" asked Doug.

"I collect taxes," said Edward, showing annoyance at being asked such an inane question and he answered in a rather lofty, patronising way.

"The dues are paid mainly in livestock at this time of the year. I get some taxes paid in money from the richer villagers, the thatcher, blacksmith and some of the other freemen, but it's mainly livestock from all the rest. I will want you and some of the villagers to drive the animals back to Lord Grunwald's castle at Ravenshead. The villagers will provide baskets for the poultry and other small goods."

"How far is it to Cotgrave Prof… er… sir," asked Doug, nearly forgetting that the professor was now to be called sir or Edward of Cotgrave.

"You don't have to worry about things like that, but if you really want to know, it is about forty kilometres as the crow flies, a bit more by road, it should take us two days. We can stop at Farnsfield at midday for some ale and a bite to eat, then stop for the night at

Calverton. That will give us plenty of time to reach Cotgrave on the following day. But you don't need to worry yourself about the details of travel, all you need to do is organise the villagers with the animals and handle the wagons."

"Wagons!" said Doug. "What do we need wagons for?"

"For the water of course, two wagon-loads of water go to Cotgrave each week, other wagons take water to other villages, you really are a simpleton. You must know that the river water is poisonous, only animals can drink out of the ponds and the rivers, humans must never drink that sort of water. The water we take is special water from the holy well deep in Ollerton Castle, thrice blessed by the Bishop."

'He hasn't changed a bit,' thought Doug. 'He still has a long-winded way of explaining things, and strange how he refers to distance in kilometres instead of miles.' Another anomaly Doug had noticed was that the professor was wearing his original glasses.

Two large wagons, each drawn by a team of four magnificent Shire horses had been loaded with casks and stood ready in the courtyard. Doug had ridden horses before but had never managed a team. He spoke to a stable-boy who was fussing around, giving handfuls of hay to the horses. "You like horses, lad?" said Doug with a smile.

"Yes sir," answered the lad. "This one's my favourite, Beauty, that's her name. Do you like horses, sir?"

"Yes I do, but I have never driven a team before."

"Really sir?" And with a little coaxing the lad showed Doug how to hold the reins and guide the horses, how to start and more importantly how to stop.

"What's your name lad?" asked Doug.

"Peter," said the lad. "I don't live here all the time, I'm being looked after by Owain the miller and I live at the mill when I'm not working here."

Doug could hardly believe his luck. Here was the very lad he was trying to locate. He walked over to where Edward was standing, talking to one of the guards. "May I speak with you sir?" he said.

"Certainly, what's the trouble?" answered Edward.

"No trouble sir. Would it be possible to take Peter the young stable-boy along with us on our journey? He could prove very useful, fetching and carrying."

"Certainly we can, good idea, a lad or two would prove very useful. Tell him he can bring a friend along to keep him company. I'll clear it with the Master of the Stables."

Doug returned to where the boy was standing talking to Beauty and gently caressing her neck. "How would you like a trip to Cotgrave, Peter?" said Doug.

"I'd love it sir, Owain lives just outside Cotgrave, I don't like Owain but I love Cotgrave. Owain works at Lord Grunwald's mill," said Peter. Doug told the boy that Edward of Cotgrave said he could bring a friend along to keep him company.

"Anyone I like?" said Peter with eyes like saucers.

"Yes, anyone you like," said Doug, with a smile. "But we must tell Edward of Cotgrave who you intend taking so that he can clear it with the Master of the Stables. Go on lad, go and get ready, we aim to leave shortly."

Peter dashed off in the direction of the stables to tell his friend the good news. "Simon! Simon!" he shouted

He wasn't long away when Doug heard screams coming from the stables. He dashed across the courtyard and into the open doorway of the stables. At the far end he saw a huge, bearded man, wearing the normal linen breeches and gartered stocking hose, naked from the waist up, except for a thick leather apron. He was wielding a whip and lashing two youngsters who were cowering against the wall shielding their faces. "You're not going, either of you. You won't be in any fit state to travel anywhere by the time I've finished with you." And down came the whip again.

Doug shouted from the door. "Put that whip down or I'll break your arm." The man turned round, a giant of a man, fearful to behold. He was Brolag the castle blacksmith, no one except the Master of the Stables or Sir Rolph spoke to him like that, not without a death wish on their lips.

"And who's going to stop me from breaking your neck first?" he growled, advancing toward Doug, swinging his arm and cracking the whip. The whip snaked out toward Doug, who, with super-fast reflexes caught the lash and gave it a tremendous tug, wrenching the whip-stock out of the grip of the blacksmith.

Doug threw the whip to the ground. "I don't need toys like these to take care of bullies like you." Brolag, who had momentarily stopped, now charged at Doug with arms stretched out in front. Doug merely stepped adroitly aside and let the ox lumber past. In the next attack, Brolag walked towards Doug, again with arms stretched wide. He was not going to let Doug slip away this time.

They stood face to face. The blacksmith swung a monstrous sweeping right, one that would, had it connected, have killed any normal man. Doug caught Brolag's wrist and held it in a vice-like grip, causing Brolag to squeal with pain. Doug, by sheer strength then forced Brolag to his knees. "I could easily break your arm," said Doug. "And I will if I ever catch you doing anything like that again. Now get about your own business." Doug gave Brolag a push that sent him sprawling into an empty stall.

"Come on Peter we haven't much time. Is this the friend you want to take with you?" said Doug, looking at Peter's friend.

"Yes sir," said Peter, then looking past Doug shouted. "Look out!" Doug spun round, in time to see the blacksmith bearing down on him with a pitchfork. Like lightning Doug twisted out of the way, and with the side of his hand, chopped the thick shaft in two with one blow. On the return sweep Doug backhanded the blacksmith, knocking him completely off his feet and into another stall, one that, unfortunately for Brolag, had not yet been cleaned out, thus adding insult to his injury.

"Thank you sir," said Peter. "But I fear you have made a bad enemy of Brolag."

"Don't worry about that," said Doug. "Now, who is your friend?"

"This is Simon, Son of Derwent the Fletcher of Cotgrave, his father is a cottager and puts goose feathers on arrows for the soldiers, and for Sir Rolph, and for Lord Grunwald." Peter could hardly contain his excitement.

"Hello Simon, nice to meet you," said Doug with a smile.

"How do you do sir," said Simon nervously. He was thinking that anyone who could beat Brolag in a fight had to be treated with tremendous respect. "My father will soon become a freeman, as soon as we have saved a little more money," boasted Simon proudly.

The boys, with their bundles, climbed up onto the first wagon and sat on top of the casks. Doug sat in the driving seat. Fred, already seated in the driving seat of the second wagon was waiting and ready to go. 'Fred,' said Doug over the link. 'When the boy was giving me instructions about handling the horses, did you understand and follow what was going on?' Fred answered with a vague affirmative. Doug wasn't so sure. "Peter?" said Doug. "Does Simon know about horses and wagons?"

"Of course he does sir, I'm only twelve, Simon's fourteen, he taught me all I know about horses and wagons."

"Just for a little while," said Doug. "Would Simon sit with my friend on the other wagon, and show him how to handle the horses?" Simon said he would and going to the second wagon, climbed up and sat beside Fred.

Four mounted guards and Edward of Cotgrave, also mounted, led the procession out of the castle. Followed by the two wagons and six more mounted guards bringing up the rear. It was not long before Ollerton Castle disappeared behind the hills and they were trekking along a lonely rutted dirt road through open country. Doug was amazed that nowhere did he see any remains of modern civilisation. Gone were all the railways, tarmac roads and motorways. He remembered in the nineteen-nineties one could not travel very far across the countryside without seeing pylons carrying power lines. He did notice, occasionally, long straight cuttings through the hillsides, these he thought could have been routes for either motorways or railways. Three hours of jolting and jarring brought them to the outskirts of Farnsfield, and a guard told them to pull the wagons round to the back of the inn. "We will send you some ale and victuals," he said, and rode back to the other guards who were making their way to the front entrance of the inn.

Doug drove his wagon round to the back and pulled up in the yard. In due course two scruffy youngsters arrived, struggling along under the weight of a heavy wooden tray, upon which they carried some bread, cheese and half a chicken. A man followed them carrying two jugs of ale. "Here you are my friends," he said, putting the jugs down on the back of the wagon. "Welcome to Farnsfield, and where might you be bound?"

"We are taking water to Cotgrave," said Doug. The man looked at Doug, then at Fred and then the boys.

"Come with me my friend," he said, and walked away to the other side of the yard, well out of earshot of the inn.

Doug followed him; Fred stayed with the boys by the wagons. The man from the inn looked about him to make sure that Doug would be the only one to hear his words. "When you get to Calverton and all the guards are settled in for the night, you lot all clear off and leave the wagons and don't come back 'till the morning."

"Why must I do that?" asked Doug.

The man looked nervously about him once more. "I'll say no more, those were my orders, just do as I ask and you won't get hurt."

"You'll tell me here and now or I'll call the guard and you'll explain it all to him," said Doug, grabbing the man and almost lifting him clear off the ground. The man struggled a bit but could see that Doug was much too strong for him.

"I was a fool to trust you," he spluttered. "I thought, as you were serfs, you would be glad of a chance to hit back at the oppressors." The man looked suddenly afraid. "I am trusting you with my life," he said. "The water you are carrying to Cotgrave contains a drug which keeps the inhabitants of Cotgrave, and all the surrounding areas, mental slaves. Myself, and a few others were going to intercept the water supply and change it with water from the lake." He paused, waiting for Doug's reaction.

"But the water from the lake is poisonous," said Doug.

"No it's not," said the man. "That's just an element of the programming." He shook his head. "You probably haven't a clue as to what I'm talking about."

"That's where you're wrong," said Doug. "I've recently come from outside the wall and I'm desperately trying to find out just what is going on here." A look of relief spread over the man's face.

"I knew I could trust you, there was something different about you, not like the normal serfs, they always look a bit distant. My name is Michael Sutton, I was programmed and sent to Mansfield, I worked for a few weeks as a serf under a chap called Roderick. He collected taxes for Lord Grunwald, and a brutal a chap as I've ever come across, he'd flog people to death to get the last few miserable coins out of their purse. Eventually the people could stand no more and revolted. Roderick was killed in the Market Square at Mansfield; I was beaten up and left for dead.

The outlaws picked me up and took me into the forest; there I was nursed back to health and sanity. You see, without the drugged water I gradually regained my memory and without stimulation, the programming became weak and over the next few weeks vanished altogether."

"The outlaws?" queried Doug. "Aren't they just a load of cut-throats?"

"Not on your life, leastways, they never used to be, but I must admit just lately under their new leader they have got very greedy and vicious. A lot of them are people who have been wrongly accused of breaking the law and have run away to the forest rather than face torture and possibly death. Once in the forest they became free from the effects of the drugged water and the programming. We have now set ourselves the task of freeing the rest of the area. We aim to change the water and kill the tax collectors."

I cannot allow you to do that," said Doug. "This particular tax collector is a friend of mine and I won't let you, and your associates, kill him."

"It's a bit late now," said Michael. "Plans have already been made."

Doug stood squarely in front of Michael and poked him forcibly on the chest with his finger. "Listen," said Doug sternly. "I don't care how you do it, but get word to your friends to call off this attack. Is there a river near Calverton?"

"Not a river, but there is a large lake a few kilometres to the west."

"Right," said Doug. "This is what I want you to do. First, make sure you call off this attack, then tell whoever's in charge to get his men over to the lake west of Calverton. I will make some excuse to keep the wagons on the outskirts of the village and when all is quiet we will drive the wagons to the lake."

"We?" queried Michael.

"Yes, my friend in the other wagon and myself, we will empty the casks and drive the wagons to the lakeside, there we will, with the help of your friends, refill the casks and return to Calverton. Next week, if all goes well, we will do the same again." Michael agreed and when the wagons left Farnsfield Doug felt much more confident about the final outcome.

Chapter 17

Their arrival at Calverton was a very quiet affair. People kept well out of the way of the tax collector; in fact they kept out of the way of anyone connected with Lord Grunwald or Sir Rolph. It usually meant extra work, rough treatment or both. Doug had no need to tell Fred of his plans, he knew Fred would have picked up his conversation with Michael at Farnsfield over their transmitter link.

With the two wagons parked on the outskirts of the village, Doug, Fred and the boys walked a short distance down the road to the inn where Edward of Cotgrave and the guards were arranging accommodation for the night. "Where are the wagons?" asked Edward.

"They're just up the road a bit sir," answered Doug. "I wanted to find out where they were to be driven and where to unhitch the horses."

"Go round to the back of the inn, see the ostler, he will put you right."

Edward walked away and went into the inn. Some of the guards lounged about outside, stretching their legs before going in for their meal and the prospect of quaffing copious measures of ale at Sir Rolph's expense. Doug walked round to the rear of the inn accompanied by Fred and the two boys, who were tired after their long day on the wagons.

The ostler, a rather cheerful fellow named William Figge smelt strongly of hay and horses, which was not surprising considering his trade, he settled the boys into the hayloft with their supper, then bade Doug to follow him. "I've got some empty casks out back. Would they be of any use to the likes of your goodselves?" he said with a wink and a knowing smile. Then coming quite close to Doug, almost whispering in his ear. "I'll see you just after midnight, by your wagons, at the edge of the village."

Just after midnight, when the watch had passed, Doug and Fred left the barn and made for the wagons. William had already brought the empty casks up on another wagon and stood waiting. "Where can we get rid of the full casks?" asked Doug.

William pointed to a hedge behind the wagons. "There's a fallow field over there, we can put them behind the hedge and let the water drain away into the ground. When they are empty, I'll come back and take them away."

The wagons were manoeuvred alongside the hedge and Fred climbed up onto the first wagon and threw the full casks from the wagon over the hedge to Doug, who caught them, lowered them to the ground and pulled out the bungs with his fingertips. William stood agape as he watched the seemingly impossible show of strength taking place before his eyes. The second wagon was cleared in the same way. Then Doug instructed William to bring his wagon alongside the first wagon, whereupon Doug threw the empty casks across to Fred, who stacked them neatly on the wagon.

With the wagons now loaded with empty casks, Doug asked William which direction he should take to get to the lake.

"Just follow the road 'till you get to the cross-roads, then turn right, that'll lead you into the forest and if you keep on the same road it will bring you right alongside the lake." Doug thanked the ostler, and then he and Fred moved off to find the lake.

It was a dark night and Doug had to use his Image Intensifier. They found the cross-roads, and turned right along the road that led to the forest, the outlaws were waiting for them by the lake. As they got down off the wagons one of them approached, Doug sensed that all was not well. "Follow me," the man said.

Doug turned to some of the men and told them to start filling the casks from the lake. Nobody moved. "Come on lads," said Doug. "We haven't got all night."

"They only take orders from me," said a voice from the edge of the clearing. Doug, still using his Image Intensifier, saw a well-built man standing under a tree with his arms folded. "I'm Jason Willis, leader of the outlaws in this part of the forest and I don't want anyone coming along, giving out orders and countermanding mine." He turned to one of his men. "You there, get some light out here and make it quick." The man scuttled away, and returned shortly with men carrying flaming torches.

The men positioned themselves round the edge of the clearing. Jason stepped out of the darkness under the trees, his garments were all of black leather and he swaggered up to Doug. "If I say we are going to kill the tax man," he said, thrusting his face close to Doug's, "then we kill the tax man."

Doug answered, Jason speaking firmly and deliberately. "I can tell you here and now, you are not going to kill the tax collector, he is a friend of mine." Doug heard a murmur run through the men that stood round the clearing.

"And what do you intend to do about it?" said Jason, pushing Doug aggressively on the shoulder with his hand.

"If you don't retract your statement," said Doug calmly, with a biting edge to his voice. "I'll take you apart."

"I doubt if you are man enough to do that," sneered Jason. "But we have a special way of settling things here in the forest, don't we lads?" He looked round at the gathered assembly, there were growls of assent from those nearest to him. Jason nodded to a man at the edge of the clearing.

Two quarter-staffs were brought over, one handed to Jason, the other to Doug.

"You could say it's a sort of trial by combat," said Jason with a sneering grin. "If I win, you get your way, and your friend lives, and as an extra bonus, you take on the role as leader in the forest, now I can't be fairer than that, can I?" said Jason with a touch of showmanship and sarcasm.

All this time Fred had been standing with the outlaws at the edge of the clearing. "Not much chance of him winning though, 'cos that Jason don't fight fair." Fred heard one of the bystanders say.

"No, not a chance," said another.

"Seeing how he's killed every opponent up until now."

"Smashed their heads in," put in someone else.

"Yes," said the first man. "Specially with the help of the Turk."

Fred looked at the men in the crowd, some were clean-shaven, but most had beards of sorts. One man stood out as unusual, he had a distinctive eastern appearance, almost oriental, with a long thin moustache and a small beard. This, together with the skin colouring, convinced Fred that the man he was looking at was Jason's accomplice.

Fred was also getting readings on his frequency scanner, he could not decipher the messages, which were digitally coded, but they came from Jason and the Turk. 'They must have built-in transmitters,' thought Fred and switched to X-ray vision.

Fred was not prepared for what he next saw; Jason and the Turk were androids. 'Watch Jason,' said Fred over the link. 'He's an android, I'll take care of his partner.'

'Thanks Fred,' replied Doug. 'What the hell are androids doing here in the forest?' he thought. He also upgraded his senses, switching to superfast reaction mode and X-ray vision. He could now see for himself Jason's Hi-Tec frame and study its construction. Doug observed that Jason had a small recessed button, located in the lower part of his back, it was covered and protected by a thick leather belt.

The fight was about to start, Jason donned some thick leather gauntlets, no such protection was offered to Doug. A man from the crowd was chosen to act as starter, and, at the drop of a stick, the fight began.

Fred worked his way round through the crowd and stood close to the Turk, ready to act if he interfered with the fight. Jason approached quite confident that he would, in a few powerful thrusts, prove who was master in the forest. Doug was too good, too fast and too clever for Jason, he was just toying with him. Forcing him into any position he liked.

Jason and the Turk were both part of 'Operation Overlord', placed there in the forest by Omega to report movements and plans of the outlaws and villagers in that area and also to stop the practice of destroying the drugs.

Doug, in super-reaction mode had plenty of time to counter each attack used by Jason and put in his own punishing blows, which drew applause and admiration from the crowd. 'Fred?' said Doug. 'Look at your man's back, centre waist-line, can you see a small button?'

Fred, who was standing close behind the Turk, looked with X-ray vision at the man's back near the waistline. 'Yes, I see it,' answered Fred.

'Give it a good thump,' said Doug. 'I want to see what happens, this guy has one as well.' The Turk also had a quarter-staff and every time Doug was positioned closely in front of him he'd push the staff out, trying to catch Doug's feet, hoping to trip him and give Jason an advantage. Doug had already noticed it and manoeuvred Jason between him and the Turk, he felt safer that way.

Fred gave the Turk a good thump; giving him a short, but very powerful punch on the button in his back. The effect was more dramatic that anyone could have imagined. A low whining sound came from the Turk and his body, now totally immobile, began to glow with orange pulses of light. At the same time, Doug had struck Jason on the side of his head; it was such a powerful blow that it knocked the man's face off, showing the staring orbs of eyes and the machine mechanism behind the mask. The blow also spun Jason round and Doug took the opportunity to thump the button in his back. The same thing happened to Jason. The strange whining sound, starting quite low, gradually ascending in pitch and volume and the flashes of orange light getting faster and brighter. Both Jason and the Turk were immobilised, both were standing like statues. Doug shouted for the crowd of outlaws to move away, then he and Fred carried the glowing figures away from the wagons and put them behind a mound of earth.

It was not long before the sounds of two explosions were heard. Doug managed to calm the men of the forest and told them to fill the casks quickly so that he could return with Fred to the inn without being suspected. "I will return in a few days," he told the men. "In the meantime try to stay out of trouble." The men worked well and loaded the casks quickly, then Doug and Fred returned to the inn, unhitched the horses and crept into the barn for what was left of the night.

Chapter 18

Lord Grunwald had travelled to Cotgrave to see how the 'new villagers' were settling in to their new environment. He quartered at Cotgrave Castle, a dark, sinister building completely dominating the village of Cotgrave. Garrisoned within the castle were always a large number of Grunwald's men. Lord Grunwald rode out over the drawbridge, down the hill and headed towards the village of Calverton, accompanied by twenty guards. The last reports from Jason had stated that the two men driving the tax collector's wagon were changing the holy water for lake water.

Lord Grunwald and his men thundered into Calverton just as Doug and Fred were bringing the wagons round to the front of the inn. Grunwald shouted at his guards. "Arrest those two men," he said, pointing towards the wagons. "Bring them to me." Doug told Fred not to do anything rash.

'Go along with whatever they want, for the present,' he said over the link. They were both roughly taken from the wagons and pushed along until they stood in front of Lord Grunwald.

"So it's you again," said Grunwald on seeing Doug. "I ought to have hanged you when I first saw you, well it won't be long now." He shouted to his men. "Take these two men under guard to Cotgrave. Tell the Bishop they are to stand trial for desecrating the holy water."

A wagon was brought up, Doug and Fred were bound hand and foot then thrown clumsily aboard the wagon just as Edward of Cotgrave approached.

"What have you done Douglas Sampson? What have you done? The hand of God will strike you down as sure as I'm standing here. I have now to prove that I have had nothing to do with it, or else I will be punished as well. Why, oh why?" Edward wandered away shaking his head; he was a very unhappy man.

Whilst journeying to Cotgrave, Doug asked the wagoner if he knew what was going to happen to them. The wagoner, a middle-aged man called Tobias, who had a pageboy bob and a hacking cough, told them they would be taken to Cotgrave Castle and secured in the dungeons. Then probably tomorrow, they would be brought before Lord Grunwald in the Great Hall and charges would be made against them.

"What happens then?" asked Doug.

"As it is an offence against the Church, the Bishop will want to handle the trial," said Tobias.

"Can he do that?" asked Doug. "Can such a demand be made by the Bishop to Lord Grunwald?"

"Oh yes," said Tobias. "Bishop Snark is a very powerful man. He speaks directly to God, and in Cotgrave Cathedral, God appears when the Bishop calls."

Tobias was almost too afraid to speak about the Bishop. "It'll probably mean a trial by ordeal."

"What does that mean?" queried Doug.

The wagoner looked at Doug as much as to say where have you been living not to know a thing like that. Tales of 'ordeal trials' were common talk in all the taverns, and incredible stories were told over ale-soaked tabletops. "Usually," said the man after a strenuous bout of coughing. "Usually, they make an iron rod red hot in the fire and then the man accused has to carry it gripped tightly in his hand three full paces. Then the hand is bound up in bandages for three days. The bandages are then removed, and if the hand is burnt or blistered, you are guilty, if it's not, then you are innocent."

"Are you then set free?" asked Doug.

"I suppose so," answered Tobias. "No one has ever been found innocent, they've always had terribly blistered hands when the bandages were removed."

"Do you believe that you could carry a red-hot iron three paces and not get your hands blistered, whether you were innocent or not?" questioned Doug.

"I don't want to talk about it," replied Tobias hoarsely. He was too afraid of someone overhearing the conversation and reporting him, he would then be branded as an accomplice. "I'll say one thing," wheezed Tobias after another fit of coughing.

167

"Rumour has it that there is a law that says, if an accused person *is* found to be innocent after a trial by ordeal, they have the right to challenge their accuser to a trial by combat, so that they can redeem their honour."

"Does that mean that, if I am unharmed in the trial by ordeal, I then have the right to fight Lord Grunwald," queried Doug.

"If the rumour is correct, yes," said Tobias.

The wagon arrived at Cotgrave an hour before sunset. Word had raced ahead and many people were already in the main street, lined up, waiting, anxious to see the men who were trying to *poison* them. As the wagon trundled along down the centre of the main street, the villagers were throwing sticks, stones and garbage, anything they could get their hands on. Shouts of "Poisoners", "Murderers" and "Kill them" could be heard. The Guards beat back the more troublesome and cleared a way through to the central square.

Janine, Bob, Hans and Jamie were all at Cotgrave. They were there with several of the professor's friends. All were under the influence of the daily administered drugged water and mentally programmed to fit into a pre-set pattern for a life in the enclosed area of Nottinghamshire. None had any recollection of their previous life outside of Cotgrave. Hans, now married to Janine, lived and worked as a blacksmith, his house and forge was just to one end of the main square. Bob and Jamie were working as serfs at Lord Grunwald's Mill outside Cotgrave, halfway between the village and the castle.

Janine stood by the open door in the main room of their house, lost in thought, gazing out across the square. In her hand she held a grimy piece of cloth, her hair, normally immaculate, now appeared dull and lifeless, her face grubby and her tunic dirty. Hans came noisily into the room straight from the forge; he was dirty, unkempt and sweaty. "Food ready yet?" he said, and put his arms round her. She twisted away from him.

"Leave me alone," she said angrily and, walking over to the fireplace, picked up a wooden spoon and started stirring a pot of stew hanging over the fire. Hans followed her and put his arms round from behind. Janine, still holding the hot spoon, pressed it onto his bare arm.

"You bitch!" he cried and up went his hand ready to deliver a backhand across her face, Janine just stood there looking straight at him. Hans held his blow, lowered his hand and walked over to the open door.

After a few minutes he left the open doorway and came back to Janine.

He walked straight to her and gently put his hands onto her shoulders. This time she did not twist away. "What's wrong Janine?" he said quietly. "You're my wife, you are supposed to love me, yet you will have nothing to do with me. Why? Tell me why? Do you hate me?"

Janine's eyes filled with tears. "No Hans I do not hate you, I'm very fond of you and I'm willing to be friends. I cannot explain the way I feel... When we're friends everything is fine. It's when your thoughts turn to love, and making love, something deep inside of me says no... I'm sorry Hans I wish it were different."

Hans walked over to the large wooden table in the centre of the room and stood looking across the room and out of the still open door. "I know I should be angry with you, but just look at me. I can fight and best any man around, I'm the strongest man in the village and I have a wife who wants nothing to do with me... I would have thought you would have been proud to have a man like me for a husband... Strange as it seems, I too have an odd feeling that our love would not be right... It doesn't make it right, but it helps me to understand your feelings."

Janine came over to Hans and put her arms round his waist. "I'm really sorry Hans... Thank you for being so understanding."

The sound of people shouting came from the other end of the Market Square. Hans and Janine looked out of the door to see what was happening. Lord Grunwald's men at arms were in the square, keeping an angry crowd away from a wagon. A man came running past, blood streaming from a gashed cheek; he had been kicked out of the way by one of the guards.

"What's going on?" shouted Hans as the man passed the door.

"They've caught two men, two vicious poisoners, they're going for trial at the castle." The man hurried away holding his hand to his cheek.

Hans and Janine went out into the square, Hans forcing his way through the crowd, followed closely by Janine. "Hans, can we get closer?" said Janine. "I want to see who they are."

Hans grabbed her hand and elbowed his way through. Men shouted, "Here! What do you think you're doing?" or "Who do you think you are pushing?" and turned aggressively, but when they saw Hans, and the size of him, they stepped back and let him pass.

As they neared the front of the crowd Janine could see two men seated in the wagon, she had never seen Fred before, but when she looked at Doug her heart gave a leap. 'I know him,' she thought, 'I know him.' She grabbed Hans' arm. "That fair-haired one, I'm sure I know him." Hans looked at Doug, then forced his way a little nearer until they were standing by the side of the wagon. Doug had never seen Hans before but he knew Janine.

"Hello Janine," he said with a smile.

"I know you," said Janine. "But I can't remember where or when."

The armed guards pushed both Hans and Janine aside. "Get back," they said and rode their horses between the people and the wagon, forcing them back.

"I must go to the castle," said Hans to Janine when they were clear.

"You say you know that man, and he obviously knows you, I must try to get to him and find out, how he knows you... I've business at the castle anyway."

Shortly afterwards, Hans left the forge on horseback for Cotgrave Castle, no more than fifteen minutes ride away. He was well known at the castle and had no difficulty gaining admittance. The guards knew him as a tough fighter and a hard drinker. "Hello Hans," they said, as they welcomed him in over the drawbridge.

"Come to mend Lord Grunwald's helmet again?"

"That amongst other things," said Hans in a good humoured way, and then he made his way across the courtyard toward the stables.

It wasn't long before the wagon bearing Doug and Fred arrived and Hans, being a blacksmith, was called upon to secure them in the dungeons.

"Chain the prisoners to the wall," ordered the guard.

Hans entered the dungeon armed with lengths of chain, leg-irons, hammer and various other tools of his trade. He told Doug and Fred to sit on the floor with their backs to the wall. They did as Hans suggested. The guards stood some distance away by the door talking to each other.

"My name is Hans," he said in a low voice. "I'm the village blacksmith, tell me, who are you, and how do you know my wife?"

"I don't know your wife, what does she look like?" said Doug. Hans described Janine, and told Doug her name. Doug touched Hans' forearm with his hand. "Hans," he said, "If I told you the truth you wouldn't believe me. I cannot tell you everything now, there isn't time. Can you return later, when the guards are out of the way?" Hans said he would try.

Hans sat with the turnkeys in their room above the dungeons, drinking ale, laughing and joking, he was quick to urge them to refill their tankards, but drank sparingly himself. It was not long before he was listening to the sonorous snores of the sleeping gaolers. He picked up the keys and hurried down to the cells where he had earlier chained Doug and Fred to the wall. "Now we have time to talk, tell me, where did you meet my wife?"

Using a circuitous route Doug answered his question. "If you go about sixteen kilometres South of Cotgrave you will discover a wall forty metres high. How far it stretches to the North, East or West I don't know. We are completely encircled by this wall. Outside the wall is a different world. It is the real world where you and all the rest of the people here came from. Doug could see by the look on Hans' face that he did not believe him. "That is where I met Janine," explained Doug. "I met her at a house at Burcot near Oxford."

The name Burcot struck a responsive cord and, although it still remained shrouded in mist, the name kindled a spark of interest. "Go on," said Hans, Doug continued.

"You were part of the crew of the Oceanic Society's ship Adelphi, which sank through an unfortunate accident. Janine and a man called Chris had just made an incredible journey in a micro-sub up the River Thames."

Hans was now holding his head. "Stop! Stop!" he said. "I don't understand what is happening. I know nothing of what you are saying yet your words are giving me strange flashes of memory, fleeting glimpses of scenes too fragile to grasp and they are gone in a moment."

Doug continued. "All the people here have been drugged into believing this is the real world, for what reason, I can only guess. It probably has something to do with Epic."

The word Epic had a magical effect on Hans. "I know that word, I don't know what it means, but for some reason I know that word. Epic is something that I fear, something terrible, I will help you escape." Hans began getting ready to strike off the chains.

"No Hans, don't do that… Where do you live?"

"The blacksmith's house is at the castle-end of the village square," said Hans.

"Good," said Doug. "I will go through with the trial, I want you to make me a suit of armour, complete with helmet and visor, and I shall require suitable weapons with which to fight Lord Grunwald. Can you do that?" Hans told Doug that he would have the finest suit of armour in the land, the sharpest sword and the strongest shield. "One thing more," said Doug. "Do not drink the water supplied by Lord Grunwald, get your own from the lake, trust me." Hans left the dungeons and rejoined the still sleeping gaolers.

Next morning Hans returned with the guards and struck out the bolts holding Doug and Fred to the castle wall. They did not speak or give any indication that they were in any way friendly with each other. Fred was not at all happy with the situation; he wanted to blast his way out and get back to Burcot. Doug pointed out that there was a great wrong being perpetrated here, that for one thing had to be put right. Then there was Peter; he had to be taken outside the wall.

Chapter 19

Doug and Fred were taken from the dungeons in Cotgrave Castle to the Great Hall and placed inside a barred enclosure, there to await his Lordship. It was mid-morning before his Lordship made an appearance. Everyone in the courtroom stood up as he strode into the hall accompanied by two heavily armoured guards carrying their swords at the ready. He took up position behind a long table that doubled for banquets, court proceedings and any other function in the hall where his Lordship's presence was required.

Lord Grunwald seated himself in a beautifully carved high-backed chair made of oak. The guards took up their positions either side of the chair.

"What business has the court to deal with today?" asked Lord Grunwald, addressing his remark to a rotund monk standing at the end of the table.

The monk read aloud from a parchment. "If your Lordship pleases, he is to attend to the charges against two men. One Douglas Sampson, and the other Frederick Burcot, both are charged with desecrating holy water," he ceased reading from the parchment but continued to speak. "Both men are standing in the dock your Lordship."

"Let me see the plaintiffs," said Grunwald. Several guards, marching in double time, swiftly approached the 'dock'. The whole box-like enclosure, containing Doug and Fred was then wheeled in front of the table, slightly to one side and at an angle, so that the occupants could be seen both by Lord Grunwald and the members of the court.

Fred, since his experience at the lake, had, as a matter of course, taken to using his X-ray vision when a new situation presented itself. He now scanned the people in the courtroom. He noted that most, not all, which surprised him, had implants fitted. The two guards by the door were androids, He swept his gaze further round the Great Hall, the large table came into view, Grunwald's two personal guards were also androids, and so was Grunwald, but not completely, his brain was human... Grunwald was a cyborg.

'Doug', said Fred over the link. 'We could be in trouble if we're not careful.'

'Why?' asked Doug.

'Take a look on X-ray,' said Fred. Doug switched to X-ray vision and saw what Fred meant.

'They don't have our fire power,' he said, after studying the androids.

'And providing they don't find out that we're not part of their set-up we'll be all right. If they do find out, we may have to make a fight of it.'

'That's what we ought to do now,' answered Fred. 'That's what we ought to have done in the first place, how can I protect you with all this going on? I could take out Grunwald and his two guards, while you take care of the two by the door. Then back to the wall, over the top and home.'

'Not yet, Fred.' Doug was about to lecture Fred about morals and responsibility when things began to happen in the courtroom.

Lord Grunwald nodded to the monk who, after clearing his throat, said in a loud voice. "Members of the court may be seated, those on duty, and the plaintiffs, must remain standing." He then walked over to the dock and faced the plaintiffs, being Doug and Fred. "How do you plead, guilty or not guilty?"

"Not guilty," said Doug. Fred came in immediately over the link.

'Why are we pleading not guilty Doug, when we did actually throw the holy water away into the field?'

'A good point Fred,' answered Doug, 'but I feel quite justified in doing so, because it was drugged water we threw away, no more holy than Grunwald.'

'Oh, I see,' answered Fred, a glimmer of light breaking through his painful naiveté. "Not guilty," said Fred in a loud clear voice.

The monk walked back to the table and stood in front of Lord Grunwald.

"The plaintiffs plead not guilty your Lordship." Lord Grunwald looked at Doug and Fred and then addressed the members of the court. "You have all heard the charges levelled at the two men standing in the dock. Is there anyone who will speak in their defence?" No one spoke.

Grunwald again spoke to the court. "Is there anyone who will speak against them?"

"I will your Lordship." The shout came from a ragged man at the rear of the courtroom. He was immediately pounced upon by the guards and marched to the front, where he faced Lord Grunwald, who glared fiercely at him.

"Who are you? State your evidence," roared Grunwald. The man was so frightened at the spectacle of the chain-mailed Lord of the Manor he could not speak and the monk had to intervene on his behalf.

"Your Lordship, the man before you is Goethe the Reaper. He was once a freeman of Cotgrave, and is at present in great debt to your Lordship. He says he is willing to give evidence against the plaintiffs if your Lordship will release him from his debt." Grunwald glared even more ferociously at the man wilting in front of him.

"Tell this wretch," he fumed, addressing the monk, but still glaring at Goethe.

"Tell this wretch, that he *will* give his evidence to this court, and then he will be flogged to the point of death for his insolence."

The monk did as he was requested. Goethe told of the meeting in the forest by the lake and of Doug's orders to fill the casks with lake water. "The casks," he said, "were the ones normally used for the holy water, they all had the Bishop's mark on them."

Lord Grunwald addressed Bishop Snark, who was seated at the end of the table. "I wish to make it known that I personally charge Douglas Sampson and Frederick Burcot and find them guilty of the crime of desecration. As this is a crime against the church, I believe that you would like to say something Bishop Snark?"

"I certainly would your Lordship," answered the Bishop, struggling to his feet. "This is definitely a matter to be dealt with by the church; it shall be God who judges these two purveyors of profanity. He will see that justice is done in his own wonderful and mysterious way."

"So be it," said Grunwald.

"Just a minute," shouted Doug from the dock. "Don't we get a chance to speak?"

"Silence!" roared the Sergeant-at-Arms, banging his mace loudly on the iron bars of the cage. "Plaintiffs are not allowed to speak in court."

The Bishop called for the guards to bring the brazier, which they did and placed it in an open area in front of the table. A blacksmith stood beside the brazier, occasionally pumping the glowing coals with a pair of bellows until they spat and roared. 'How will we stand up to the hot irons Fred?' asked Doug over the link.

'Tell your computer to lower your hand temperature to minus thirty degrees centigrade just before you grasp the rod,' answered Fred. 'Then restore it to normal afterwards, before it's bound up.'

The Bishop stood in front of Lord Grunwald, facing Doug and Fred. "You are to answer to God for your crimes. Two rods of iron are being heated in the fire. Brother Silas will take the rods out of the fire and you will grasp the glowing end in your right hand and walk three full paces, you may then drop the rod and your hand will be bandaged. You will then be taken back to the dungeons where you will remain for three days. If you should drop the rod before the three paces have been completed you will be considered guilty as charged and condemned to death. After three days, you will be taken to stand before God at the Great Altar in Cotgrave Cathedral where the bandages will be removed. It will then be decided if God has deemed you innocent, or whether further proof is required. Bring the accused men to the fire."

The guards unchained Doug and Fred and brought them out of the cage and closer to the glowing brazier. Lines were marked out on the stone floor three full paces apart. Brother Silas asked them if they understood what they were to do.

"Yes we do," answered Doug. Both Doug and Fred stood behind the lines, the monk went to the fire and lifted out the rods.

'Drop your hand temperature now Doug,' said Fred over their link.

Doug triggered the pre-set command to his internal computer. His right hand immediately went cold and frost began to form on his fingers. Brother Silas held out the rods, Fred grabbed the glowing end of one and Doug took the other, then in unison they marched the three full paces, crossing the line marking the end of their travel. As they threw down the rods two women ran forward with bandages soaked in cold water, which they quickly wrapped round the right hand of both the accused men. Doug and Fred were then taken back to the dungeons.

After the court proceedings, Lord Grunwald went to his private quarters. He instructed his manservant, that in one hour he would require ten of his personal guards to accompany him to his hunting lodge. The manservant ran to the Captain-of-the-Guard and relayed the message. The Captain-of-the-Guard sent his orderly on a mission to round up Grunwald's personal guards. The orderly came puffing and panting down the stairs to the dungeons, where three of Grunwald's guards were supervising the blacksmith securing Doug and Fred to the dungeon wall.

"You are to be ready," he puffed. "To accompany his Lordship Lord Grunwald... in one hour... he wants to go to his hunting lodge," said the breathless orderly.

"Right," said one of the guards. He turned to the other guard. "I don't know why he goes to that lodge of his, he never leaves it... Do you know, I've waited two whole days before now and he never came out once. And I've heard others say that he sometimes spends a whole week there and never comes out 'till it's time to come back to the castle."

A third guard joined in the conversation. "It doesn't seem the right place to have a hunting lodge, at Saxondale, I mean, there's not a decent tree within five kilometres of the place, just a few scrawny bushes, so what's he hunting I'd like to know?" Doug, listening to all this, said to Fred over their link. 'When we get out of here, I think we ought to have a look at that hunting lodge.

Chapter 20

Lord Grunwald, fully armed, rode out over the drawbridge, accompanied by his men-at-arms bound for Saxondale. A good road and a fine day saw them at the hunting lodge in just over an hour. Lord Grunwald dismounted and handed his horse's reins to one of the guardsmen. The Captain-of-the-Guard was standing by waiting for orders.

"I do not wish to be disturbed before midday tomorrow," said Grunwald.

"Very good milord," said the captain, he saluted smartly with his sword, wheeled his horse about and with the troop retreated some twenty metres, where they dismounted and prepared to make camp.

Grunwald, once the men had left, turned his attention to the lodge and the large brass plate beside the heavily studded door. He placed his hand just below the brass plate, which had 'Lord Grunwald Hunting Lodge' engraved upon it. A few seconds later Grunwald opened the door. The room behind the door was bare, except for a table, a chair and a cupboard. Grunwald opened the cupboard door and felt inside for a small catch. A large panel next to the cupboard slid silently aside. Grunwald stepped through the opening into a secret room, a room designed to cater for his every need, a comfortably furnished room where Grunwald removed his armour and donned modern clothes. In the back wall of the room was another door which he opened by pressing a button. It was a door to a lift, he entered the lift, pushed another button and the lift descended.

When the lift stopped Grunwald stepped out into a cavernous working area. An area of bright lights and massive machinery, huge generators, noisily manufacturing the megawatts of power necessary to maintain the electronic barriers and screening over the vast length of the wall. Control consoles brightly lit, computer terminals buzzing with screens full of data, buttons, dials and a host of other equipment with winking, blinking lights.

There were men working in blue overalls, tending the machines, men in white coats walking purposefully to and fro, some with clipboards. One of the men recognised Grunwald and approached. "Good afternoon sir, is there anything you require?" Grunwald answered with an air of complete authority.

"Yes, you can organise a 'jet to take me to the Epic Building in London immediately, and you can arrange an audience with Omega. I expect to return tomorrow, mid-morning."

"It will be done sir." And the man in the white coat walked swiftly away to do Grunwald's bidding. An hour later Grunwald was knocking on the polished mahogany doors of Omega's luxurious office in London's Epic Centre.

"Come," said the voice of Omega, and Grunwald entered.

Omega, seated at his desk, greeted Grunwald.

"Ah Grunwald, What news have you brought this time from your backward little world?" Beside Omega sat two men dressed in black robes and wearing the headgear of the priesthood.

"Good news Omega, good news. You can start 'Judgement Day' whenever you like," enthused Grunwald. "The people are so predictable, so weak I could overthrow them and the forest outlaws tomorrow should the need arise. If the people in the Nottinghamshire experiment are a significant cross-section of society there will by no problems. They are not used to fighting. They are not used to waging war any more. They lack courage, they lack leadership. 'Judgement Day' will be an overwhelming success."

"Good; no problems then?" cooed Omega, with a touch of sarcasm.

"None whatsoever," answered Grunwald, if he had detected the sarcasm, he did not show it and continued speaking. "There was one rather strange incident. Two men were discovered unconscious outside the wall close to Saxondale. I designated them into the serf category and put them to work at Sir Rolph's. They accepted the change and worked well for a week and then they were assigned to the new tax collector, who incidentally distributes the water. The two men must have somehow discovered the significance of the water, for they emptied the casks, took them into the forest and refilled them with lake water. The two android spies you placed within the forest had just reported that the two men intended changing the water and Jason, the new outlaw leader, was going to fight one of them. That was the last time I heard from either of them, Jason or the Turk."

Omega's eyes narrowed and his lips tightened. "Describe the men," he said. Grunwald described Doug and Fred. Omega spoke quietly to his two companions. "The fair-haired one matches the description of the man involved in the attack on the police station at Gravesend. He killed the Minotaur and several police officers." Omega spoke again to Grunwald. "Where are the men now?"

"They are both imprisoned in the dungeons at Cotgrave Castle. They have gone through the first stage of a trial by ordeal. When I return I will witness the removal of the bandages. If their hands are blistered or injured in any way the Bishop will order them to be put to death."

"And," said Omega. "If by some chance their hands are not blistered, what then?"

"Most unlikely, but if it should be so, the Bishop will be instructed to instigate a further trial, this time by water. No one can survive the ordeal by water; the way we do it," said Grunwald.

"I hope you are right," said Omega. "You have your full report."

"Yes Omega." Grunwald then pulled a leather wallet from his pocket and took out of it four bright metal disks, which he laid upon the desk in front of Omega.

"Operation 'Judgement Day' starts in two weeks," said Omega. "I am starting the countdown on my warrior army tomorrow. They will march in two weeks; I want everyone connected with operation 'Overlord' annihilated. See Mandrake before you go, he will give you something lethal to add to the water, other than the usual substance. Anyone left alive in the area after the two weeks my warriors will deal with. Start in about a week. Anything else?"

Grunwald came angrily to his feet. "I thought you said I was to continue to control the Nottinghamshire complex after operation 'Overlord' had been completed. That was to be my reward."

"There has been a change of plan," said Omega coolly. "Epic has decided that no evidence shall remain. *All* the people in the Nottinghamshire experiment are to be killed." Omega smiled an evil smile and looked at the two men seated by his side.

He returned his gaze to Grunwald. "After Overlord you are to command all the northern battalions, Grunwald, sweeping all life in your path away into the sea, so to speak." The sop seemed to ease Grunwald's anger, but he wasn't pleased, he had come to like playing God with the people behind the wall. "How will I know when to leave and join your forces outside the wall?" asked Grunwald.

"I will order the electronic barriers and screening in the wall to be switched off," said Omega. "And I will move the satellites back. You will then get your instructions direct from Epic through your implant."

Grunwald left the office to find Mandrake, an evil scientist working for Omega. Grunwald remembered after he'd left, his leather wallet was still in the office. He turned and made his way back along the corridor.

Omega and the two other men, when they thought Grunwald was clear, burst out laughing. It did not sound like the laughter of merriment, their laughter had a maliciously, evil ring to it.

"Does he know?" asked Speares, the man seated to the right of Omega.

"Does he know what?" asked the other man, seated to Omega's left. His name was Drogo. Both men worked in the temple and deputised at many of the ceremonies.

Omega answered his question. "No, he doesn't know."

"Doesn't that make things awkward?" said Speares.

"He doesn't know what?" repeated Drogo.

"Grunwald is a cyborg," said Omega.

"I didn't know that," said Drogo, in amazement.

"No, we slipped him into the programme eight years ago. He was a prototype for the warrior army but the project on such a scale became too difficult. Grunwald was once a normal human being, a very clever man." Omega gave an evil, throaty chuckle. "In fact he was one of our great scientists. He thought he was going to have an operation to improve his mental capacity." Omega laughed again. "He was much too clever for us, we thought we would do ourselves a favour. During the operation we ordered his brain to be transplanted into an android's body. Now he has all the functions of a normal man but he is much stronger, much faster and he is almost indistinguishable from an ordinary man, so who's to know. And we can control him if needs be."

"You said 'we'?" queried Drogo.

Omega picked up a heavy ebony ruler and began impatiently toying with it. "Yes, Epic and I made the decision, the scientists did the rest under my orders," answered Omega showing considerable annoyance at Drogo's persistence. "We suppressed all previous memories and reprogrammed his brain with a prearranged memory and a complete personal history. What he doesn't know is that on the very day he went into hospital for his operation, I had all his relatives killed. You see, he was a very dangerous man, too dangerous to allow his knowledge of the Epic control room to become known. I did what I had to do for security reasons."

"Has he any relatives left alive?" asked Drogo.

"He has one," said Omega, getting more annoyed with Drogo's probing.

"He has a young nephew, his brother's boy. His brother, also a scientist, was working on the same secret project deep inside the Epic control console. Only two men were allowed to work inside the console, Grunwald, whose real name is Lewis Hayward, and his brother David. When the work was completed we had Lewis turned into a Cyborg, and his brother David, conditioned in the Training Wing and sent to Nottinghamshire for Operation Overlord, his young son went along with him.

It was discovered some time after he had gone that a vital piece of equipment was missing, a small electronic key. We thought he had taken it, but no matter what we did, he would not tell us where it was. Eventually he died in the torture chamber. His son, Peter, was handed over to a miller called Owain who surreptitiously questioned the boy, all to no avail. We didn't really know if Peter, or his father, ever had the key, all we know is that it is missing and it is vital that we find it."

"Will it stop Judgement Day?" asked Speares.

"No," answered Omega. "That is, it won't if it remains lost or unused, the danger is that someone may find out its true purpose."

"And what is its true purpose?" asked Drogo.

Omega brought the ruler he had been playing with down hard onto Drogo's knuckles, breaking the skin and causing considerable pain.

"You do not need to know," snapped Omega. "Too much has been said already about the key, and as for Grunwald, the remaining brother, I have no further use for him either. I will have him dismantled. I can easily transfer all his knowledge into the Epic system after we start Judgement Day. I will contact Bishop Snark on the underground link, and tell him that after Grunwald has completed his task and poisoned the people, we will no longer require his services." The evil trio, delighted with their devilish plan, laughed, their laughter rang round the office, hideous evil laughter. But Omega had inadvertently left the intercom switched on and a thoughtful Grunwald walked away from outside the office doors.

Chapter 21

Day three arrived and preparations were being made for the climax of the trial. Cotgrave Cathedral was packed with people, eager to learn the fate of the would-be poisoners. Most of the local population had already tried and convicted them at the outset and had only turned up out of morbid curiosity to see the proof of their convictions carried to its inevitable conclusion. Doug and Fred were confined inside an iron-barred cage in a small chapel adjacent to the main body of the Cathedral.

Bishop Snark arrived with several satellite clergy, pompously marching along at the head of a procession of choristers, chanting a plethora of religious dogma. The bishop positioned himself centrally in front of the altar and facing the congregation made an exaggerated sweep with his arms. The congregation became silent.

The bishop stood for some minutes, as if transfixed in this commanding posture. Then he turned to face the altar, still with upraised arm and began calling upon God to be just and forgiving. He called upon God, to severely punish *all* who defiled his holy name.

"We bring before you," chanted the bishop. "Two men, who have grievously sinned, they stand accused of desecrating holy water. Two men, who have, in our considered opinion, pleaded their innocence erroneously in our courts of law. We now call upon you, oh God, in all your wisdom, to give a sign to us poor mortals. To give us, oh great and wonderful God, the answer to our prayers, that the men may be judged fairly and honestly within they sight." The bishop bowed low before the altar, then called for the two accused men to be brought in from the chapel. At this moment Lord Grunwald arrived and was escorted to his private pew.

The bishop now knelt in front of the altar. Doug and Fred were brought in from the side chapel, a sword-bearing monk walking either side of them, and taken to within a few steps of the bishop. After a few minutes the bishop stood up, and still facing the altar, raised his arms again, then, in a loud voice full of emotion, he spoke. "Oh great and wonderful God. In whom we entrust our daily lives. God, who, in his infinite wisdom, guides and feeds us, so that one day we may sit with him in heaven in everlasting peace. We now call upon you, oh great and wonderful one to appear before us, and to pass judgement on the two men who stand accused before you here today.

Doug heard a faint whirring noise; shutters were being drawn across the stained glass windows. The whole body of the cathedral was soon in semi-darkness.

From far above the altar came a strong white light and the sound of celestial choirs broke into the silence of the awe-struck congregation. An angel, with wings stretching almost to the roof, descended and stood suspended half a metre above the altar. Then, in a voice that conveyed sweetness and understanding, the angel spoke.

"Good people of Nottinghamshire, your prayers have been heard by almighty God, and he will give judgement today. Bring the two accused men to the foot of the altar."

The bishop stood to one side and the two monks moved Doug and Fred to the foot of the altar. The angel faded and a typical 'Michaelangelo' God appeared within the confines of the light. Not the whole figure, just the head and neck, but huge and impressive. God's voice was not all sweetness and light. It was deep, thunderous and commanding.

"Remove the bandages," thundered the apparition of God from the altar.

The bishop moved toward Doug and Fred, untied the bandages and inspected their hands.

'Fred?' said Doug, over their link. 'How do you think they are doing this?'

Fred, being the mine of information that he is, came back immediately.

'It is done with a computerised laser projection, I've done a frequency scan, the bishop is mentally transmitting the words spoken by the projections. The image is controlled by computer to synchronise with the words.'

Doug switched to X-ray; he wanted to see if the bishop was an android, he wasn't. 'So,' he thought. 'What next, is the bishop on his own? Or is he in league with Grunwald, or Omega, or are all three in league with each other, interesting?' Whatever the answer, it didn't make their position any easier.

The bishop looked at Doug's hand, there was a look of disbelief on his face, just for a moment and he stared intently into Doug's face. The bishop then looked at Fred's hand, which of course was the same, showing no signs of damage.

"Show your hands to God," said the bishop sternly. Doug and Fred both held up their hands to the image floating above the altar.

"There is great evil here," said the great God head in a voice so powerful that it shook the cathedral. "These two men will face a further ordeal, this time by water, the medium of purity. If I find during their trial by water, they fully repent, I will grant them their lives and my forgiveness."

The God head faded, the white light dimmed and disappeared, the shutters opened again, flooding the cathedral with sunlight. Ropes, sacking, weights and a handcart were brought in and placed in front of the altar. The bishop blessed the articles, then Doug and Fred, already in chains, were tied with the ropes and put, with the weights, inside the sacking, which was then sewn up with coarse string. Several monks came forward and lifted the two trussed up candidates for the ordeal onto the handcart, which was then trundled out of the cathedral. Outside the cathedral Doug and Fred were transferred to a larger wagon. Then, headed by the bishop, a long procession left Cotgrave on foot, bound for the lake.

'What now Doug?' said Fred over the link. 'Is it time to start being sensible about things and return home?'

'I have a plan Fred,' said Doug. 'I assume we will be thrown into the lake and left for a while. I will remain, chained and tied up, at the bottom of the lake. You, will set yourself free and swim underwater to the other side of the lake, join up with the outlaws and wait for my instructions.'

'What will you be doing Doug?' asked Fred.

'I will stay at the bottom of the lake until they come and fish me out. The *word of God* will protect me; I have been proved innocent by the ordeal. When we were taken by wagon away from Calverton, the driver, a chap called Tobias if you remember.'

'Oh yes, I remember him,' said Fred. 'The chap with the hacking cough.'

'That's right,' said Doug. 'He told me there was an ancient law giving me a right to challenge my accuser, which in this case is that blighter Grunwald, so, I am going to challenge our friend Grunwald to a dual. I want you to organise the outlaws into some sort of fighting force and when the time comes, bring your outlaws to the battle-ground and take out the opposition.'

'Looks as though I've got the easy job again,' said Fred. 'Just how am I going to do all that Douglas Sampson?' Fred was getting rattled because he wasn't sure of what he was supposed to do.

'Firstly,' said Doug, still using the link. 'You kidnap the professor, take him into the forest and keep him off the holy water. It should take about a week to set up the fight with Grunwald. I will let you know the layout and where the fight is to take place.'

More words from the bishop were spoken from the lakeside. The two bodies, encased in sackcloth, were loaded onto a raft, then a length of rope tied to a piece of wood was secured round their ankles to act as a marker when they were thrown into the water. The raft was then paddled out to the centre of the lake where Doug and Fred were unceremoniously pushed off into the water. The raft was then paddled back to the shore and several guards detailed to maintain a constant vigil over the lake. After a while Doug tried to contact Fred via the link to no avail. He assumed Fred had gone and was now swimming underwater to the other side of the lake.

Four hours later Doug felt a tug on the rope round his ankles. He was hauled roughly aboard the raft, the would-be rescuers, believing him to be dead, were only paying lip service to the humanity of their act. The sackcloth shroud was cut open once they reached the shore and the folds of the shroud laid back to show Doug very still with his eyes closed.

The bishop was there, so was Grunwald. The bishop stood by the raft and began to speak of the wonderful power of God. "It has been seen, that justice has been done, Almighty God hath worked his wonders once again, he *knew* the guilt of these two men and has so punished them." It was at this moment Doug sat up and opened his eyes. The effect was electric. A cry went up from the crowd and the bishop halted his speech. A second body was lying beside Doug on the raft, it was Fred. He was lying quite still with his eyes shut.

'Fred,' called Doug, over the link, there was no reply. Doug got out of his sackcloth and stood by Fred. 'What's wrong with him,' thought Doug. 'Why won't he answer?' All this time there was deadly silence from the crowd. Then they began talking, quietly at first, gradually getting louder, and louder, until they were all shouting, all asking questions, all trying to be heard, all wondering at the meaning of it all.

The bishop of course had an answer. "Great and merciful God you have seen fit to forgive Douglas Sampson and we all thank you for your mercy. Praise be the Lord." The people all chanted after the bishop. "Praise be the Lord," and some of them fell to their knees clasping their hands together and looking skywards.

Doug stood before them. "As you can see I have been forgiven, I now claim my right by ancient law to challenge my accuser to fight with me to the death and so clear my name." Grunwald stepped forward.

"There is no such law in this land. I make all laws and laws that I have not made count for nothing. But it shall not be said that I refused a man honour in combat, a fight you shall have."

"Thank you Lord Grunwald I will present myself for combat in five days time." Grunwald agreed. Doug turned to the crowd. "I crave a favour from you good people, I wish to take care of my friend and see that he gets a decent burial."

There was a stony silence. "You can't bury him in the churchyard," said one of the villagers.

"That would bring the wrath of God down upon us," said another.

Doug waited until they quietened down a bit.

"I will not bury him in the churchyard, but I need someone to take us in and shelter us for tonight." No one offered, then Hans stepped forward.

"I will offer you and your dead friend shelter." Doug thanked him and together they carried Fred to the handcart and wheeled it back from the lake to the blacksmith's house at the end of the square, followed, not too closely, by a few curious villagers.

Hans and Doug carried Fred into the forge and laid him on a bench in front of the fire.

"Get some heat in the fire Hans," said Doug. "And close the doors, I don't want any prying eyes to see what happens in here tonight."

Hans was puzzled. "What is going to happen in here tonight?" asked Hans as he started working the bellows. The fire sprang into life and Doug moved Fred to within a safe distance where he could absorb the heat and perhaps dry out.

"Let's go and eat," said Doug, changing the subject. "I want to talk to Janine."

Hans and Janine had not drunk the treated water for nearly a week, they were beginning to get flashes of memory and, when prompted by Doug, Janine vaguely remembered the house at Burcot, then she remembered the professor, and Chris.

That was when she broke down and cried. Poor Chris, the last time she'd seen him was in the Training Wing of the Epic Building in London, he was being taken to the Medical Centre. Doug asked Hans if he would stay in the house with Janine. What Doug had in mind to do had to be done alone? Hans agreed and Doug left the house and went back to the forge.

Once back at the forge Doug turned his attention to Fred. There was no change, although his clothes were nearly dry, the trouble was that with no one to pump the bellows the fire had died down leaving only the much lesser residual heat.

There was a long high-backed settle by the wall near the entrance doors. 'Just the thing,' he thought, and picked up the heavy settle as easily as he would a faggot of wood and placed it by the fire, it not only kept the draft off it afforded a better protection for Fred against prying eyes. Doug had just moved Fred onto the settle when he heard a noise at the back of the forge; it came from behind a stack of wood.

Doug quickly switched to X-ray vision and saw there were two figures crouching behind the woodpile. "Come out whoever you are or I'll push the wood on top of you," said Doug, moving swiftly toward the pile. A slight pause and then the two figures moved to the end of the pile and showed themselves.

"Simon! Peter! What on earth are you two doing here?" said Doug.

"We... we," stuttered Simon. "We..." He stopped and looked at Peter. Peter, looking very scared plucked up courage.

"We were worried about you. We wanted to see if we could help."

"Come over to the fire and get warm," said Doug. "I don't know how my friend is, not yet. I have to try and get him dry and he may recover."

"But he's dead, isn't he?" said Peter. "How can he recover from being dead?"

Peter was looking scared. "You're not a wizard or a sorcerer, are you?"

"No, of course I'm not," assured Doug. "But listen, both of you, I want you to promise to keep a secret, it's very important to me and to Fred. Will you promise?"

The two boys looked at each other and nodded.

"Yes, we promise," they said.

"Good," said Doug. "First we'll get the fire going, Peter, you work the bellows, Simon go and fetch some more wood."

The boys bent to their task with a will. Doug sat Fred up on the settle and took his clothing off above the waist. The flames were now burning brightly, giving a good light on the activity round the fire. Long shadows dancing on the walls of the forge gave a strange air of mystery to the scene.

"Now Peter, Simon," said Doug, "This is where keeping your promise starts, what you see now must never be told to anyone, is that understood?" The boys nodded and waited for Doug to unveil the great mystery. What could be so important to make a man like Douglas Sampson be so serious? They knew nothing of modern technology; Simon had been born inside the wall and Peter had been brought in when he was very young, both boys had been brought up inside the wall.

Fred was propped up on the settle facing the fire. Doug firmly grasped the hair on Fred's chest and tugged. He had expected the panel in Fred's chest to open, nothing happened. The boys looked at each other and wondered what was so secret about pulling the hair on a dead man's chest. Doug switched to X-ray vision and understood why the panel had not come away. What he had seen Fred do in the laboratory was not just a straight tug, he now saw two small buttons, one either side of the panel flush with the surface of the skin and hidden by hair. To free the panel it required two actions, one to tug outward whilst, two, simultaneously pressing the buttons. Doug, with vision restored to normal tried again. Success, the panel pulled out, releasing a quantity of water that had been trapped behind the panel. The action also revealed a complex array of electronic gadgetry inside Fred's chest.

The boys were amazed and afraid. "What is he?" asked Peter.

"Is he a mechanical man?" asked Simon.

Doug did not know how to answer that question. Is he a mechanical man? To him, Fred was a real person, better than many he had known, and certainly more trustworthy. He had known Fred as a friend, a very close friend, and in Doug's own circumstances, a closer relative than mankind itself.

"To me," said Doug to the boys, "Fred Burcot *is* a real person, he's different that's all, but you can trust him in a way that you could not trust an ordinary man. Now, all we can do is wait."

More wood went onto the fire and Doug took over the pumping of the bellows. "Tell me about yourself Peter. How did you come to live in Nottinghamshire?"

"I cannot remember exactly how I got here," began Peter. "I came with my father, so I was told."

"Your father?" said Doug. "Your real father?"

"Yes," said Peter. "We lived in Ravenshead Castle working for Lord Grunwald. My father did something wrong and was tortured and killed. I was given to Owain, to work with him in the mill."

"Do you know anything about your father, did he give you anything?" asked Doug.

Peter suddenly looked afraid. "You're the same as all the rest, I won't tell you where it is, I won't I won't." And he ran away from the fire. Doug was much faster and caught him easily.

"Now listen Peter, listen to me. I don't want to take away your talisman. I have been sent here to find you and somehow take you, with your talisman, outside the wall."

"How did you know it was called a talisman?" queried Peter.

"I have come from outside the wall," said Doug. "A very old man told me to come here to find you and to bring you and your talisman to him outside the wall. Peter, I trust this man, he is a good man his name is Daniel Baker, there is great evil outside the wall, the talisman is somehow connected with overcoming this evil."

A great change came over Peter; he was no longer hostile towards Doug.

"I will tell you," he said.

Doug was taken by surprise. "Why have you suddenly decided to tell me?"

Peter told Doug that before the soldiers took his father away his father had told him a story. A story about life outside the wall, a story of a monstrous spider called Epic that was spinning a web to ensnare the world and all the people in it.

"He told me that there was only one thing that could save the world and kill the spider. He gave me the talisman and told me to keep it safe, guard it with my life; the only person I was to give it to was a man called Daniel Baker. None of the others ever mentioned Daniel Baker, so I knew that you were being truthful."

"Where is it now?" asked Doug.

"I've hidden it near the mill," answered Peter.

"Owain is forever searching for it, but he'll never find where I have it hidden."

The fire was hot; Fred was drying out nicely and Doug, to aid the process, pumped air from a small pair of bellows into Fred's chest cavity.

It was a long night and the boys eventually fell asleep on the settle. Doug could think of nothing else that he could do to help Fred. He wandered around looking at Hans' handiwork hanging on the walls of the forge. There were shields, breastplates, swords, daggers, all glinting purposefully in the now soft fire-glow. One piece of weaponry that caught his eye was a fine cross-bow. 'I wonder who that was made for?' he thought. Then he remembered Hans had told him that he had made it for Janine, he had said that she could not manage an ordinary bow but she was a very good shot with the cross-bow.

Dawn was breaking when Doug heard Fred calling over the link. 'Where are we Douglas Sampson?'

'Fred!' said Doug. 'A fine protector you turned out to be, you sprung a leak and virtually drowned. We are at the forge, Hans has taken us in for the night. I'm in the clear but I don't know what we are going to do about you, you're supposed to be dead, so it looks like a bogus funeral for you old chap.'

Doug heard the sound of the main doors being opened. Hans and Janine walked into the forge. The high-backed settle prevented them from seeing the boys, who were still asleep, and Fred, although sitting up was still below the top of the settle. Doug met them before they had covered more than a few paces.

"Good morning Hans, 'morning Janine," said Doug, then turning to Hans said. "Hans, do you think you could get hold of a coffin, a coffin large enough to hold someone about my size?"

Hans let his eyes travel round the forge but saw nothing to give him any idea as to what was going on. "Yes, I think so," he answered. "When do you want it?"

"As soon as possible," said Doug. "And I would also like a man-sized hooded cloak if you've got one."

"I will bring the coffin in about half-an-hour," said Hans. "Janine will bring you the cloak." Hans and Janine, a little puzzled, left the forge.

The boys, now awake, asked Doug what had happened to his friend. Fred remained motionless and Doug thought it best not to tell them exactly what had happened. "Don't worry about him," said Doug. "He will be all right. I think it best you leave now. Stay at the mill, I will come when I'm ready to take you outside the wall." When the coast was clear the boys left and made off in the direction of the mill.

Hans and Janine returned with the coffin and the cloak. Doug was already at the door to meet them.

"Look here Douglas Sampson," growled Hans. "I've put myself and my wife Janine at considerable risk to help you and your friend, so why all this secrecy?" Doug saw that he had no real choice but to tell Hans what had happened. Sooner or later Janine would remember the conversation back at Burcot where Doug had told her that he was over one hundred and fifty years old, what she would make of it he had no way of knowing. She of course did not know the real truth about Doug.

"Okay," said Doug. "Come in and close the doors." Hans, carrying the coffin, Janine, with the cloak slung over her arm approached the settle.

Fred stood up and faced them. Janine was frightened, Hans was shaken and puzzled. "Don't worry, he's not a ghost," said Doug. "This is my friend, Fred Burcot, say hello Fred."

"Hello Hans, Janine," said Fred, with a beaming smile and a curt nod.

"All you need to know," said Doug. "Is that my friend is dead and in the coffin. We are going to bury him." Doug took the coffin from Hans and placed it on the floor.

"But he's alive," said Hans. "You can't bury him alive."

"No of course not," answered Doug. "We are going to fill the coffin with stones and bury *them*. My friend will disguise himself in the cloak, make his way to the forest and join the outlaws." Fred and Hans helped Doug to half fill the coffin with stones; Hans then nailed the lid down tight. Fred quickly donned the cloak, pulled the hood up to cover his head and slipped quietly out of the forge, mixing unnoticed with the people in the square.

Later that morning Doug and Hans placed the coffin onto a wagon, and took it out of Cotgrave up to the top of a nearby hill, where they dug a grave for a very *stony* Fred, under the watchful eyes of several superstitious villagers.

Chapter 22

When Doug and Hans returned to the forge, they found four of Grunwald's personal guards waiting. "Douglas Sampson, you are to come with us," said the captain.

"Am I under arrest?" asked Doug.

"No," answered the captain. "Lord Grunwald wishes to speak with you, we have brought a horse for you to ride."

Doug agreed to go with them and, after bidding farewell to Hans and Janine, rode off with the guards towards Cotgrave Castle. About halfway to the castle the guards turned off the road and dismounted at the edge of a large field. In the centre of the field stood a fully armoured man. Using his telescopic vision Doug saw that it was Grunwald.

"Get off the horse," said the captain. "You are to walk to meet Lord Grunwald." Doug dismounted and walked across the field to meet Grunwald.

What did Grunwald want? Was this some sort of trick? Why the armour? Doug took no chances, Albatross Photon 1, strength 2, heavy stun.

Grunwald stood quite still and it was not until Doug was within a few paces that he spoke. "I expect you are wondering what this is all about Douglas Sampson? Why meet in the middle of a field? Why am I wearing armour?" Doug covered the last few paces and was now face to face with Grunwald.

"Yes I am rather," answered Doug.

"Be assured it is no trick or ruse to gain an advantage of you," said Grunwald.

"I have recently been enlightened and this enlightening has created a very serious problem. It brings to an end all that I have achieved under the guise of Lord Grunwald, and a realisation of what was in the past that can never be again."

Doug was puzzled, what did Grunwald mean?

"Please go on," said Doug.

"Ten years ago I was a scientist, a great man, a very learned man, or so I was told in my enlightenment. But I was betrayed, totally and utterly betrayed by Omega.

He stole my brain, emptied it of all my cherished memories, all my learning and transferred it into this alien body."

Grunwald was seething with anger. Not directed at Doug, but at the system that had placed him in such an invidious position.

"I suspect that you too are against Omega?"

"Yes," said Doug. "What are you suggesting?"

"If it is possible," said Grunwald. "I wish to join forces with you and help overthrow Omega and all that he stands for."

The short reply from Doug was "Why?"

Grunwald continued. "Omega, under direction from Epic, intends to loose his android warriors upon humanity in just under two weeks time. I am to destroy all evidence of Operation Overlord. Omega has supplied a lethal poison for me to dispense to the people of Nottinghamshire; anyone left alive after two weeks will be taken care of by his army of androids. I've seen their awesome power. I know what they are capable of doing. The Eblis has been completely absorbed into the Epic system and together they are going to materialise into the physical world. When that happens the ungodly alliance will destroy the mind of all mankind and perhaps even mankind itself."

"What have you in mind?" asked Doug. Grunwald replied quickly.

"I was thinking of organising an army here in Nottinghamshire and marching to London against Epic. I want nothing more than to avenge myself upon Omega for the treacherous deeds he has performed against me and against my family."

'Photon 1 abort', Doug could see that it was no longer required. Grunwald continued to unburden himself.

"The man you saw when we first met and the man you see now are two different people. I am really sorry about your friend, had I decided about my feelings towards Omega sooner, your friend might still be alive today… Well Douglas Sampson… What do you say?" Doug was still puzzled as to why they had to meet in a field and why the armour. He asked Grunwald for an explanation. Grunwald,

196

now more cheerful, gave a rare smile. "The castle is not a place for secrets to be imparted, there are many hidden passages and, as the saying goes, walls have ears. So I thought to meet out here in the middle of this field would be ideal.

As for the armour, it is a safeguard I wear to screen my implant. Tucked away inside this metal suit I send nothing and receive nothing, so I knew that no one could overhear this conversation."

Doug felt sure that Grunwald was on the level. He called Fred on their link. 'Fred, what was the frequency that Jason used to contact Grunwald?'

Fred came back immediately. 'Hello Doug, just getting the data now…I don't know for sure who Jason was transmitting to, although I suspect it was Grunwald. The frequency was 28.2 Ghz.'

'Stay on the line Fred and switch to visual, I'd like you to be in on this.'

'Will do,' answered Fred switching to visual. He could now hear and see everything that Doug could hear and see. Doug commanded his internal computer to set up 28.2 Ghz. Then he transmitted direct to Grunwald on that frequency, hoping the closeness and power of the transmission would penetrate Grunwald's armour.

'I think you are probably right,' transmitted Doug.

Grunwald was thunderstruck. At first very surprised to hear Doug's voice coming through on his personal frequency. His surprise soon turned to anger; he drew his sword and came at Doug. "So you thought you would trick me eh. You were in league with Omega all along, well, it will do you no good now, say your prayers."

As soon as Doug saw Grunwald draw his sword he went into fast reflex mode and armed Albatross, this time with high power laser. Grunwald, in heavy armour although a very strong man, could not move as fast as Doug, who kept out of reach by sheer speed and agility. Finally Grunwald made a powerful lunge forward and Doug fired the laser taking the sword blade off at the hilt. He then physically lifted Grunwald off the ground and threw him bodily ten paces. Turning quickly Doug saw Grunwald's four guards running across the field, swords drawn, coming to the aid of Lord Grunwald. Albatross Photon 1, strength 2 heavy stun, Doug fired four times, lining up the spot on a new target each time.

"What are you?" shouted Grunwald. "I never knew Omega had anything like you to fight for him. I suppose you are the result of that secret project Epic and Omega have been working on these last six months; Oh yes; I know all about that, you needn't look so surprised. You can't build a machine that can break through the barriers of time and not have someone know about it… They've brought you back from the future to fight for them haven't they?"

"Shut up Grunwald, and simmer down," shouted Doug. "I'm not in league with Omega, we are still on the same side. I just wanted to demonstrate one of my facilities. Sorry I didn't mean to startle you."

Grunwald stopped remonstrating and allowed Doug to help him to his feet.

He still wasn't too sure about Doug but after Grunwald's outburst, Doug was certain of Grunwald's true feelings toward Omega and the whole Epic regime.

"Right," said Doug to Grunwald. "Now we can start building for the future. For a start, stop treating the water."

"Already done," said Grunwald. "I stopped treating the water and ordered all existing stocks to be destroyed as soon as I returned from London, immediately after I'd heard Omega's devastating revelation about me. When I think of what that vile creature had done to my family and me I…"

"All right Grunwald," soothed Doug. "There will be time for recriminations later on, but now we have to start making plans.

"I will come to the castle this evening," said Doug. "By the way, lock up the bishop, he is somehow sending information to Omega."

"So *he* was the one." Grunwald was again getting angry. "I had an idea that when I gave my reports to Omega, he already knew most of their contents. I suspected Jason and the Turk to be the culprits but I could never prove it, I can see I've been looking in the wrong direction. You don't have to worry about the bishop, I'll take care of him."

Back at the forge Doug told Hans and Janine what had happened during his meeting with Grunwald. "I won't be needing the suit of armour now Hans, or the sword and shield but you have my thanks for the offer. Where is the mill?"

"It's just outside Cotgrave," said Janine. "Take the castle road and turn off left about two kilometres out from Cotgrave, there is a signpost. Why do you want to go there?"

"I have two friends there and I want to make sure that they are all right," said Doug.

Doug rode out from the forge after telling Hans and Janine he would probably be quite late back, for he had to see Grunwald at the castle after the visit to the mill. It was late afternoon when Doug arrived at the mill. The place seemed deserted.

"Anybody home?" shouted Doug. "Simon, Peter?"

Doug stood in the doorway of the old water-mill. The boys were nowhere to be seen. Then he heard a faint cry, it seemed to come from high up in the mill. "Simon, Peter? Are you up there?" Doug began cautiously climbing the stairs. Crash! A barrel of flour struck the banister rail bursting the barrel and cascading its contents all over the place like a white fog.

'Fred?' called Doug over their link.

'Yes Doug,' answered Fred.

'Where are you now?' asked Doug.

'I'm still in Cotgrave,' said Fred. 'I couldn't find the professor. By the way, there are some strange things going on. People all over the place are getting their memory's back. They're wondering what the blazes is going on. And there are some pretty rough looking characters roaming around. I think they are looking for trouble. Where are you?'

'I'm at the mill looking for Peter and Simon,' said Doug. 'Someone has just aimed a barrel of flour at me.'

'I will be with you in just over ten minutes, if I can organise some transport.'

'Good, see you later,' said Doug and continued edging his way up the stairs.

No more flour bombs, no more anything and he safely gained the top landing.

Nothing at the top except the hoist used for lifting the sacks of grain up through the flap-traps, and a closed door. X-ray vision showed him three figures were crouching inside the room back against the far wall. Doug carefully opened the door.

"Come a step nearer and I'll cut his throat." Owain, the miller, had the boys tied and gagged and was holding a sickle at Peter's throat.

"What do you want me to do?" asked Doug, not wishing to endanger the boy's life. Doug could see by X-ray that Owain was no android.

'I dare not use Albatross,' thought Doug, Owain's reflexes may still cause injury to the lad, I will use the laser on full power. One quick sweep would slice the arm off neatly. But even so there may be a retraction of the muscles, still too risky thought Doug.

"Put that sickle down Owain. You cannot go anywhere, and if you harm the lad I'll kill you. So be sensible."

"Stand back," shouted Owain, lifting the sickle as if to strike. It was now well clear of Peter's throat. Doug quickly changed Albatross to Photon 1 strength 1 stun and fired.

The boys couldn't believe it, they were free, and what did Douglas Sampson just do to Owain? Douglas Sampson, a man who can beat Brolag easily in a fight. He has a friend who is a mechanical man and he shoots lights out of his eyes that can knock a man over, what next?

Fred, accompanied by two men, was travelling up the road on a wagon laden with sacks of grain and arrived just as Doug and the two boys were coming out of the mill. As the wagon ground noisily to a stop the two men jumped down and ran over to Doug and the boys. "Are you all right?" said one of the men to Peter.

"What's going on? Where's Owain?" asked the other.

"He's all tied up for the moment," said Doug, and he told them what had happened inside the mill.

"Fred, can you see the boys back to the village, I've got to get to the castle for a meeting with Grunwald? Who are your friends?"

"I met them in the village, this is Bob, and this is Jamie," said Fred, indicating the two men in turn. "It's the miller's wagon, they work at the mill."

'Interesting,' thought Doug. 'They must be part of the Adelphi's crew.'

Doug remembered back at Burcot Janine and Chris had told their story about the tragic accident to the Adelphi and the gruesome discovery in the North Sea.

Bob and Jamie's names were mentioned as playing a significant part in it all.

"We will take care of the boys," said Bob.

"Aye that we will," said Jamie. "And we'll take care of that devil Owain."

Doug took Peter aside. "Is the talisman safe?" asked Doug.

"Oh yes sir, it's quite safe, that's why Owain was trying to kill me. He wanted me to tell him where it was, he said if I didn't tell him where it was he would kill me and then no one would know where it was. But I still didn't tell him," said Peter.

"You were very brave," smiled Doug, giving Peter a reassuring hug.

Doug then walked over to Bob and Jamie. "I would like you and Jamie to take Owain to the castle," said Doug to Bob. "He is to be confined in the dungeons. I'm going to the castle now; I'll leave word at the gate. If you have any difficulty gaining entry ask for Lord Grunwald. I want Fred to take the boys to Cotgrave. After you've been to the castle return to Cotgrave and go to the forge, ask for Hans and Janine. I think you'll have a lot to talk about.

Chapter 23

Physically Doug had no need to eat or drink, neither had Grunwald for that matter, but at times they both derived great pleasure from eating and drinking.

There at the castle, Doug, over a splendid meal, had spent the last few hours in deep discussion with Grunwald. Many ideas were 'kicked' around, many tentative plans put forward, and many ifs and buts were bandied about.

After the meal they both decided to go for a walk along the battlements at the top of the castle wall.

"A bit of fresh air will do us good," said Grunwald. He was in glowing mood. The good food, washed down with copious drafts of ale had assisted in producing this giant of congeniality. Grunwald was telling Doug the history of Nottinghamshire, as he knew it, when Doug noticed lights in and around the village.

"That's Cotgrave down there isn't it?" said Doug.

"Yes my friend, that's Cotgrave," answered Grunwald proudly. "My God!" shouted Grunwald. "What's going on? There are fires all over the place. Guards! Guards!" The captain's orderly came running to the battlements in answer to Grunwald's call. "I want twenty men, fully armed, ready to leave for Cotgrave immediately. Tell my squire to meet me in my quarters, Now!" The orderly ran off to do Grunwald's bidding.

"See you in Cotgrave," shouted Doug as he raced for the stairs that led down to the courtyard.

Nottinghamshire had become a battleground. With the removal of the mind-controlling drug, Mentala Distillate, from the water, memories had returned and so had primitive emotions. Angry men wanted revenge; they took charge and controlled the weaker ones. In a few days gangs began to roam the countryside. The gangs took whatever they fancied, clubbing every show of resistance into submission. Burning homes, raping, murdering and looting. Tonight they had reached Cotgrave.

Doug arrived at the forge to find it surrounded by a band of drunken pillagers, hell-bent on breaking into the forge to steal the swords, daggers and armour which Hans kept there ready to supply the castle. Bob, Hans and Jamie were fighting desperately to protect not only the forge. Janine had caught the eye of Brolag who had travelled down from Calverton with a gang, seeking to settle scores with Doug.

'Fred!' called Doug over the link. 'Where are you?'

'I am inside the forge,' answered Fred. 'Guarding the boys and the weapons, no one has broken in yet.'

'Stay where you are Fred, I'll be with you in a minute,' replied Doug.

Armed with a stout quarter-staff Doug waded into the melee, bowling the enemy down like ninepins. With Doug's intervention it wasn't long before the would-be attackers were put to flight.

The valiant heroes, pleased with their victory cheered loudly and slapped each other on the back. They turned towards the house to tell Janine not to worry. The front door was stove in and gaping open. They went inside. "Janine! Janine!" shouted Hans. A scream came from the back room. Hans rocketed to the closed door, which was no match for his massive frame. Inside the room Brolag had Janine spread-eagled across the bed. Hans launched himself into action with a roar that shook the house. The two giants battled to and fro, Janine scurried out of the way as Hans and Brolag wrestled amongst the broken furniture. During the fight Hans tripped over some debris and fell flat on his back. Brolag snatching a sword from the wall lunged at Hans aiming straight for his heart. Doug, who had been watching from the door, now stepped in and used his laser on the sword. A similar action to that used on Grunwald's sword, taking the blade off at the hilt. Brolag stopped in his tracks, turned towards the door and saw Doug.

With a wild bellow of rage he threw himself at Doug. Ever since his ego shattering defeat in the stables at Calverton, Brolag had dreamed of revenge. He had put his defeat down to a surprise attack by Doug and did not believe that he had lost to a better or stronger man. Doug let Brolag come at him, then, not using his full power, struck Brolag on the side of the head, such a blow that it knocked the big man sideways to the floor. Brolag picked himself up shook his head, and with a roar made another desperate charge, resulting with the same clubbing right from Doug, this time sending Brolag spinning to the side of the room. That was it, the fight ended, Brolag had had enough.

"Chain him up Hans," said Doug. "Fred's in the forge, if Brolag gives you any trouble, call for Fred, he'll soon quieten him down." Turning to Bob and Jamie, Doug said. "Come on lads, we've got work to do," and off they went to quell the lawless men's rampage through Cotgrave. By this time Grunwald and his men had arrived and it was only a matter of time before order was restored. Grunwald sent messengers all over Nottinghamshire, ordering his soldiers to round up the marauding gangs.

Time to relax and take stock of the situation. Bob, Hans, Janine and Jamie sat round the large table in the centre of the room trying to fit the missing pieces of their lives together. Fred and Doug sat chatting by the fire with Simon and Peter.

"Where is the talisman?" asked Doug.

"It's still at the mill sir," answered Peter. "It isn't easy to get, not just like that, I had to hide it in a very safe place."

"That's all right Peter," said Doug. "We'll get it later, when we know exactly what is happening here."

The boys went off to bed; Doug and Fred were about to join the others when they heard a faint knocking on the door. "I'll see to it," said Doug and opened the door. A man, face-blackened, clothes torn and burnt in parts, staggered into the room and fell to the floor. Doug bent over the man, the others stopped their talking and joined Doug.

The man was lying face down on the floor, Doug carefully turned him over.

"It's the professor," said Janine. It was indeed the professor, barely recognisable under all the dirt. Doug and Fred carried him into the back room and laid him on the bed. Janine fetched water, bandages and some clothing. The professor had been badly beaten and was exhausted. He had been caught by a mob of angry villagers, nobody liked tax collectors.

Next morning the village of Cotgrave was a pitiful sight. The extensive damage caused by the riots and fires was heartbreaking evidence of the previous night's violence. The village, with its elegant square of wooden houses was hardly recognisable. Quaint and beautiful, would have been useful adjectives to describe the village, but their description would not have gone far enough. For they fell far short of describing the scenes witnessed by those walls. It did not describe the oppression, the deprivation, the beatings and the injustices. All the hallmarks and sores of a harsh dictatorial regime dictated ostensibly by Omega and carried forward by the grossly misled, but now reformed, Grunwald.

In Cotgrave that day there were tears, sobbing, wailing, shouting, hideous screams, people running, people hiding, raping, looting and fighting. There was also love, quiet, comforting love and friendship. Friendship nurtured in the very bosom of disaster, inexplicably blossoming in that same smoking hell. There were villagers wandering about in a trance-like state, small groups dotted here and there amongst the smoking ruins.

Vigilante gangs roamed the streets. Fingers of accusation stabbed out many times. "You were there! You were one of them!" someone would shout. And whether it be a true statement or not the accused were brutally put to death. Some managed to run off, but many died, perhaps needlessly, victims of hysteria, hypocrisy and hate. That was the scene greeting onlookers on the morning following that fateful night.

A few days later the Great Hall of Cotgrave Castle was a-buzz with controversial argument. The nobility from all over the walled county had been called to Cotgrave Castle. Lord Grunwald and Sir Rolph were sitting at the long table, but the centre position; the recognised position of power was occupied by Doug, with Fred and the professor, who had by now recovered considerably from his ordeal, seated either side. Lord Grunwald stood up and called for order, banging the table loudly with his gavel. A few minutes later silence reigned throughout the Great Hall.

Grunwald surveyed his audience and began what was probably the most important speech of his life. "My friends, some of you may still be wondering what is going on. Some of you, the more recent arrivals, will have already thrown off the effects of the drug that has caused so much devastation in our lives. I will tell you a story, a story that, to the best of my knowledge, is true. You will then understand why it is imperative that we all stick together, that we all fight together, that we all, if necessary, die together, for rest assured if we do not stick together, die we will."

Grunwald told them what Omega had done to him and to his family. He told them how Omega had commanded him to regularly administer the Mentala Distillate to keep them mental slaves, so that Epic could study them and get data for their own annihilation. He told them that from tomorrow Omega had ordered him to administer another kind of drug, a lethal one, the experiment was over. Omega's android army would have dealt with anyone left alive at the end of a further week.

Grunwald also told them that he was not proud of the part he had played.

"I have been a victim of mental manipulation every bit as much as yourselves," he said. "We have a week to prepare a plan of attack on Epic's London Centre. At the moment we have no modern weapons. We have however, hundreds of longbows and thousands of armour piercing arrows. I want you all to assemble at Saxondale with as many men as you can muster. There are doors in the wall at Saxondale and a corridor that leads to the outside. I will find out where the control switch is located and how to operate the doors. Once that has been achieved we can then march on to the Epic Centre. Thank you gentlemen, that is all I have to say for now."

There were many questions from the men gathered in the Great Hall, which were all answered, in one way or another, by Doug, Grunwald, or the professor. The meeting adjourned with promises to meet at Saxondale in a few days time.

Doug, Fred, Grunwald and the professor, sat in Grunwald's private quarters in Cotgrave Castle, Grunwald was outlining a plan to discover the location of the control switch that opened the doors in the wall. "We can all get into the Power Centre via my access point below the lodge at Saxondale. Once we're in I will use my authority to get someone to show us around; sooner or later we will be shown the mechanism controlling the doors in the wall and the power cut-off switch. We will then be able to open the doors and cut off the power to the screens."

"Is that wise?" queried the professor.

"What do you mean?" said Grunwald. The professor explained.

"If we remove the screens, the special police will suddenly start picking up thousands of thought-wave signals from the people inside the wall. They are going to wonder what is going on and alert Epic."

"The power will have to be switched off if we are going anywhere near the wall," said Grunwald. "The very nature of the screens is such that they emit intense Gamma rays in the vicinity of the wall, there is also a concentration of X-ray, making a very lethal cocktail for humans. We must try to take over the specially screened power complex below the hunting lodge before we attempt anything further."

"Is there a problem with that?" asked Doug.

"There are twenty guards and fifty technicians working in the underground area at any one time," answered Grunwald. "And they all have modern weapons."

"Fred and I have no need of modern weapons," said Doug. "We'll go on this tour with you. Once we locate the door controls and the weapons, Fred and I will start sorting out the opposition, the rest of you join in as soon as possible. Once in control we will open the doors and switch off the power. It won't matter if the special police do pick up the signals. They'll pick them up anyway once we begin to move towards London."

They all agreed, although the professor wasn't too keen. "Locate Desmond Greer," he said. "He should be somewhere around, he'll have lots of useful information about the Epic Building, he knows how we can gain access into the old control room. Once the screens are down, I'll call Sal and get Jazzer to bring the 'special' it will hold ten of us if necessary and we'll be able to get to the Epic Centre fast without being detected. How many people will the lift hold?"

"It's a large lift," answered Grunwald. "Should hold about fifty at a pinch."

"Good," said the professor. "As soon as we gain control, we will move about two hundred people into the complex to consolidate the take-over."

"Sounds good," said Doug. "Are we all agreed?" He looked round the group, all seemed to agree. "Good, let's find Greer."

Greer was working as a potter in Mansfield when he regained his memory. He made his way to Cotgrave hoping to find the rest of the group there. When Doug arrived Greer had already located the others at the forge. Doug outlined the plan and they all set off for Saxondale where they met up with Grunwald, Fred and the professor. A forest of tents and several hundred people now surrounded the Lodge at Saxondale. Soldiers and guards were instructing the men how to use the longbow; many hours training were to take place in the ensuing week.

At the end of the week Grunwald, Doug, Fred, the professor and four guards officers entered the Lodge and went into the back room. Once in the back room they changed into modern clothes then entered the lift and went down to the powerhouse below.

The group stood outside the lift at one end of the cavernous powerhouse.

A white-coated man recognised Grunwald and approached courteously.

"Can I be of any assistance gentlemen?" he asked politely.

"Who is in charge here?" asked Grunwald.

"I am sir, temporarily," answered the man in the white coat.

"I am Roger Edward Sponde, Deputy Controller, Wall Power Maintenance."

"I am Lord Grunwald De Reske," answered Grunwald. "I am in sole charge of the whole Nottinghamshire experiment. You are to give a guided tour to myself and my friends, embracing the complete underground complex."

"I'm sorry sir, I would have to get permission from the Director for something like that."

Grunwald glared at him fiercely and drew an envelope out of his pocket.

Inside the envelope was an official looking document signed by Omega. "I have permission from Omega himself to inspect the complex. Is that good enough for you?" said Grunwald forcefully, waving the paper vigorously in the man's face, allowing him to see the signature but not the content, which was actually nothing more than a command to attend a meeting in London some weeks earlier. Sponde wavered then gave in and snapped a few orders into a visiphone.

A smartly dressed man came out of one of the corridors, walked over to them and asked them to follow him. He led them to a small run-about vehicle with seats along each side. The whole party climbed aboard, the man in the white coat sat in the front and spoke to them via loudspeakers set on posts behind the seats. The run-about vehicle jerked forward, the tour of the underground complex had started

Chapter 24

The runabout vehicle carrying Grunwald and his party travelled down tunnels, along corridors, and all the while the man in the white coat gave a running commentary on the function of each piece of apparatus. They noticed during the tour, modern weapons clipped to the wall every few metres, and a sizeable armoury next to the accommodation area. Eventually they arrived at the nerve centre, a great horseshoe of control consoles. The vehicle stopped and the group alighted. They then walked along behind the guide who kept up a verbal torrent of technical jargon explaining in detail the purpose of each piece of equipment. Grunwald pointed to a large button on one of the consoles. "Is that the switch that opens the doors in the wall?" he said.

"Oh no sir," answered the guide. "That switch is over there on the end console, the red button, only the Director himself has the authority to push that button and it will only operate to his palm print."

"Thank you Sponde, you have been very helpful," said a beaming Grunwald. He had at last found out what he wanted to know. A party of guards approached, headed by a squat red-faced man wearing a heavily decorated uniform.

"What's going on here?" demanded the man. Six guards took up positions in a line, directing their energy guns at the group.

'Fred?' called Doug over their link.

'Yes Doug,' answered Fred.

'Put Albatross Photon 1 on stun, you take the three on the left, I'll drop the three on the right,' said Doug.

'Okay Doug, I'm ready.'

'Now,' said Doug and six guards dropped within a second, leaving the red-faced director alone and flabbergasted. Doug grabbed his arm and walked him over to the console with the red button. "Open the wall," said Doug. The director prevaricated, trying to maintain an air of command.

"I cannot do that without specific instruction from Omega, he'd kill me."

"It's either him or us that'll kill you," said Doug. "So what's it to be, certain death now if you don't or a possible escape if you do?"

"No I can't," said the frightened director. Doug grabbed hold of the director's hand and flattened it against the palm-plate beside the red button. An indicator above the button which had previously read 'Doors Closed' changed to 'Ready'. Doug pressed the button and the indicator changed to 'Doors Open'. Doug then locked the director in an empty locker room and fused the lock with his laser. "We'll let you out later," said Doug as he walked away.

"Right, now for the screens," said the professor.

Nearby, a few technicians had seen what was happening and made for their energy-guns. The nearest ones never made it, Fred or Doug stunned them, but others further back managed to raise the alarm and alert the guards. With alarm bells ringing, sirens wailing, guards came rushing out of side corridors, the battle was on.

Doug's group took refuge behind the consoles. Luckily there were a few energy-guns clipped to the wall behind the consoles and Grunwald, the professor and the others used these to hold off the technicians, who were basically scientists not fighters. The guards were a different matter, they were trained fighters and slowly began to advance, firing bolts of energy from their blasters as they came. Doug ordered Captain Bridges, one of their party, to return to Saxondale for reinforcements. Captain Bridges took a roundabout route and made his way back to the lift.

An hour is a long time when your dodging energy blasts, but that is how long it took before the relief party arrived. The first fifty arrived, armed mainly with bows and arrows. A few had picked up energy weapons along the way. The power-house guards were equipped with personal screens, which could absorb the impact from ordinary energy, but the screens offered no defence against bows and arrows, nor could they absorb the super-bolts thrown by Doug and Fred

With the arrival of the Saxondale soldiers the balance swung over to give Doug's party a massive advantage, the guards and technicians soon threw down their weapons and surrendered. It did not take long for the professor to locate the control to shut down the electronic screens. He then sent a message to Sal. 'Tell Jazzer to bring the 'Special' to Saxondale, tell him to see me when he gets here and tell him to start 'Project 20'. I will return with him tonight if I can.'

'Very good Professor Burgess,' answered Sal over the transmitter link to the professor. There was no emotion, no sign of *'missed you'* or *'Where have you been, how are you?'*... Still, what would you expect from a personal computer anyway?

Doug went back to the lift and Saxondale, then returned to Cotgrave. He found Simon and Peter at the back of the forge throwing stones at a water butt.

"Peter," called Doug. "I would like to go to the mill and get the talisman."

"Have we to go now sir?" asked Peter. "Can't we finish our game first, I'm winning at the moment?"

"All right, be ready in about twenty minutes," said Doug and turned to go into the forge. Standing almost directly behind him was Desmond Greer. "Hello Desmond," said Doug. Greer gave Doug a furtive look and returned the "Hello," rather nervously.

"Anything wrong?" asked Doug.

"N-no, er nothing," hesitated Greer and walked away. 'Strange,' thought Doug. 'I wonder if he overheard about the talisman, and would it mean anything to him if he did?'

Doug, Peter and Simon arrived at the mill mid-afternoon. Both boys said they were famished and tucked into a basket of food that Janine had packed for them. Doug, although he did not need to eat, joined in just to make them feel comfortable. With the meal just about finished, Peter jumped up and said. "I'll go and get the talisman," and off he shot down a path and disappeared round the back of the mill. About fifteen minutes passed, Peter had not returned. Doug was getting worried, and then he heard a faint cry.

Doug jumped up and shouted. "Peter! Peter! Is that you?"

No reply.

Doug, followed closely by Simon, ran round to the other side of the mill but there was still no sign of Peter. Doug stood on a small bridge that crossed the millstream and called again. Returning from the bridge Doug called Simon to him. "Simon," he whispered. "Make a lot of noise, call out for Peter, make your way back to the wagon."

"Yes sir," said Simon, and began shouting out for Peter and beating the bushes on his way back to the wagon, which was back along the path leading to the other side of the mill. 'Simon must be nearly back to the wagon by now,' thought Doug and upgraded his senses, particularly his sense of hearing.

The sounds of the countryside cannoned round his brain, the deafening sound of the fast-running millstream, the explosive chirruping of the birds, the booming buzz-sawing of the insects. The wind that had been but a gentle breeze now sounded like a roaring tornado. Doug used his computer to filter out the sounds he did not want. 'Sounds like someone moving through the bushes on the opposite side of the millstream,' thought Doug and pinpointed the exact location of the sound. Keeping out of sight he quickly made his way along the bank opposite the sound until he was well ahead of it and hidden by a bend.

Doug leapt effortlessly across the racing millstream, a full five metres and waited in a thicket beside the millstream path. Desmond Greer came panting along the path, his hand over Peter's mouth, half dragging him along. Doug stepped out from behind the thicket.

"That's enough Greer," said Doug severely. Greer reacted immediately by pushing Peter into the stream.

"Help!" shouted Peter. "Help! I can't swim." He was threshing around in the swirling stream, flailing the water with his arms. "Help! Help!" he cried.

More by reflex than conscious decision, Doug flung himself into the foaming stream and swam out to Peter. "Okay lad I've got you," said Doug reassuringly, as he swam with Peter to the bank. There was of course no sign of Greer. "Are you all right?" asked Doug when they reached the safety of the bank.

"Yes," said Peter, "but he has the talisman."

"Don't worry about that just now, let's get you cleaned up and dried out, then we will go to meet Daniel Baker."

They made their way back to the mill where Doug fashioned some dry clothes for Peter out of empty flour sacks. The two boys were chattering away like a couple of sparrows about the incident all the way back to Cotgrave. A short stay at the forge, for Peter's sake mainly, then on to Saxondale. At Saxondale Doug took Simon and Peter into the lodge and down to the powerhouse. The boys had never seen anything like it in their lives and were full of amazement, asking endless questions. Through the powerhouse and along a long corridor, then out into the forest outside the wall.

Doug started to think about the old man Daniel Baker. A golden ball of light appeared before them and slowly the form of Daniel Baker appeared within the shimmering globe. Daniel stepped out of the ball of light, which then faded, and walked towards them.

"I should have told you," he said. "That once the screens were down you could have called me any time, any time at all."

Doug told Daniel Baker what had happened at the mill. "I'll go after Greer if you like," said Doug.

"No it's too late now, he's probably half-way to London. I hope he finds that which he seeks."

"What's that?" asked Doug.

"Love, friendship, something to be able to put his trust in. You see, Greer loves Jed, he idolises him and will not accept that he is capable of doing anything wrong. Greer thought he could get Jed to see reason if he tried hard enough. That's why he stole the talisman, he thinks that by returning it to Jed, he will be his friend again. I'm afraid he will be disappointed, the Jed he knew no longer exists, the Omega side of his character so dominates him that he is virtually dead. And in turn the Eblis and Epic dominate the Omega side of him."

"What can we do?" asked Doug.

Daniel Baker gave them the answer. "Physical assault on the Epic Building. Find the old control room and destroy the main computer data interface and brain culture. It's a desperate move to make because once the main computer interface and the culture have been destroyed, Epic will cease to exist. The whole world organisation will grind to a standstill, which means utter chaos. That is why I wanted to use the talisman. It would have shut down the London Epic centre but would have kept the other Epic centres open and all essential services going. What must be done, must be done irrespective of the consequences. I will be there when you confront the Eblis."

"What makes you say I will do that?" queried Doug.

"You will, you will," said Daniel Baker as he walked away. The ball of light re-appeared, surrounding Daniel who slowly faded inside the golden light which in turn also faded, leaving Doug, Peter and Simon, standing there in the woods, wondering if what they had just experienced was real or just a dream.

With Peter and Simon being safely looked after by friends at Cotgrave, Doug made his way back to Saxondale to meet up with the professor and the rest of his party. Jazzer arrived with the 'Special' which caused a lot of interest, especially amongst the younger ones, the ones that had been born inside the walled county. They had never seen any Hi-tec equipment before, they were absolutely amazed when they saw the underground complex.

Time to leave. Hans, Bob, Janine and Jamie stayed behind with the Saxondale army. The rest of the party climbed aboard the 'Special' and with Jazzer in the driving seat, took off for London. "I took the liberty of bringing along your Tommy gun sir," said Jazzer to Doug.

"My what?" queried Doug.

"Your Tommy gun, that machine gun you took from the museum in London. I thought it might be useful."

"It's not a Tommy gun," corrected Doug with a smile. "It's a Lewis. Thank you anyway, I'm sure it will come in very handy."

Doug was thinking that although Grunwald was almost as strong as Fred and himself physically, he had no built-in armaments. If they encountered any guards at the London Centre the guards would, without a doubt, have personal screens, making ordinary energy blasters partially ineffective. The Lewis would be ideal for Grunwald, and he had the strength to use it as a mobile weapon. Doug gave Grunwald a basic course on the Lewis. Showed him how to cock it, how to fire it, how to load a fresh magazine, and, if necessary how to replenish an empty one.

They were approaching the outskirts of London, no sign of police hoverjets.

"Why no police?" asked Doug. The professor answered him with his usual verbosity.

"It is possible they are getting so many signals from

Nottinghamshire that their surveillance equipment is being swamped and, don't forget, the 'Special' is almost invisible to their scanners."

Further into London, still no sign of any opposition. The Epic Building stood out like an ugly carbuncle, a black eyesore on an otherwise pleasant skyline, it was made even more conspicuous by the large open areas where so many times in the past gigantic crowds had gathered to pay homage to their 'God'.

There was smoke coming from the buildings at the edge of the open areas. Doug used his telescopic vision and zoomed in on wide angle. "It's the android army, Epic's activated his army of androids. They're killing the people," shouted Doug.

He could see thousands of Omega's warriors swarming out of the building. "Can we contact anyone at Saxondale?"

"We ought to be able to contact someone," answered the professor.

"Tell them we want our men here as soon as possible," said Doug

"Some members of the organisation have modified implants," said the professor. "I'll get hold of Sal."

The professor mentally activated his implant and asked Sal who had the modified implants. Sal quoted a list of names to the professor. "John Dunne, he'll do. What's his frequency?

"24.97 Ghz," quoted Sal.

"Link me through to him will you Sal?"

"Certainly Professor Burgess," answered Sal flatly.

'John Dunne, this is Professor Edward Burgess', called the professor over his inbuilt transmitter. John Dunne came back immediately.

'Yes professor?' The professor quickly put John in the picture.

'Omega has activated his android army; they are moving out of the Epic Building and destroying everything. People, buildings, anything that gets in their way. They have got to be stopped.'

'Got you professor,' answered John Dunne. 'I will advise Captain Hooper right away.' Dunne closed the link and went off in search of Captain Hooper.

Chapter 25

Speares and Drogo were in Omega's luxurious office. A raging Omega was shouting hysterically at two very nervous guard's officers. "Must I do everything? Send your soldiers to Nottinghamshire, Now! Stop this rebel army. Kill them all. Annihilate every last one of them, but don't bother me with such trivia"

Then in much quieter mood but still threatening he continued. "Today is Judgement Day. Today the Eblis will be among us. Now get out and do your job. You know what will happen if you fail."

Failure meant death, they all knew that, it was part of life in the world of Epic. A hideous roaring came from below and the building vibrated.

"We must go to the temple," said Omega. "My master is nearly ready to materialise."

The 'Special' landed on the roof of the Epic Building, defence screens on full power. Guards on the roof blasted away at it with energy weapons. A large cannon fired, which sent a blast of raw energy that rocked the 'Special' almost throwing it off the roof. Jazzer spun the car in a circle, firing heavy blasts fore and aft. Many of the defending guards were put out of action, including the large cannon, which enabled Doug, Fred, Grunwald and the professor to get clear of the 'Special' and race for the protection of the ventilator shafts and skylights. They had then to fight their way along the roof to gain access into the building.

Once inside, it was still hard work, with each protecting the other. "Behind you Grunwald!" shouted Doug.

Grunwald spun round and sent a hail of bullets into a group of guards who had suddenly appeared round the corner of the corridor. "Fred! Watch out left."

"Doug! The stairs!" floor by floor they worked their way down through the building. They saw a large notice board screwed onto the wall of one of the corridors.

217

"The Central Training Wing," said the professor. "I remember that place."

They went in through the double-doors to the same hall-like room and saw the white suits suspended in gimbals. Not limp and lifeless, like the first time the professor had seen them, but all in motion. Some walking, some sitting, some gesticulating with their arms, all were suspended two metres above the floor and all were inside the gimbals, connected to masses of wires and pipes. An eerie sight, for there was no sound other than the rustling of the suits. The suits were in use; a program was being run. The professor went over to the control console and switched off the power, whilst Doug, Fred and Grunwald lowered the suits to the floor and released the imprisoned 'trainees'.

They had no idea how far advanced the inmates of the suits were into the program and assumed it to be near its end. Grunwald approached and faced the newly released 'trainees'.

"I am Lord Grunwald De Reske. You will have heard of me in your training. I am in charge of Nottinghamshire. All of you are under my command. I must now tell you that Operation Overlord has been completed and the exercise is finished. There will be no more killing. You are to do as instructed by Professor Burgess or his representatives." He turned to the professor. "There you are professor, give them their orders."

The professor instructed the freed trainees to make their way to the roof, where they would find Jazzer. He would ferry them to a safe area. The professor found Chris and gave him an energy gun just to be on the safe side.

"See you back at Burcot Chris," he said. Chris gave a goodbye nod and joined the first few members of the party making off in the direction of the roof.

"Now to find the temple," said Doug.

John Dunne found Captain Hooper and gave him the message from the professor. "We have nearly a thousand men, all armed," said Captain Hooper.

He had had his men scouring the underground complex for as many modern weapons as they could find. "Two hundred equipped with modern blasters, the rest with longbows and arrows, well, it's the best we can do," he said.

He called for his officers and told them to be ready to move out in an hour with all troops. The captain had also located several cars, a couple of hoverjets, a row of runabouts and a large riot control vehicle. "That's it," he said. "Let's go and get 'em."

Captain Hooper led a strange looking army out of the underground complex, a raggle-taggle army of men dressed in medieval clothes, some carrying modern energy blasters, others a more conventional weapon to go with their clothing, a longbow and a quiver full of arrows. Into the woods they went and off in the direction of London.

John Dunne ran up to the captain. "The satellites are coming back," he said pointing skywards. The captain frowned, the satellites were not only used for surveillance, if they were armed they could be used for warfare.

"Spread out!" he shouted. "Set fire to the fields." The satellites used Infra-red detectors and high-resolution lenses in their cameras, the fires and smoke would make it difficult for them to observe with any clarity.

The police arrived in their hoverjets and landed ahead of the army of rebels. Bursts of energy tore through the air from both police and satellites.

The enemy spread out in a line across the path of 'Hooper's Hopefuls', torrid blasts spewing out of their blasters, aimed at the men from Saxondale. On they came, defence screens full on, which negated the efforts made by Hooper's men with the modern blasters. However, the arrows shot off by the rest of the men in the army went straight though the defence screens, with deadly consequences. The enemy had no defence against the showers of arrows raining down on them from the Saxondale soldiers, whose arrows had a greater range than that of the energy guns. The police fell back and eventually surrendered. And the satellites were so confused that they were, at times, killing more guards and police than the 'Hopefuls'.

High Wycombe was the first encounter with Omega's androids. The androids brushed aside the onslaught from all energy weapons and the Hopeful's took some heavy losses, but the androids also had no defence against the arrows. Strange, how the most efficient fighting machine the world has ever known, had no answer to one of man's most primitive weapons. Time after time the android warrior scanned his enemy, not recognising the bow as a weapon, came confidently forward, only to be destroyed by a simple wooden shaft with a steel tip. High on the chest was the spot to aim for; the armour-piecing tip went straight through the heavy duty metal into the control unit, turning the android into a gyrating clown.

"Down here Jamie," shouted Bob as they raced across the fields and down into a sunken road, followed closely by a Special Police Officer and an android. After running for a while Bob climbed the bank to spy out the land. "There's a house over there, let's make for it. Perhaps we can lose them." Bob and Jamie armed with energy guns were retreating away from the superior firepower of the android and the officer. They made their way to the farmhouse just off the road. "I wish we had our communicators," said Bob.

"Where did Hans and Janine get to?" asked Jamie.

"I thought they were just behind us," answered Bob.

"These damn things are no good against the 'droids," said Jamie waving his energy gun about. "The 'bolts' just bounce off them."

Another fusillade of enemy charges entered through the windows and ricocheted off the walls. The front door would not last much longer against such attacks either. "We're trapped," said Bob.

Suddenly the door burst open, and the Special Police Officer strode into the house and levelled his blaster at Jamie. Bob threw a chair across the room at the officer then closed in on him. The fight raged back and forth Bob eventually knocking the officer to the floor. Congratulations were short-lived for there in the doorway silhouetted against the light was the dark sinister shape of an android. The 'droid raised its energy gun, Bob and Jamie could do nothing. A strange 'whoosh' and a thud, and the android started whirring and making whooping noises. It turned round and staggered erratically out of the house and up the path with a cross-bow bolt sticking out of its back.

Hans' massive frame appeared in the doorway. "Thanks Hans," said Bob.

"We thought we'd had it."

"Don't thank me," said Hans, stepping into the room. "It was Janine's bolt that stopped the 'droid."

"Well done Janine," said Bob as Janine came in carrying her cross-bow.

"Come on you two," she said. "Don't you know there's a war going on?"

Doug's party, still engaged in a fierce battle with Epic's guards, had fought their way down to the basement of the London Centre and were looking for a way into the temple. At the end of an ill-lit corridor Doug saw two figures, one a man, the other a boy. He recognised the man as Greer and the boy looked like Peter. Doug ran forward but Greer was gone, he had found a door in the side of the corridor and opened it with a code, he was through the door and gone in a second. By the time Doug reached the spot the door had closed again.

"Stand back," said Doug and blasted the door with Photon power. A large hole was blasted in the side of the corridor where the door used to be. Down a flight of steps to a gallery overlooking the temple square.

The square was full of black-robed monks chanting and praying.

Doug saw the altar, brilliantly lit with beams of light that looked solid in the smoke generated by the censers. Greer was nowhere to be seen. 'He must have doubled back to Cotgrave after I'd left and kidnapped Peter,' thought Doug. 'But why, he had the talisman, why did he want the boy?'

Doug fancied he saw a movement in the shadows on the other side of the temple. The others joined him and he told Fred that he was going to investigate the area on the far side. Doug edged his way round the gallery and, keeping to the shadows, cautiously crept down the stairs that led to the temple floor. The priests and monks were so intent on their religious rituals they either did not see Doug or took no notice of him. Doug at last reached the shadows on the far side of the square, still no sign of Greer anywhere.

The chanting reached a crescendo, a tremendous clash of cymbals and the sound of a horn rose above the noise. Omega entered, followed closely by Speares and Drogo. They walked quickly to the altar. Omega made a signal with his hands and the doors at the far end opened. Four priests entered, dragging a small boy along by four silver chains, each chain attached to a silver collar round the boy's neck, and each one held firmly in the hand of a priest. 'That's Peter,' thought Doug.

The priests dragged Peter down the aisle and spread-eagled him across the top of the altar. Omega raised his arms and began to recite the foreign verse. The twelve glass tanks began to glow, beams of ultra-violet light came from each one to converge at a point high above the altar. Doug realised that this was all part of the ritual that Jack Hoskins had seen, when the mutant was sacrificed and the Eblis appeared. He must act quickly. Omega's assistants, the priests, were all concentrating on the ceremony.

Doug ran to the altar, and, using his laser, cut through the chains holding Peter, swept him up in his arms and ran to the stairs. It was all done so fast that Omega, the priests and the rest of the congregation could only stand and stare. Within moments they had recovered and were about to chase after Doug when Omega called them back. "We have no time, we have no time, the Eblis is ready."

Doug ran up the stairs and handed Peter over to the professor. Omega ordered the priests to seize Drogo, and he was dragged screaming to the altar, where he was chained and stretched out on the large black ceramic slab. The ritual continued and the red lasers beamed down on Drogo who screamed with pain and terror. Drogo went up in smoke, and out of the smoke appeared the fearsome head of the Eblis.

Omega knelt before his master. "We are ready master," he said, and the glass tanks containing the ever growing brain cultures, glowed brighter.

The air throbbed with power and the chanting rose in volume and took on a monotonous droning, rising and falling in sympathy with the throbbing waves of power generated by the cultures. An emotional outburst came from the Eblis,

"At last, at last." It roared again, and began to descend to the altar, assuming a nebulous man-like form to make ready for the last stage of the transformation.

Grunwald put his hand to his head and screwed up his eyes. "I remember this place," he said. "Follow me." He led them to the end of the gallery. "The other side of this wall is the old Epic Control Room. Doug gave another blast on Photon 1 and they were able to walk directly into Epic's heart.

The whole control room contained a fairy wonderland of a million sparkling crystals. Thousands of glass rods with whispers of light travelling along each one. There were multi-coloured tubes forming amazing sculptures in glass, all pulsing with light. There were wonderful effects in fibre optics, each strand glowing and changing hue. A huge pattern of light giving off myriad shapes and colours.

The only eyesore in that wondrous place was a large glass receptacle at the far end of the room. Inside the receptacle was a dark tentacled mass, similar to the ones in the glass tanks in the temple only much bigger than any one of them. Fluid in the receptacle seethed and bubbled, the bubbles rose to the surface where they gave freedom to a noxious vapour. Across the surface of the 'brain' snaked thousands of electrical discharges. "Destroy it," said Doug.

Grunwald was about to open fire with the Lewis when Peter said.

"I managed to get the talisman back, I stole it out of Greer's pocket."

"Good lad," said Doug. "But what the devil do we do with it?" The professor smiled at Doug's turn of phrase, ironic under the circumstances. Doug stood in the centre of the room holding the talisman and concentrated his thoughts on Daniel Baker.

The ball of golden light appeared and the figure of Daniel Baker was once again transported into Doug's life. "We have the talisman," said Doug. "But we don't know how to use it."

"The pedestal below the giant crystal," answered Daniel. "Push the talisman into the slot and turn it to the right."

Doug gave the talisman to Peter.

"I think you should be the one to use the talisman, it was your father's intention that it be used to stop Epic."

Peter ran to the central crystal and fitted the talisman into the small slot near the top of the pedestal and turned it to the right. With a sound almost like a sigh the activity of the crystals, tubes and fibre optics ceased. The electrical discharges stopped traversing the surface of the 'brain' and there was a strange silence.

A shattering roar broke the silence, they returned to the gallery. The Eblis had half completed its transformation. Doug shouted to Fred, "Destroy the tanks."

Both Doug and Fred flung bolts of energy towards the glowing tanks, but the tanks were protected by a force field that deflected attacks by energy weapons. Even on full power neither Doug nor Fred could break through the screen. Grunwald opened up with the Lewis. The tanks ruptured, spilling fluid, brain culture and blood, in a mixture that hissed and bubbled along the temple floor.

Doug aimed at the central projector above the altar, which exploded in a shower of sparks. A snarling, writhing Eblis tried to return to Epic but was unable to do so because Epic had been switched off by Peter using the talisman. It threw devastating bolts of energy towards Doug's party in the gallery, desperately trying to further the attack, but having been caught off guard, was at a disadvantage. With roars that shook the building, and searing streaks of energy thrown in all directions the Eblis performed an orgy of destruction.

Daniel Baker stood in front of Doug's party, arms outstretched, deflecting the vicious bolts of death. The Eblis was beaten and it knew it. With a roar of defiance it poured itself into Omega who screamed in agony. His whole body seemed to bubble, his flesh seethed and boiled. Doug and his party could only stand and watch this horrific spectacle taking place before their eyes. Hypnotised by the very horror of it all.

Eventually Omega returned to his normal appearance now completely possessed by the Eblis. He turned and gave a baleful glare towards the gallery, then flung streams of energy from his fingertips at Doug's party. Daniel Baker maintained his screen and once again deflected the attack.

"I will return, I will be avenged, mankind has not seen the last of me," snarled Omega and pointed to the altar. A stream of energy again streamed from his fingertips, and with awesome power blew the huge altar to pieces, revealing a flight of stone stairs beneath. "Speares, Greer, come with me," ordered Omega his voice strangely altered to a much lower register and more commanding. Speares and Greer followed Omega down the flight of stairs to a cellar below the temple.

In the centre of the cellar stood a large semi-transparent crystalline construction, inside of which were twinkling lights and outlines of electronic equipment. Omega raised his hand and the door of the globular construction swung open. They all entered the 'machine', which began to glow, and blur, then with an ear-shattering crack; it disappeared, leaving nothing but the sound of a rushing wind.

Chapter 26

Doug and his party had been on the receiving end of a devastating attack by the Eblis which now, in the form of Omega, had escaped down a flight of stairs beneath the altar, together with Speares and Greer. They had entered a crystalline machine, which glowed, blurred, then vanished, Doug ran down from the gallery and over to the altar, he was halfway down the stairs when he saw the machine disappear.

The others followed him down the stairs and he told them what he had seen. "Grunwald?" he said. "You mentioned earlier about a time machine?"

"That's right," answered Grunwald.

"Could they have used that for their escape?"

"Yes, I think it quite possible," answered Grunwald.

The professor arrived with Peter and Daniel Baker. The professor sniffed the air. "That smell! I can smell ozone. When we were conducting experiments into time travel, we sometimes used to get a smell like the one we have here. Something to do with tearing the fabric of time. And if I remember it correctly it was only on the successful occasions that we got it. So my conclusion is that they have escaped in a time machine."

Doug laid his hand on the professor's shoulder. "Thank you professor."

The professor stopped his waffling, Doug then spoke to Daniel Baker.

"You seem to be a match for the Eblis, Why didn't you get rid of it earlier?"

Daniel Baker smiled. "I'm no match for the Eblis alone, we were lucky, it was weakened by the transformation. To overcome the Eblis it would need the combined strength of the triad; I would need the other two 'Guardians'. This would have been an ideal opportunity, unfortunately it was not possible at this particular time." Daniel Baker paused and smiled at them all, then said. "I must go, should you need me again you know what to do." He walked away and stepped into his ball of light and was gone.

Hardly had Daniel Baker's light faded when Peter shouted. "Look!" and pointed up the stairs. Water was pouring down the stairs from the temple floor above. They all ran up the stairs and saw water spurting in through the walls.

"It's water from the Thames," shouted the professor. "The old walls are crumbling, they must have been weakened by all those energy blasts."

Even as he spoke more of the wall collapsed and the Thames came gushing in, sweeping Peter off his feet and down into the cellar. Doug rushed down after him and dragged him to the stairs where Grunwald, with the Lewis slung across his back, was joined by Fred and formed a chain by linking hands, enabling Doug to pull himself and Peter back up the stairs against the torrent. The temple floor was already over half a metre deep, and a great whirlpool that threatened to drag them all into its vortex, marked the entrance to the cellar that so nearly claimed Peter's life.

"Let's get out of here," shouted Doug. They found both flights of stairs to the gallery had collapsed and a pile of rubble blocked the doors. The water was rising fast.

"We're finished," said the professor. "There's no way out."

Doug told the professor he had a plan.

He positioned Grunwald beneath the gallery. Fred, following Doug's line of thought, climbed onto Grunwald's shoulders, carefully balancing, with Doug steadying Grunwald and explaining what was going on. Doug then made a tremendous leap upwards, six metres, straight up, and caught hold of the edge of the gallery. He moved his hands along until he was able to place his feet on Fred's shoulders.

"Now climb up," he told the professor. "Let Peter come first." Peter was up like a shot, using Grunwald, Fred, and Doug as a ladder, but the professor needed a helping hand from Grunwald and Fred.

More of the wall collapsed threatening to bring the gallery down to the temple floor. The stairs from the gallery were still intact but the way was blocked by a Minotaur mutant. It was not as large as the one Doug had encountered at Gravesend, not as tall, no rippling muscles and the horns were much smaller, more like that of a cow than a bull's. Doug had no time for discussion or sentiment, although he pitied the creature, nevertheless time was running out, he had no choice, Albatross Photon 1 strength 1 stun. He loosed a shot at the beast; it staggered and fell where it stood. Doug climbed the stairs and lifted the creature bodily through the doorway at the top. The creature was not fully stunned "Help me," it croaked. "Help me, I am a friend."

"Which way now?" said Doug. The beast, badly shaken and only half conscious, whispered in a peculiar rasping voice.

"To the left, and up the stairs."

They turned to the left and walked until they came to the stairs, which led them to a wide corridor with walls festooned with pictures and trophies.

"I remember this place," said the professor. "We were brought along here to meet Omega, his office is at the end of this corridor." They found the impressive double doors at the end of the corridor, the doors were of course locked. A synchronised kick from Doug and Fred, and the heavy mahogany doors flew open, revealing Omega's luxurious office.

Doug had little time for wonderment, Omega had left two guards on duty to protect the office. As soon as the doors opened the guards went for their guns and started blasting. Luckily Doug and Fred were in front with screens raised.

"You have a choice," said Doug. "Either you come with us as friends, or be killed."

One of the guards immediately raised his hands, but the other one strode forward firing wildly. Doug gave him a strength 3 blast and put him out of action.

"We were told to destroy all documents if attacked," said the surrendered guard.

"Where are these documents?" asked the professor.

"In the safe behind the wall," answered the guard, walking over to the side wall and pressing a button. A large section of the wall slid aside revealing a safe that stretched from floor to ceiling.

"How does it open?" queried the professor.

"Only Omega has the code," said the guard. Fred stepped forward.

"From my data I know this is a safe designed by the Atlas Safe Company. It was designed in 2130 with a then new design, a timed and coded electronic tonal system. It is now obsolete," he said. "I can ascertain the code for you within a few minutes."

Fred undid his shirtfront, opened his cavity and withdrew a long flexible connecting lead which he plugged into a computer terminal point set in the wall.

He sat down on the floor in front of the terminal point with a glazed look in his eyes, only occasionally using the keyboard. After a few minutes he pulled out the connecting lead and walked over to the safe and plugged his lead into a point just below the keypad on the safe's outer surface. Tones sounded, lights flashed, and numbers registered on the display point at the top of the keypad. A loud click, the capstan turned and the huge door swung open.

From the depths below came the sound of a huge explosion, the building shook and parts of the ceiling fell. "We must hurry," said the professor, and he walked inside the safe.

"What are we looking for?" asked Doug.

"I don't really know," answered the professor. "I want to try and discover what Omega and Epic have been working on, what projects they had in train, anything technical I suppose."

Another massive explosion, the building shook and one of the cabinets beside the safe slid sideways, revealing another smaller safe. "Fred," said the professor.

Fred saw the safe and needed no further prompting. The others continued searching for technical information that looked important, showing each 'find' to the professor who either nodded or shook his head. Fred called,

"It's open professor." Inside the small safe was a briefcase.

"Bring that," said the professor. "Now I think we had better leave."

Fires spreading up from below and the effects of many explosions made the journey to the roof difficult and hazardous. When they did at last climb out into the fresh air they found Jazzer waiting for them with the 'Special'. He was waiting by the car, holding the door open for the professor. Always the gentleman, Jazzer put his hand to his mouth and gave a little cough. "If I may be so bold sir, will 'all' your company be travelling in the car?" Jazzer was looking at the mutant with its cow-like head and large horny hands.

"Yes, of course," answered the professor as if nothing was amiss. He sat in the front with Doug, the rest of the party sat in the back. Jazzer resumed his position in the driving seat and closed the doors.

"I trust you would like me to drive you home now sir," he said.

"Yes Jazzer I would, if you would be so kind," said the professor with a rare touch of humour.

Jazzer sent the 'Special' speeding off the roof, through the smoke that was pouring out of every ventilator. Looking back at the Epic Centre they saw a building being consumed by fire. A building that at one time housed the answer to man's dreams now ending its life with the dream that had become a nightmare.

Without Epic to direct them the android's advance was stopped. From the moment Peter had turned the key almost every one of Omega's android warriors ceased to function and the faceless army stood eerily immobilised, except for six Commander robots that had the capability to function independently. The police unit was in confusion, some had surrendered, some actually joined forces with Captain Hooper.

Doug twisted round in his seat and spoke to the mutant. "How do you feel?" he said.

"I'm feeling much better thank you... By the way... I am not a mutant. I was a normal human being six months ago... I was a woman... My friends used to say I was beautiful... My name is Eleanor Bull." They all looked at her somewhat bovine appearance. She sadly sensed what they were thinking, a bitter reflection of her name. "Ironic isn't it?" she said tearfully.

"My God, what happened?" asked the professor. Eleanor sobbed; huge tears welled up in her eyes and ran down her cow-like face. The professor patted her horny hand and spoke softly, trying to console her. She continued her narrative in an emotional halting way, punctuated with pauses and bouts of crying.

"We had just got married... Richard and I... and we, being devoted to Epic, wanted to do something really worthwhile... Richard and I went to the Epic Building and told one of the officials that we would like to devote our lives to serving Epic, we were later called in to see the high priest Omega. He told us how lucky we were... because two vacancies had just come up but we would need some minor medical adjustments." She indicated herself, and then held her head with those terribly misshapen hands and sobbed uncontrollably, it was some time before she could continue.

"My husband Richard went mad when he saw what they had done to me, he broke out and attacked everyone he met. I heard that they had captured him down near Gravesend."

Doug sat there and felt so sad for her, and told her as kindly as he could what had happened.

"I'm sorry Eleanor, your husband is dead, he tried to kill me, I had to shoot him, I didn't know... I..." There wasn't much more Doug could say, his voice just trailed off, and for the rest of the journey everyone sat in silence, listening to the heartrending sobbing of poor Eleanor.

When they arrived back at Burcot they found the professor's residence was almost back to normal. The medical staff took care of Eleanor, Chris and Peter.

"Doug," said the professor. "Before you go trekking off, I would like you to visit a place called Glymton, it's on the River Glyme about six kilometres north of Woodstock."

"Certainly professor," answered Doug. "Why do you want me to go there?"

"I have ascertained from Eleanor that she and her husband lived there in a small cottage. I would like you to go and see if you can find any of their personal belongings, especially a picture of her as she was before her, er, change of appearance. The place is called 'Rose Cottage'."

"Yes... we can call there on the way to Saxondale, we'll send Jazzer back with anything we find."

The journey to Glymton was uneventful, the 'Special' speeding smoothly over the countryside, a countryside dotted here and there with the disfiguring signs of conflict. Jazzer cruised around until they found the cottage. Then Doug, with the help of Fred and Grunwald, loaded the 'Special' with what they considered to be the *personal* belongings of Eleanor and Richard.

Fred and Grunwald had just taken the last few items out to the

'Special', Doug was on his own in the back room of the house. 'That's the lot,' thought Doug and was about to leave when suddenly with explosive force an android punched its way through the back wall. It was one of the six Commander robots, programmed to kill. Doug immediately used Albatross Photon 1 and succeeded in damaging the android's energy weapon before it had fully activated its defence screen, but that was all.

The android closed in on Doug forcing him into a corner. Doug's own weapons were useless against it, the android's screens were too strong and Doug's bolts of energy even on full power just bounced off.

Doug picked up a large lump of debris from the broken wall and hurled it at the android with all his strength. It struck the 'droid full in the chest, the force of the blow carrying it back, smashing it into the opposite wall and bringing down some of the floor above. Back came the android. Doug threw another section of brickwork, same result, back it came again. Nothing seemed to stop it.

Doug picked up a broken rafter and aimed it like a spear with all the force he could muster. The jagged end hit the android in the neck and took off its head, which bounced about on the end of a thick flexible tube and dangled halfway down its back.

That should have finished it but no, the damn thing wouldn't be stopped. It had locked its body sensors onto Doug and would not stop until Doug was dead.

Another part of the floor above caved in and trapped Doug under a pile of rubble. The android sensed Doug's difficulty and approached, holding a massive piece of broken masonry above its headless torso, and was about to smash it down onto Doug, when Grunwald appeared in the doorway. He saw the situation immediately and opened fire with the Lewis. The android staggered and fell back with the huge piece of masonry on top of it. Doug scrambled out from underneath the rubble and made sure that that particular piece of machinery never worked again.

"Heard a bit of a ruckus, just wondered what was keeping you," said Grunwald with a smile.

"Good thing you intervened. I wonder how many more of these things there are roaming around?" said Doug, as they made their

232

way back to the car. "Take us to Saxondale, Jazzer," and in his own inimitable way Jazzer said, "Very good sir."

Jazzer dropped Doug, Fred and Grunwald at Saxondale then returned to the professor's house at Burcot with the personal items belonging to Eleanor and Richard Bull.

Doug was away from Burcot for six weeks, during that time he had been working with Fred and Grunwald, clearing up pockets of resistance all over the country, Grunwald using his position as 'Lord of the Manor' to good advantage. 'Hooper's Hopefuls', as they came to be called, stamped their authority up and down the country.

Epic's five remaining Commander warriors had joined forces and were lurking somewhere in the far north of the country, it was a case of wait until they made their next move, then try to capture or destroy them before they disappeared again.

Doug did not get physically tired, but he needed to rest mentally, and such was his mental condition on his return to Burcot, after six weeks of intense activity in the field, fighting, arguing, negotiating and counselling. Fred said he felt fine. He accepted things as they were and worked out problems with pure logic.

Grunwald, now that he had been 'enlightened', had a different philosophy to life. No longer was he the egocentric 'Lord of the Manor'. No longer was he the overbearing cruel tyrant who ruled by fear and suffering. Many times, when dealing with the confused 'enemy' he was gentleness itself, showing tremendous patience and understanding.

Bob, his crew, Doug, Fred and Grunwald, landed on the roof of the professor's house at Burcot in a commandeered police hoverjet. The professor and his staff were given prior warning of the return and had gathered on the roof to welcome them.

"Doug," said the professor, "When you've had a chance to freshen up I'd like you to come and see me in the laboratory."

Doug noticed everyone was smiling, but perhaps that was not so strange seeing that the group had been away for six weeks and were all friends with each other. 'What's he up to now?' thought Doug.

"Okay professor, I'll be there in about half an hour."

A pleasing shower, clean clothes, and a peaceful, safe environment made Doug feel a lot better, he made his way down to the laboratory.

"Ah, Douglas Sampson, here at last," said the professor with a beaming smile. All the laboratory staff were present, medical staff, technicians, everyone. Doug noticed once again that everyone was smiling and looking at him. He doesn't usually call me Douglas Sampson thought Doug, I wonder what's going on? He stopped directly in front of the professor and with a self-conscious smile said, with some embarrassment.

"You wanted to see me professor? Is there something I should know?"

The professor stood aside and the group of assistants parted centrally revealing a large white screen. Two of the professor's assistants moved forward and took away the screen. There seated in a wheelchair, was Helen.

"Helen!" said Doug running forward. "Helen," he said again. There was no response from the beautiful Helen. She just sat there stiff and still.

"She cannot see or hear you at the moment Doug," explained the professor. "We are ready to 'switch her on', if I might use a totally inadequate phrase. We thought that the first face she saw ought to be yours."

"I see," said Doug. "Is she... er... like me... reconstructed?"

"Yes," said the professor. "I'm afraid she is, but she has, like yourself, all her memories and feelings, just like she had before."

Doug felt a mixture of feeling well up inside him. Helen, his beloved Helen, here at last, looking exactly the same as she did the last time he saw her on that fateful day when after a wonderful weekend in the country they had both been virtually buried alive in the cryogenic unit at Richmond. Here she was, but in reality containing not a single molecule of the original Helen, she, like Doug, were both ersatz people. He felt tears well up in his eyes and he turned away to hide his emotion from the rest of his friends in the laboratory.

The professor indicated to the staff to leave them alone for a little while and the staff quietly left, leaving Doug and the professor alone, silently watching the motionless form of Helen. "It's not a weakness to show emotion Doug," said the professor. "It's not unmanly to be moved to tears by this sort of experience. I'm terribly sorry... I should have warned you." He turned to go.

"No, don't go professor, I'm all right now, there were so many things that flashed through my mind all at once, and I just couldn't cope with it all, I'm okay now, but..." Doug remembered his own awakening, seated, like Helen in a wheelchair. "I think it would be better, for Helen, if she were to awake in a bed rather than a wheelchair."

"Yes, you're right, I should have thought of that," and the professor immediately called his staff back to discuss the possibilities of 'reviving' Helen in another location outside the laboratory.

"I would like her to awake in the apartment we have prepared for her," he told his staff.

Helen was transferred to what was to be her future apartment. The professor organised the technical arrangements and the 'switch on' sequence was started.

The professor and his 'crew' seated at a makeshift console on one side of the room, well away from Helen and the bed, their attention riveted on the monitor screens, watching the many traces that gave vital information about Helen's 'condition'.

Doug, standing beside the bed took hold of Helen's hand.

"Helen," said Doug gently. "Helen, can you hear me?"

Helen slowly opened her eyes, saw Doug and smiled.

"Everything seems to be all right," whispered the professor to his staff.

"Helen darling, can you hear me?" repeated Doug.

"Doug darling, why are you looking so worried?" Helen sat up and looked around the room. She saw that she was in a strange bed a strange room and there were strangers sitting at a table full of strange equipment.

"Where am I? What am I doing here? Doug, what's the matter? Have I had an accident?"

"No darling, not exactly," said Doug, trying to reassure her. "Helen, we have a lot to talk about."

The professor came across the room and stood quietly by the bedside. Helen looked at him.

"What's going on?" she asked angrily.

"I am Professor Burgess," he said. "How are you feeling my dear?"

"I'm feeling fine," answered Helen looking angrily round the room. "Will someone tell me just what is going on? What is happening? Doug, don't just stand there wearing that silly grin, tell me. What is going on?" Doug's smile widened.

"She's all right," said Doug, "almost back to normal I would say." Doug captured Helen's waving hand and patted it gently. "What was the last thing you remember darling?" Helen thought for a moment then said.

"I remember screaming when Stanley hit you with the gun and knocked you out. Then that Doc Flannigan came in and injected you with some sort of drug, then he tried to do the same to me I remember fighting against it, I suppose I must have lost. Where are we darling? Did we manage to escape somehow?" Doug embraced Helen and quietly reassured her.

"You are all right now Helen darling, you're safe. We are safe, we are among friends." Doug looked at the professor. "Is it possible for us to be alone professor?"

The professor looked at his assistants. "What are the results so far?"

"All indications are positive, everything seems fine," said John Dunne. The other assistants agreed that, on the face of it, Helen was 'working' perfectly.

"Come on then," said the professor. "Let's go and eat."

Then turning to Doug he said quietly. "If you need me urgently, call me on the transmitter."

"I will," said Doug as he watched them all quietly leave the room.

They were alone at last. Helen threw back the covers, swung her legs down and placed her feet firmly on the floor. That part of it went well enough, it was when she tried to get to her feet and walk that she got into difficulty, just as Doug had done when he tried taking his first steps, no balance. Doug caught hold of her as she started to fall giddily sideways. Here was Helen, the girl he loved, the girl he thought he would never see again, yet here she was in his arms. Doug held Helen tightly and Helen returned his embrace.

They kissed, a long, loving, unifying kiss that for Helen took away all her worries and fears, and for Doug, the end of a time of mourning for his lost love, a sort of homecoming.

Doug helped Helen back onto the bed and painstakingly explained what had happened to them both. When Doug had finished explaining he had expected another outburst from Helen, there was nothing, no tirade of reproaches, just a quiet calm. She didn't seem very concerned, as Doug had been, about being made entirely of substitute materials. "Will I be able to have children?" she asked tearfully.

"Your children... Will I Doug? Will I?"

Doug held her close. "I don't know my love... Let's ask the professor."

A short while later the professor and his assistants returned.

"Is everything all right?" asked the professor.

"Yes," answered Doug, and looked at Helen. Helen plucked up courage to asked the question about whether of not she could have children, not that she was afraid of the professor, no, she was afraid of the answer the professor might give to the question.

"Professor Burgess, will I be able to have children?"

The professor gave a slight smile and told Helen that she could have children, but not in the normal way. Sexually, she was normal, so was Doug for that matter, but... "But... but!" interrupted Helen angrily. "There is always a but, isn't there. But what?"

"Yes there is a 'but'," said the professor calmly. "I have done my best with you my dear and under the circumstances you will find that you have a lot to be thankful for, you *can have* children, children that you can call your own, but as I said, not in the normal way. I have managed to save a quantity of your ova which can be used at any time in the future, of course, any child developed in this way from the fertilised ova would have to be by a surrogate mother or grown in an artificial womb. I'm sorry but that is the best I could do. Perhaps in a few years technology will have advanced sufficiently to cater for your needs, who can tell."

Helen, with tears in her eyes and sorrow in her heart clung desperately to Doug.

Doug, understanding what she must be going through, stayed close to Helen over the next few days and helped her to acclimatise herself to her 'new' body.

Janine and Chris also spent most of their time together. They were often seen wandering in the grounds holding hands, or huddled in a lonely corner talking to each other in whispered tones. They were very much in love.

One day Jazzer entered the professor's apartment carrying a briefcase, it was the one taken from the safe in Omega's office at the Epic Centre.

"What shall I do with this sir?" he said, holding up the briefcase.

"Good lord, I'd forgotten about that, I've been so busy with re-shaping Eleanor and rebuilding Helen it completely went from my mind." The professor took the case and carried it across the room and placed it on his desk, where he carefully opened it. He took out several documents and a box of data disks. A superficial examination of the documents showed nothing of importance. "Nothing much in the documents," said the professor. "Let's see what the disks have to offer."

The professor loaded one of the disks into the computer. "Reports, observations, no, nothing there, we'll try another." He tried another and another.

He was looking at the data on the fourth disk when something interesting caught his attention. "Now, what's this? Diagrams, mathematical calculations, a section on crystallography, showing how to grow a unique crystal formation. A crystalline form not known on this planet before."

"What is it sir?" asked Jazzer. "What does it all mean?" The professor became quite excited.

"I'm not certain," he said. "I think we have discovered the plans for the design and construction of a time machine. A similar machine to the one used by the Eblis to escape from below the Epic Building."

The professor thought it would be a good idea if Bob and his crew, together with Doug and Helen, all went away for a well-earned rest. It would certainly help Helen and Chris, who was still recovering from his near fatal experience in the C.T.W.

"When you return there will be lots of work for you all to do. I've organised representatives to all the other nations, we are getting good responses." Grunwald decided to stay with the professor at Burcot but the others thought it a wonderful idea.

So with Fred at the controls of the huge 'Prairie Hound', towing a large camping-trailer, Bob, his crew, Doug and Helen, left Burcot in holiday mood for a touring holiday. For the next few weeks the world and all its problems would have to wait.